FULL CIRCLE

WILL HISTORY REPEAT ITSELF?

ALEX J FISCHER

For my Family and Friends

1

Rachel threw open the door to the apartment she had started calling home. "I'm back." She took off her shoes and left them near the door. She whipped her blonde hair back behind her and called out. "Where are you two?"

Lauren stepped out from the kitchen, holding Roger in her arms. "We're in here just getting him a bottle ready." She disappeared again and beeps from the microwave replaced the silence.

"I'm sorry for coming home so late." Rachel turned the corner and leaned against the wall to her right, watching Lauren test the bottle on her arm. "Come on in here. It'll be more comfortable feeding him in here than standing." She led Lauren and the baby Roger into the main living room and over to the couch.

Lauren cradled Roger and started feeding him as they talked. "How was it today?"

"Today?" Rachel asked. "As peaceful as could be hoped. If you ask me, it's just a matter of time before the Crag Cartel makes themselves known. It's been over a month, so we're waiting and watching. I can tell Dad doesn't like that plan. He won't ever admit it to anyone, but I can tell." She flexed her new prosthetic right ring finger.

Lauren used her free hand to place a towel on her shoulder. "Are you getting used to that yet?" Lauren momentarily took away the bottle as Roger coughed. She raised him to her shoulder and patted his back until she heard a burp.

"It still feels off. I can kind of still feel my finger, but I know it isn't there. This replacement serves its purpose well enough. Is it vain of me to have gotten this because I didn't want people to see my hand otherwise?"

"For a young woman like you?" Lauren smiled, replacing Roger in the crook of her arm and resuming feeding. "Not at all. It makes you a normal woman. Every woman wants to look her best. That's just normal."

"How about you two?" Rachel asked, digging the remote control out of the seat of the sofa. "Everything go alright here today?"

"Normal as always. Girl to girl, I was honestly looking forward to hearing about the group. You know, to break up the day-to-day routine."

"Sorry to bore you." Rachel smirked. "We're still on red alert preparing for war. You know the drill. We're squirreling away guns in various storages around the city, setting up numerous groups of personnel around the city, and doing our best to establish intel sources."

"Wait, setting up groups of personnel?" Lauren asked. "What's that mean?"

"According to Dad, it's how it was done back in his day. You set groups of three to four men or women up in an apartment, give them turf to guard and collect from, and it helps solidify your hold on land. If you ask me, it's outdated; but you know him - set in his ways."

"Spreading personnel out on your turf does make sense," Lauren said, taking the empty bottle away and burping Roger again. "It should help against the inevitable attack."

"It also makes whoever they do attack more vulnerable though if they only have four."

"Better than one, which would be the case if we weren't mandating where people stay. Strength in numbers and all that." Lauren handed Roger off to Rachel before taking the expended bottle back to the kitchen. "Where is the boss anyway?" she asked as she rinsed out the used bottle in the sink.

"He said he'd be home a little late tonight. I didn't ask why. I've learned not to ask unless I want more work."

"He's busy preparing for the inevitable," Lauren said, walking back into the room. "To be honest, I'm surprised the Crag Cartel hasn't made themselves known yet."

Rachel held Roger in her lap as she spoke. "We know they're in the city. We even have an idea where they're holed up, but we haven't heard of them starting up their new business. I wouldn't be surprised if Dad doesn't send a squad to their place and start the war officially soon. He's not one to wait to get hit first from what I've learned."

"You really think he'd attack a larger group like that?" Lauren sat down beside Rachel. "That seems risky."

"Risky, but he wants to be the only group in town. We'll see what he does. Whatever it is, it'll be soon…"

Meanwhile at the Warehouse…

"Davis!" Daniel overlooked the floor below, his hands clutching the guard rail. "Get up here for a minute." He disappeared back behind the door into his office as he slammed the door shut.

"I'll be right there," Warren said from below on the ground floor. He looked at the two men by him. "We'll get started with your trials afterward. You'd best prepare yourselves."

"Yes, sir," both men answered.

"Now go make yourselves useful somewhere. I don't care if you're assembling rifles or carrying shit. Do something besides standing here like jackasses." He turned and marched up the stairs. He entered the office and moved in front of Daniel's desk. "Yes, sir?"

"How is the perimeter?" Daniel asked, pulling a pack of cigarettes out of his coat pocket. "Are there any disturbances I should know about? I just know those cartel fucks are going to try something soon."

"I haven't seen anything out of the ordinary. I was preparing to administer another trial for our two newest recruits tonight."

"We'll need all the damned muscle we can muster." Daniel put the end of the cigarette in his mouth, brought the lighter up to it, and flicked the wheel, engulfing the other end in flame. "We've split our forces around our turf, accumulated weapons, and have more numbers. We're nearly ready. I've heard word from Oleg that they're planning something. Do you know what that means?"

"It means we should take the fight to them first if you ask me, sir," Warren said, placing his hands clasped together behind him. "If we let them strike first, they set the pace. We can't let that happen."

"Exactly." Daniel breathed out a cloud of smoke. "We have an idea where they are, but we need solid intel to make our move. Is Lee here yet? He should have arrived today."

"He's downstairs trying to find a place for his office. Shall I get him up here?" Warren asked.

"Yes."

Warren moved and opened the door. "Hey, Lee! Get up here. The boss wants to talk to you."

The pudgy thin haired man looked up and jogged as fast as his form allowed. He climbed the stairs and went past Warren on his way in.

"It took you long enough to get here, Lee," Daniel said to the man now across his desk. "I take it you brought your equipment with you?"

"Of course," the fat young man said, wiping his brow. "Where shall I set up to get started?"

"You have your living quarters if you want. If you want an office in this building, we can make that happen. Wherever you want it. I'd recommend your house though. This place doesn't have fast internet."

"Got it. I'll set up in my apartment."

"Just make damned sure you reply when I send you an encrypted email, and get what I tell you done," Daniel said. "For now, we need you to look up where our new rivals are in the city and report to us. They're called the Crag Cartel. They've recently moved here." He pushed a slip of paper across the desk toward Lee. "That's what we know about where they are. Use that as a jumping off point or whatever. You know more about it than I do. It should go without saying, but they probably have a tech specialist as well. So cover your tracks."

Lee grabbed the paper and looked at the writing. "Crag Cartel? I've heard of these guys before. What are they doing here in Toledo?"

"They're looking to expand their gun trade up here purposely to run us out of business. I will not allow that to

5

happen, which is why I need their locations. I'd prefer if you found their business locale, but personal addresses wouldn't be bad if you can find them. This is a time sensitive assignment. At this very moment, they're probably looking for our places. They know this warehouse, but that's about all. I want that playing field even. You are my ace in the hole."

"Finding a group that size in this town shouldn't take too long. The max would be a day if I really have trouble."

"I want it faster than that. Their tech people won't take their time, and neither will you. Is that clear? Make no mistake - this is a war, and information is power. You will be getting us said power. Do not let me down, son. I invited you for a reason. Now earn your keep. Head on home, get set up, and find them. Once you do, send me an encrypted email to the address I put on that paper."

"It will get done immediately," Lee said, face reddening. "So, about my getting my own place?"

"Denied." Daniel took in a lungful of smoke and exhaled billowing clouds. "It's for your own protection. I don't want you by yourself in case they track you down. I did instruct them to give you a private room, so don't worry. You'll have your privacy and peace while working. Now get going, and get to work. I expect an email tomorrow."

Lee stood up and gave a formal bow. "Yes, sir." He immediately left the room, leaving Warren and Daniel.

Daniel looked up at Warren. "I know I put you two in the same place. My apologies. Try to put up with him."

"I'll keep him in line, sir." Warren smirked. "Our household has upgraded our internet infrastructure as requested."

"Good. I always keep my men and women well equipped. I consider it business expenses. Now I know you have a busy schedule. I won't keep you. Keep up the good work, Davis."

"Yes, sir," Warren said. He turned around and headed for the door. He stopped after opening the door and looked back at his boss. "Oh, there's one more thing I should mention."

"What's that?" Daniel asked, leaning back in the extravagant chair.

"The last of our initiated have now moved into their assigned domiciles around the quadrant we discussed."

"How many more hopefuls do we have besides the pair I saw you with earlier?" Daniel snuffed out the cigarette in the nearby ashtray.

"There are six right now. More show up every week."

"Good. Then we can have them in two more houses. The more mini-bases we have around our territory, the more secure it is. In fact..." Daniel got up with a wide smile and planted his palms on the desk, looking at Warren. "Do you know of anyone else that would be qualified to test the recruits?"

"Adams is reliable. I know he could."

"Then get him to speed up the process. I trust you'll answer any questions he may have. I want this done perfectly, Davis."

"It will be, sir."

"I know. Now get to work, you lazy bum," Daniel said, a tinge of sarcasm tinting his voice.

Warren nodded and, without further words, left and closed the door behind him.

"I'll have to keep my eye on him," Daniel grunted, moving around the desk and looking out the windows. He spotted Warren talking to Ben on the ground floor. "He's a hard worker, ambitious, and capable. I need to keep him in his place. He can't get ideas above his station."

A ringing from Daniel's jacket pocket interrupted him.

He recognized the ring tone as one his daughter installed on his phone of pop music playing. "I hate this damned tone." Daniel dug out the phone...

2

Rachel switched channels and tossed the remote control onto the nearby end table. She looked over at Lauren in the kitchen. "Hurry up. The show's starting in like a minute. I just put Roger to bed, so let's relax."

"Popcorn's almost ready." The telltale beeping of the microwave followed. "I take that back. It's done." She opened the microwave, brought the bag over to the table with a bowl on it, and emptied its contents into it. She brought the bowl over to the couch and sat down beside Rachel.

"I bet you never imagined you'd be watching television with the boss's daughter when you joined the Morris Syndicate, did you?" she asked, a knowing smile on her face as she grabbed some popcorn.

"Not really. I expected more illegal activities if I'm honest. Not that I'm complaining. I love babysitting Roger. Not to mention the pay's out of this world for what I do."

"I figured you'd like this gig. Aren't you glad I picked you out when I did?"

A loud noise from the front door interrupted the pair's talk.

"What was that?" Rachel asked, already reaching for her gun. She stood up from the couch and readied her weapon.

Lauren placed the popcorn forgotten on the kitchen counter and pulled her weapon out. She came up beside Rachel, shoulder to shoulder. Both women pointed their weapon toward the front door.

"It could have been the neighbors," Lauren whispered to Rachel at her side. "You know, slamming doors is pretty loud."

"Shh," Rachel shushed her friend. "Do you hear that?"

Muffled male voices, obviously frazzled, could be heard behind the front door. "Just open the door, man. Let's get this over with. I want my debt paid off already. Besides, this place gives me the creeps for some reason."

"I'm trying damn it," a different male voice responded with another large noise and the door shook momentarily.

"Well try harder," a third voice said. "I want to get home sometime tonight."

"We got some real winners it seems," Rachel said, sarcasm dripping from her words. "I hope you don't have any priors."

"Why?"

The door burst open on the third try. A man fell forward into the narrow hallway after losing his balance. The two girls didn't waste any time. As soon as the door was thrown open, they squeezed the triggers repeatedly. Beyond the muzzle flashes, two men could be seen falling backwards into the hallway in front of the doorway.

"That's why," Rachel said before angling her firearm down to execute the lone man inside the apartment struggling to get to his feet."

"What?" Lauren asked in a loud voice. "I'm sorry, my ears are ringing."

"I said, that's why." Rachel repeated in a louder voice. She inched down the hallway, keeping the weapon at the ready, and closed the door. She peeked into the nearby room and dashed over to the crib near her bed. "Thank Christ."

Roger laid in the crib crying his eyes out.

Rachel holstered her weapon and reached into the crib. "Come here, baby." She placed Roger's head on her shoulder. "Shh, everything's alright now, sweetie. You're okay," she said in her best soothing voice.

Lauren moved to the open doorway. "Someone had to have called that in. The police will be here inside fifteen minutes."

"Which is why I asked if you had priors."

"I technically do not. I was never caught or brought up on charges if that answers your question."

"Good. Then when they get here, tell them it was self-defense. We feared for our lives and defended ourselves. I'm pretty sure this state has a presumption of self-defense. Look, they broke the door down, and there's a guy inside holding a gun. It'll be fine. It'll be boring for you and a little nerve wracking, but trust me when I say it'll be good."

"You're leaving?" Lauren asked, moving to the side allowing the pair to pass her into the hallway.

Rachel packed a nearby bag with baby powder, formula, a bottle, diapers, wipes, and assorted other materials as she talked. "I have to go tell father what happened. We can't have him coming back here with the police here, can we? It'd be the end of the syndicate."

"Right," Lauren said. "I'll call him and let him know not to come over here while you two get out of here."

"No, don't," Rachel said. "You act like a scared little maiden in a corner, and when the police get here they'll buy that hook, line, and sinker. They'll treat you with kid gloves. I'll call father on the way."

"Alright."

"Sorry about girl's night in being ruined, but shit happens. We'll reschedule," Rachel said with a laugh in front of the door.

"Right," Lauren said, watching Rachel open the door and step over the bodies.

Rachel got out into the hallway and looked both ways, seeing no one. "I'd be scared too if I heard that much gunfire," she muttered to herself before jogging toward the door containing the stairwell. She ducked inside, still trying to comfort the crying child in her arms.

"I'm sorry about the loud noises, baby," Rachel cooed. "Mama had to take care of the bad men." She went down the stairs as she soothed him. Once she reached the bottom floor, Roger had stopped fussing as much and quieted down, his eyes closed again. "There you go," her soothing voice said.

She opened the nearby door and made her way out of the lobby and into the parking lot. She strapped Roger into the back seat baby chair and got into the driver's seat. She pulled out of the parking lot and into traffic. "I can't believe they found our place. We'll have to move." She pulled into a nearby shopping mall's parking lot and pulled out the phone from her pants pocket. She input Daniel's number and brought it to her ear before pulling back into traffic.

"Yeah?" Daniel asked after a few moments. "What is it, princess? Wasn't this your girl's night in thing? Why are you calling? Did you run out of popcorn?"

"Stop being a condescending ass. No," Rachel said,

biting her lip. She looked out the glass window to her left at the passing traffic. "We were hit."

"Hit?"

"Crag sent guys to our apartment, Dad - as in they busted the door down and tried to kill us. Do you still feel like being a smart ass? Your daughter and grandson were in mortal danger. Does that drive the point home?"

"That means the police will be there soon," Daniel's voice said. "Are you still there?"

"I left Lauren there to plead self-defense. Me and Rog got out of there in case they came back. She should be fine. They busted the door down. Self-defense is a rock solid defense in Ohio."

"I'm not worried about that. I'm worried about where we'll bed down from now on. That new house I bought technically can be moved into, but it's barebones. You know where it is?"

"Yeah, Dad. I went along with you. We'll be good. I still can't believe you spent all that money on a big ass mansion. Now we need another score, right when the war's started. Nothing can go wrong there."

"Can it." Daniel's voice turned stern. "Do not second guess me. I prepared it for this case especially. I knew they'd find our place eventually. I didn't expect it to be so soon. So we'll meet there tonight."

"You knew we'd get hit and didn't tell me?" Rachel asked. "Gee, thanks, Dad."

"I told you to expect anything. It wasn't a meaningless platitude. Pay attention when I tell you something. That's on you."

"Right," Rachel braked for the upcoming stop light. "I'll be extra careful and over examine everything you say now."

"Better than the alternative," Daniel's sarcastic voice

said. "Now hurry up and get over there. It should be safe. I'll send some guards over there. They'll patrol around the perimeter. Just have them set up rotations. Do you remember how I taught you?"

"Sadly I remember that night."

"Then do as I taught you, and always stay armed just in case."

"In case they get by four men?"

"I've done it before with your oh so delightful, deceased Uncle figure. It can happen if they're good enough or the patrols are sloppy. Always be ready for an attack at any time, just to be safe."

Rachel frowned, her eyes narrowing. She grit her teeth before she spoke. "Sure thing. I learned that lesson tonight, first hand."

"Good. Then go. Make sure to double and even triple back in case they're still tailing you. We want to keep the new place secret," Daniel's voice said before the line went dead with a click.

"That bastard," Rachel hung up with a scowl. "Rubbing Roger's death in my face like that. He lies to me about killing him then waves it in my face."

A cooing behind her distracted her. She looked in the backseat. "I'm sorry, baby. Mommy's just a little angry at your grandpa. Let's go to our new house then, yeah?" She continued down the road leading out of the city.

A while later at the new mansion...

"I think this was the place." Rachel pulled off of the main road onto a gravel path with woods on either side. "The place is certainly out in the sticks. It's a bit creepy if I'm honest." She could barely make out the fence ahead of her, thanks only to her headlights being set to bright piercing through the suffocating darkness. She slowed to a stop at the large fence. "Right, there's no one to let me in. Guess it's time to do it manually." She looked into the backseat. The soft breathing indicated the rhythmic bumps of the car ride had lulled Roger to sleep.

She got out of the car as quietly as she could and closed the door behind her. She jogged up to the large gate and gripped it. She pulled the gate open. "Thank God they left it unlocked for us." She pushed the gate open fully and got back into her car. She pulled the car inside the normally enclosed property. She noticed headlights in her rear-view window and immediately stopped the car. She reached down to her waistline, pulled out her weapon, and got out of the car. She kneeled behind the now open car door.

When the car behind hers stopped in front of the now open fence the door swung open. "Whoa, easy there." Daniel stepped out of the sports car with his hands up. "It's just me. I got here as soon as I could." He looked to the side. "I see you were able to get the gate open."

Rachel stood up and holstered her firearm. "Jesus, Dad. You scared the shit out of me."

"At least you took my advice and are always ready now." Daniel got back in the car and pulled his car up beside Rachel's before getting out again. "Close that gate, and we'll head inside and get settled in." Without further words, he reached into the back of Rachel's car, unbuckled Roger from his car seat, and pulled him out. "We'll be waiting inside."

"Yeah, just make me do everything myself," Rachel said, watching her father already walking off in the direction of the mansion. She sighed and turned around. She closed the gate and locked it. She hurried across the large front yard to catch up with her father and son. She caught up with them in front of the stairs leading to the front door.

"That was fast. You're sure it's secured?" Daniel asked, climbing the stairs.

Rachel climbed alongside her father. "As best as I can figure. It won't move unless unlocked from inside."

"Good." His free right hand reached into his back pocket and picked out a key. He inserted it and twisted, unlocking the door. He pocketed the key and opened the door, revealing a nearly pitch-black interior. "Here. Hold him." He handed off Roger to Rachel and moved inside, feeling around the wall just inside until he felt a light switch and flicked it on, illuminating the massive entryway.

"I still don't think we needed the chandelier." Rachel stepped inside and gazed up at the massive light fixture. "How much did that cost again?"

"Focus on the more immediate problems we have." Daniel closed the door behind the group. "I have men on their way here. I told them to call you when they got here and that you'd let them in. They'll patrol around the property in groups of three. That should be adequate to secure this place for now. When we make the big move, we'll have multiple groups."

"At least then we can use the six bedrooms here instead of half the place being empty." Rachel patted Roger's back as he cooed and pointed across the massive foyer. Four rooms to divide how many men total?"

"Ideally we'd want nine." He led the pair through the left door, leading into a large living room. A large seventy-inch television was mounted on the wall in front of the room. A large sofa, and multiple recliners flanked it. "Each room has two beds. Someone will have to sleep on this." Daniel leaned on the couch and patted the exquisite material. "This is exactly why I got all these. Just in case we need more personnel posted here. They can sleep in the recliners too. It'd be just like the old days."

"Old days?"

"I used to have to sleep on the couch in our first post. Sis and," Daniel sneered, "Roger had their own room."

"Right." Rachel's phone chirped in her pants pocket. "Here." She handed Roger off to her father and answered. "Yeah? Alright. I'll be right out." She hung up and looked at her dad. "You must have put the fear of God to get them over here so quickly."

"No," Daniel said, circling around the couch and sitting down, placing Roger down on his knees. "They don't want us to die. You know why?"

Rachel stopped at the door and turned back. "We sign their paychecks."

"Exactly."

Rachel shook her head and exited the room. She left the house and undid the metal gate, allowing the two cars to enter and park as she closed and locked it back. She turned around and saw the three men exit their respective cars.

"Ma'am? Why are we here?" the oldest among them asked. He scratched a grey patch of his beard as he spoke. "The boss didn't really tell us anything. I mean, I just joined proper, and I'm a little lost."

"What's your name again?" She looked the middle-aged man up and down, mentally noting how in shape he was.

"It's Chris, Chris Bristol."

"Well, Chris, you guys are the first round of patrols. You do know how to patrol around outside, yes? I hope so. More men will be coming soon enough and relieve you. So far as rooms go, once you come in from duty, we'll get you settled in."

"Understood," Chris said. "We'll get to work." He placed his hands on both men's shoulders at his sides. "Now let's go. I'll take point." He guided the three away from Rachel and trailed the fence.

The man on his right said as they were walking off, "I'll bring up the rear."

"At least that's settled now. It's one less thing to worry about." She watched the group of men's suit clad forms disappear into the darkness and went back inside.

"You get them to work?" Daniel asked as Rachel opened the door.

"They're patrolling around as we speak," Rachel said, taking a seat in one of the nearby recliners. "This feels more like a temporary place though."

"It will for the next month, but this is our new house."

"I sort of remember your dad having his place out in the sticks too." Rachel said, looking over. "Is that why you bought this? Trying to emulate your dad?"

"I did this because it makes sense," Daniel snapped. "Not because of tradition. It just so happens my old man made good decisions most of the time. Think about it. With enough manpower, we'll know when anybody gets close. There are no neighbors to call the police, and I've made this place like a fortress with bullet resistant windows. They'd have to bring military grade explosives just to break them. It's as safe as we're going to get." He leaned forward and grabbed the television remote control sitting on the coffee table in the middle of the furniture and turned it on. "Now tell me all about what happened to you. I want to hear everything. How did they get in? Were they professionals?"

"Thankfully no," Rachel said, pulling the control at her right, elevating her legs in front of her. "They tried to kick the door down a few times, alerting us they were there. After they realized that wouldn't work, one tackled through the door and landed face first in our hallway. We put them down. From what I could gather from listening and watching, they were probably some junkies who owed the Crag cartel. They were probably trying to pay their debts the only way they could. They sure weren't trained from what I could tell, or disciplined for that matter. I think one ran away after he saw the others die."

"He'll be killed for his cowardice is my guess," Daniel said with a smirk. "He deserves no less going after my family like that. Still, that means this cold war just turned red hot. Technically they have deniability since their own men didn't go. I know better though."

"On the off case it wasn't them, you know we'd be igniting a powder keg while someone else wants a piece of us."

"There is no one else who'd do this."

"You don't think the hood rats would try for some petty revenge?"

Daniel shook his head. "Not with Brent's final command of squashing the beef. The only way they'd get involved is if the cartel ordered them to. I'm one hundred percent sure it was the Crag cartel who is behind this. I have our tech man searching for them. In fact, I've also sent for him to stay here. It's the safest place we can give, and they'll go after him."

"I guess someone's sleeping in a sleeping bag on the floor then."

"The men will figure that part out. Worst case scenario is we can buy a damned cot and put it somewhere. I doubt any of the men will bitch about that though. It'd make them look like a wimp."

"Fine," Rachel said. "Ignoring the practical concerns,

what are we going to do to respond? I assume we're not going to just take this on the chin and hide in our little mansion."

"You are correct." Daniel tossed the remote from his left hand to his right in one fluid motion as he spoke. "We're firing back tonight."

"Tonight? Don't you think they'll be expecting that?"

"No. If anything they'll anticipate we'll run and defend. A counterattack will be unexpected. It's what we always expected when we initiated."

"How often did that work?" Rachel asked.

"Quite often," Daniel said. "Once our tech division gets us a location, we'll send a counterattack. Not just a run of the mill raid, but one they'll remember before they fuck with us again."

Rachel leaned forward and removed her dress shoes and put them beside the recliner. "Big words, but what does that mean? I'd hope that doesn't mean a full-on siege."

"Not quite. They go after my daughter, we go after their money making locales. For them, it's the same importance. We don't just go in and kill them all. We do it smarter. A little arson never hurt anybody."

"Except if anyone is inside."

"They'll pass out from smoke inhalation first anyway. It won't hurt them."

"Just kill them."

"Exactly. It's a merciful way to go if you think of it that way."

Rachel looked away from her father, toward the television. "Whatever you say. I'm just glad I don't have to go do such things anymore."

"Yeah, about that. I have bad news."

"There is no way you're about to say what I think you are." Rachel narrowed her eyes and glared over at him.

"You don't have to exit the car like the strike force, but I do need you to accompany them. You know, keep the engine running and all that. It won't be a crippling blow to an organization that big, but it's a nice deterrent. You come at us, you lose money kind of thing. Money is the only thing people like this understand."

"Seems like messing with their income would just make them more aggressive then."

Daniel smirked. "That, or they'll realize we aren't worth fighting. I don't mind making a truce with them. They won't agree to one unless we make them realize that's the better option. Do you understand?"

"I understand we're planning to be stubborn with a giant cartel that smuggles drugs, humans, and God knows what else."

"Good."

Rachel looked away and rolled her eyes when her phone rang again. "What now?"

"Probably our hacker and extra personnel. Go let them in and give them their orders."

"Yes, sir." Rachel hopped out of her chair and headed toward the front door...

3

"Lee, tell us what you found last night," Daniel said from the front of the room behind the podium. He looked left and right at the numerous members sitting in the rows of chairs and settled on Lee's large shape right in front of him. "I expect you had to have found something after searching all night, or I'll be disappointed."

"Disregarding last night's whirlwind," Lee stood up and cleared his throat, "yes, I did find something you could use I think. I found where numerous traphouses of theirs are located, but the bigger game is their supply line."

"You found their supplier?" Daniel asked, an eyebrow raised, a smile inching its way onto his face. "That's actionable intel right there. Enlighten us."

"After a lot of virtual digging through numerous local online message boards, breaking into the guy's phone and viewing his texts, I've found one of their delivery men. Now he's one of many, but this guy is the one they go to for their big shipments. He's never lost a shipment from what I've found. I'm not just talking trucks full of drugs either. I mean on top of that, he also has been known to smuggle people, guns, and any manner of things for them. He's an old school member of the cartel. His name is Harvey Neville."

"That sounds more like a college professor than a cartel member," Rachel spoke up from Daniel's side with a snicker. She saw her father send her a dark glare, causing her to clear her throat and shut up.

Daniel turned back to Lee. "Continue."

"Your daughter makes a good point. He's an American that joined them. Don't make any assumptions though. He's as bloodthirsty and callous as any of them. He's a psychopath. There are rumors that say he's been known to kill those that try to mess with his duties. It's all hearsay online, but I'd assume the worst to be safe." He opened the manilla envelope and stood up. He stepped forward and handed it over to Daniel. "Here. Take a look."

Daniel placed it down on the podium and flipped it open. "If people online are talking, it means he's been sloppy somewhere before. Civilians don't just get that kind of intel on their own. Can you pinpoint the incident in question while we deal with this?"

"Sir?"

"Can you track it down? If you can, we can use that against them. No group wants their exploits being talked about on the street."

"No, sir. There's no concrete evidence online. There's no recordings of it - not on traffic cameras, not on any video hosting websites, or even on social media. Like I said, it's all rumors."

"Damn," Daniel said, still thumbing through the pages.

"Sir, if I might make a suggestion." Warren raised his right hand.

"Go ahead, Davis," Daniel said, not looking up from the papers.

"Instead of doing what we normally would, why not be more subtle this time?"

"Elaborate further."

Warren cleared his throat. "Instead of sending a strike force to this Neville's house, why not simply make it look like an accident? For example, his house could have a gas leak, or his house could burn down in a tragic accident while he was in bed. We'd accomplish two things by doing so. One, we wouldn't be directly tied to it when the police and fire department investigate. Two, the cartel could only guess we were the ones involved. For all they know it was him being sloppy."

"They're not stupid, Davis. They're going to know it was us after they hit us." Daniel looked up at the relatively full room of men and women sitting on the assorted chairs in lines. "We're answering back, and they're going to know it was us. Having said that, we need them to know we don't mess around. We're going after this Neville. I need three volunteers." He looked around the room, waiting.

Ben raised his hand. "I'll go, sir."

"Good man," Daniel said, browsing the rest of them. "Who's going with him?"

Two of the men Warren was seen talking to the day prior raised their hands. The taller of the two spoke up. "We'll go."

"Now remind me. Who are you two again? You're new, yes?" Daniel massaged the bridge of his nose.

"I'm Jeremy." The taller one pointed toward himself. He gestured with his thumb toward the man to his right. "This is Drew, my little brother."

"I like the cuts of your jibs, Jeremy and Drew. You'll be going with Adams."

"Who, sir?"

"Ben there." Daniel pointed at the young man. "You three will be accompanied by my daughter."

Rachel's eyes widened, but she dared not speak out of turn.

"You three will report to her, follow her plan, and get this done. Is that understood?"

Jeremy and Drew nodded with enthusiasm. "Yes, sir."

"Good. While they're doing that, I'm going to fine tune the roster here. The current patrols aren't extensive enough. You four, head out." He pointed at his daughter, then towards Ben, and finally toward the new pair. "The rest of you will be staying here."

Rachel hefted herself out of the chair and motioned for the door. "Come on then, you three. You heard the orders from the boss." She left, gesturing for them to follow her out into the ornate hallway of the mansion. She flung the door open and left it open behind her. She turned and leaned back against the wall. Once the final man had exited the room she spoke again. "Follow me. We're going to do this right, and that means planning every bit of it out. I have just the room for this." She led the group throughout the sprawling mansion until they came to a room. "Here we are." She opened the door and led them inside.

A large round table was in the middle of the medium sized room. A large desktop computer sat on a wooden table in the corner, an office chair sitting in front of it. A manilla folder lay atop the table. "I had Lee leave us a copy in here before the meeting. We have all the intel we need here." She picked it up and opened it, browsing through the papers until she picked one page out and tossed the rest on the table.

"We're just starting a fire, right?" Drew asked.

"Not quite. Weren't you paying attention, new guy?"

Rachel asked, a look of bemusement crossing her features. "We're going after this Harvey. How we go about it is up to me. Dad never said we have to make it look like an accident. There's no point. They'll know it was us anyway. Now according to this, his place is near their other operations."

"Which means?" Jeremy asked.

"It means we need an escape plan to get out quick," Ben answered. "If we're going in loud, we need to leave quick since they probably have men nearby."

"Which is why I'll be the driver. You all can go inside and get it done. I'll make sure you have a getaway driver. Ben," she turned to the young man, "you'll be leading the assault in there since I know you can take care of it. Now we want them to know about it, so going in quiet is off the table. That makes it easier and more difficult at the same time."

Ben walked over to Rachel and looked over her shoulder at the paper. "It says he lives with a few bodyguards from the cartel. How did he find that out?"

"Dude probably looked through their webcam. It even says they have one on their pc. Too bad they didn't put black tape over it. They got sloppy. I want you three to go in locked and loaded. Think smash and grab, but instead it's a smash and shoot job. Go in loud. Surprise them. Going in like swat would help too, meaning go in from the front and back at the same time. That should give you enough of a tactical advantage to shoot first while they're reacting."

"What are you going to do?" Drew asked. "Sit in the car and keep the engine running?"

"That," Rachel said, "and play overwatch for the lot of you. Basically, I'm keeping your asses alive and out of prison with support. I'll bring my laptop. Ben here knows what I can accomplish with it. Remember our little kidnapping mission when you were new? The one where dad and Warren went with us?"

"If I recall correctly, you called the guards, distracting them," Ben said, smiling. "It made it a lot easier. Don't worry, boys." He placed both hands on Drew and Jeremy's shoulders.

"Now if we're done with the male bonding exercise, let's go over exact details and then head out. I want to be done with the planning and meet back here tonight."

That night...

"I don't like this," Jeremy said from the back seat of the car. "We're in their turf, right? Any one of these houses could have armed men ready to file out at any time. They're expecting retaliation too I bet."

"Stop your belly aching," Ben said from the front passenger seat. "You two did bring suppressers like I said to, yes?"

Drew nodded. "Yeah, but the neighbors will still hear the noise. Especially if we shoot more than once or twice.

"You need to make peace that this is happening. Take this as a lesson. Don't volunteer unless you know what it means. Just know you probably made a name for yourself with Daddy doing this. Risk versus reward, and you risked it tonight. Now pay attention and stop bitching." Rachel pulled the car over to the side of the street and parked. "We're nearby the house you're hitting. She pointed down the alley. "It's down there and to the left. Now before you boys leave, let me work my magic. Hand me my laptop." She held out her right hand as Ben handed the device over. She plopped it on the dashboard so everyone could see.

"What's a laptop going to do?" Jeremy asked.

"Clearly you've never seen someone who knows what they're doing," Rachel said, bringing up the time-honored app Roger gave to her. "I can see who has phones in there. I see two downstairs in the main room. Hell, I can time it so they get a phone call when you three bust in there to add to the chaos. I can even use their cameras against them to get an idea of the layout of the place. To boot," she minimized the window and brought up a web browser, "with this I can just get the damned floor plans." She typed away for a few minutes until a diagram popped up on screen. "There. Now memorize this so you don't get lost in there."

The two men in the back leaned forward, staring intently at the screen. "How did you even manage this? Aren't floor plans like confidential and stored in the county office or something?" the older brother Jeremy asked.

"Sure, if you want to go the official route. Nobody smart goes the official route though. You'd be amazed what you can find if you search more ambiguous sites. Now I can guide you three through the place. It looks like they also do in fact have a webcam inside. Let's see what they're doing in there." She typed for a few moments with furious abandon until a video feed appeared on the screen. "Ew, that's like four hundred eighty pixel shit right there. They're cheap with their security vulnerabilities."

"I only see one guy from that," Ben said. "The other one who's downstairs isn't visible from that vantage point.

"I'm still searching for devices. Give me a minute. Here we go. We've hit paydirt." A different video feed appeared. This time the camera was facing down toward the floorboards.

"What is this?" Drew asked.

"The floor," Jeremy said.

"It's a phone camera. Quiet. I hear someone talking."

Sure enough with the chatter in the car dying down, a male voice could be heard whispering to himself. "Fucking idiots down there," he was heard muttering to himself.

"He's a real ray of sunshine," Rachel said. "So we know there's a guy upstairs. I'm not seeing any surveillance cameras in the place."

"It's just a normal house. I doubt they'd spring for such things."

"Of one of their top smugglers, though they do have two guards downstairs that we saw. That's a total of three hostiles. That makes it a fair fight," Rachel said, turning around to look at the three men.

"Are we just walking up to the door and smashing it open or something?" Drew asked.

"You could, but I wouldn't," Rachel said. "The cartel tried that exact thing when they ambushed me. It didn't work well for them. One guy should go in the back first. That will distract the front room. Then when I give the say so, the front room team should head inside. Ben," she looked over to the young man, "you still remember how to pick locks?"

"I remember a bit."

"Then you're going in the front. Sorry, boys. You two will have to split up. Who has more strength between the two of you?"

The two brothers looked at each other and back to Rachel. "Me," they both said together. The two devolved into petty arguing, each disagreeing with the other.

"Boys!" Rachel said, an air of authority enveloping her words. "Quiet. You," she pointed at the taller of the pair. "You're going in the back door. Don't try to be an action movie hero either. That means no trying to kick the damned thing down. Just use your shoulder and tackle through it.

Get a running start if you have to. I'll be watching downstairs and seeing when they turn to the back. That's when the front door team opens the door and starts shooting. Needless to say you," she pointed at Jeremy, "are going to have to find cover in case they're quick."

"I feel like I'm being used as bait," Jeremy said.

"You are," Rachel said. "Get used to it. I had to do it too, and I'm the bosses daughter. I paid my dues. Now stop bitching. Does everybody understand the plan? Once the job's done, run back here and I'll get us out of here."

"Wait for the back door to distract them, bust in and shoot, then get back. It seems easy enough," Ben said. "Shall we go and get this over with now?"

"That would be great. I'd like to get at least six hours sleep tonight before our meeting with Oleg tomorrow morning," Rachel said, swiping a strand of blonde hair out of her face. "Before you all head out, we're doing a comms check." She reached over and opened the glove compartment to pull out a headset. She hooked it up to her laptop and pressed a few keys. "Join the call and see if you can hear me."

The three men followed her orders and placed their respective ear buds in their ear.

"Testing, can you hear me?"

"We're good," Ben said. "What about you two?"

"I can hear," both said.

"Good. Then get going, and only go in on my signal. Remember that," Rachel said.

Without further ado, the men in the car filed out. Rachel switched to a local satellite feed, watching the men's cell phone signals move. "I need to tell them to destroy those burners after this. I can't forget that." She watched as two orbs moved around to the side of the target house and slowly made their way to the front door while the other orb continued around the back of the house. "I see you're all nearly in position. I'm going to call the two on the lower floor. After that, Jeremy, I want you to cause an absolute ruckus near the back door. It doesn't matter if the door actually opens or not. Ben, I want you lockpicking that door now, but don't open it until I say. Let me know when it's picked."

Silence filled the car cabin for a few minutes until Ben's voice spoke up in her ear. "I think that's got it. The knob turns so we're ready up front."

"Roger that," Rachel said. "I'm calling the two downstairs. Count to ten and then, Jeremy, ram into that door as hard as you can. I want them thinking they have a swat team at their door." She pressed the necessary buttons and heard Ben's voice.

"I hear ringing."

"That's my cue," Jeremy said over the call. A loud banging noise sounded off over the digital medium.

"Someone has a hot mic, and I have a pretty good idea who it is," Rachel said with a wince at the loud sudden noises. She witnessed the guard turning around toward the back door. "Front team, go now. They're facing the back door."

Without further coaxing, Rachel could hear gunshots echo across the local neighborhood. A veritable cacophony of cracks met her ears. She looked away from the screen and out the window toward their target. "How many shots do they need?" she muttered under her breath. "I knew I should have went in there with them." She saw dark figures sprinting toward the car. She looked back at the screen, one dot still inside the house. "What the hell?"

The doors flung open. Jeremy and Ben got in. Ben immediately said. "Get us out of here."

Rachel complied and asked. "Where the hell's Drew?" The car tires squealed at the sudden jerky movements of the vehicle as it got back on the road.

"The plan only half worked." Ben turned around in his seat and peered out the back window as he spoke. "The guy came downstairs at the wrong time."

Rachel looked up into the rear-view mirror at the unchanging, stoic face of Jeremy in the back seat. "I see."

"We got the two guards, but the main target got Drew. We got out of there as quick as we could. If we hadn't, there'd have been more of us hit."

"I'm going to kill that motherfucker." Jeremy's voice was filled with rage.

"You'll have your chance if I know my father," Rachel said. She returned her gaze to the road ahead. "We retaliated, but he'll want more. If he wants that guy again, I'll volunteer you to go on the job." Silence filled the dark cabin as flashing lights passed by outside the window from the many storefronts. "For what little it's worth right now, I'm sorry. I was so focused on providing the distraction I didn't see the guy moving toward the stairs. I was sure I had everything accounted for."

"The plan was good," Ben said. "Shit doesn't always go according to plan. You know that as well as I do."

"Let's just get back to base and pick up the pieces," Rachel said, sparing one more glance at the fury filled face of Jeremy in the mirror above. She shook her head with a sigh and drove on...

4

Rachel led the pair behind her through the mansion's hallways until they came to a large pair of double doors with an ornamental lion's head on each door, with large ornate handles below. "Come on then. Let me do the talking in here."

The group entered the room and saw Daniel leaning back in his giant office chair, his feet propped up on his desk. He had a cigar in his mouth, puffing away, a smile on his face. He waved the group in. "Get in here and report already so I can get to bed."

The three formed a line in front of the desk, Jeremy and Ben on either side of Rachel. She took a step forward and cleared her throat.

Daniel interrupted her, a solemn look crossing his features at the realization. "Why are there only three of you?"

Rachel spoke up. "We came up with a plan to assault the house and carry out the objective."

"Elaborate."

Rachel relayed the plan of attack she came up with to

her father. "Once I distracted the guards downstairs, I orchestrated the distraction and assault team I thought perfectly. There was one oversight and it cost us Drew's life. I didn't see the dot of the guy upstairs on my screen moving." Her voice lost its commanding edge. "It was my fault he's dead."

Daniel bit his lip and looked behind his daughter towards Jeremy's angry face. "First," Daniel said, getting up and moving around the desk. He moved to his daughter's left side and came face to face with the remaining brother. "I want you to know I am deeply sorry about this, son. You rest assured I'm going to make that right by taking the bastards out." He placed a hand on Jeremy's shoulder, looking him in the eyes.

Jeremy blinked, keeping his face stoic. "Yes, sir."

"Good man. As far as what happened there - that's the reality of a battlefield. I'm not trying to be callous. People live and die at the whims of fate. You did your best to minimize casualties. Sometimes it's not in the cards. What is in the cards is revenge." He backed up and paced in front of the three as he spoke. "They started this war, and we're going to finish it. I didn't survive all those battles just to be pushed around by some cartel. They think they can bully me and my men? Fuck that."

"What's the plan then, Father?" Rachel asked. "Go after them again?"

"Yes, but we need something a little more sophisticated instead of a breaking and entering. You said you got the two guards?"

"Yes, sir," Ben said, his hands behind his back. "The only one who survived was the target since he was upstairs."

"Right, so he knows he's a target. He won't be available for the next attempt, so we need another guy. Thankfully our newest member, our resident tech specialist, prepared a list for me while you all were out there." He opened a nearby drawer on his desk and pulled out a piece of paper. "This here is five names we can choose from. We have a dealer, a local businessman who chose to align with them, another smuggler, one of their lower ranking members, and the same guy as last time. So out of those four, I say we pay a visit to the local businessman. See if we can't change his decision."

"Sir, may I go?" Jeremy asked.

"Of course. I want you to work out a little of that rage. Just don't kill him. We could use what intel he has on his newfound allies. If possible, I want to question him personally."

"Do we know where the guy is?" Rachel asked.

Daniel slid the paper over to her. "Take a look. I made copies. He's not too far away."

Rachel picked up the paper and looked to the right of each name to see addresses. "We should be able to knock that out inside an hour from the looks of this."

"Kidnapping's harder than straight elimination. If you need to, question him on site. Just be sure to cover your tracks. You know the drill - masks, gloves, and watch for cameras near the place so your license plate doesn't get caught on camera. I want this done by the book." He got up and came face to face with his daughter. "Is that understood?"

"Yes, sir," Rachel said. "When are we to do this?"

"Whenever you're ready. Tonight if you're able."

"Understood."

He poked her shoulder, narrowing his eyes. "Be careful this time."

Rachel glared at him. "I get it."

"Do you?" Daniel asked, leaning back on his desk. "Because a man is dead." He pointed at Jeremy. "His brother is dead because you missed a detail. Make sure it doesn't happen again."

Rachel gritted her teeth but only answered with a nod.

"I didn't hear you."

"Yes, sir," she said through her teeth.

"Dismissed then. Be more careful, and get this done. I'm relying on you all. Take any personnel you need or materials."

All three members in front of the desk bowed in unison and turned around to exit. Ben left first, followed by Jeremy, and finally Rachel.

Rachel closed the door behind her with a sigh and a shake of her head.

"I don't blame you, Miss Morris," Jeremy said, looking down the hallway. "I want you to know that. It was my fault. If I'd been quicker, he'd still be alive. I just had to hesitate."

"Sorry," Rachel said. "Don't tell anyone I said that." She let out a large breath. "Let's just focus on our new job. Father said we're going after a shop owner. How hard can that be?"

"Never underestimate a blue-collar working man," Ben said. "They can be stubborn and can surprise you. I know a guy who robbed a local business. Dude pulled out a gun and shot at him. He was lucky to get away alive."

"What a happy story," Rachel said, sarcasm tinting her voice.

"Not really. Dude got caught on cctv and picked up later that night. The last I heard he joined a gang in prison, so he's probably never getting out."

"Ignoring your friend's poor choices, let's get this thing on the road. We don't need a bunch of preamble for shaking down a store owner." Rachel took off walking and motioned for them to follow her.

A bit later on the side of the road...

"Is that the place?" Rachel asked, rubbing her eyes and blinking. "It looks like a trash heap."

"I doubt he entered into an alliance with the cartel for fun. Dude's probably desperate," Ben said. "Which is both good and bad. There's nothing more dangerous than a scared desperate man."

"Who cares?" Jeremy asked. "He's going to do what we say or else."

"Follow my lead when we go in there. He's going to be scared when he sees three masked people in suits walk in unless he's stupid. He knows his newfound buddies are at war with us, unless they kept him in the dark. That is a possibility too. So just follow my lead. I'd rather not have another body to dispose of later."

"Understood," Ben said, gripping the door handle. He looked to his side at Jeremy in the backseat. "You good with that?"

"Yeah, follow her lead." His eyes were looking out the windshield, his voice distant. "I got it."

"Alright then. Let's not dawdle here." She exited the driver's seat and walked toward the store in question. She walked in the middle with the men on either side of her. She stopped in front of the glass door. Ben reached ahead and opened it for her.

"Welcome to..." the man paused, his eyes bulging. "I don't want any trouble now." He put his hands up in front of him in a placating gesture.

"Trouble? Us? We wouldn't dream of it." Rachel slithered

up to the counter and leaned on it. "We know who your newfound business partners are."

"You do?" the man asked.

"Yeah, Wayne. We do."

"How do you know my name?" Wayne asked.

"We know a lot of things." She gave him a smile. "We know your name, your address, your new business partners, and how much debt you're in. We also are aware you don't really want to be allied with the Crag Cartel. Who would? They're a bunch of savages - not like us." She motioned toward Jeremy and Ben at her sides. "We're civilized. We don't want to hurt you. We just want to talk to you."

"Talk to me?" Wayne wiped his brow and flicked a strand of brown hair out of his face with a gulp. "What do you want to know?"

"They probably told you to fear us, to not talk to us. They're scared is all it is." Rachel took a step forward and paced left and right in front of the counter. "We just want to know about your business partners is all. You tell us, and we go away. Everybody will be happy." She tapped Jeremy on the shoulder.

He stepped forward with a snarl. "If you don't, we will take it out on this nice store of yours. See, I need something to relieve some pent-up anger. I'd love a good excuse."

"You don't want that," Rachel said with a grin. "We don't want that. It's a pain in the ass for everybody involved. Let's skip it entirely and go right to the part where you tell us whatever we want."

Wayne's nervous glance shifted between the three in front of him. "I know who you are," he said, his voice shaking. "You're who they warned me about. They said you might come and try to talk."

"Yet they left no protection," Ben said. "I don't think they care so much about you, buddy."

"Please don't do this."

Rachel slammed both palms of hers on the counter beside the register and leaned forward. "Let's get down to brass tacks. You joined forces with the Crag Cartel. Don't bullshit us. They no doubt gave you a lump sum to help out with your little debt situation. We get it. Look, they don't even have to know we were here, sir. We won't go trying to get you in trouble," she said through gritted teeth and a forced grin. "Just answer a few questions, and you can go about your night happy and normal as can be. Don't force our hand for your own good. See, these animals you allied yourself with have angered my associate here." She gestured toward Jeremy with a thumb and a sly smile.

"What did they do?" Wayne asked with an almost stutter, shifting his attention to Jeremy.

"They killed my brother," he said with sharp inflection. His eyes were locked with Wayne's, burning with unbridled, barely held rage. He fell into silence for a few seconds. "Now give me a reason," he said with a snarl.

"I wouldn't if I were you." Rachel pushed off the counter with a smug look. "See, my boy here is a proper savage. I'm trying to save you an ass kicking, but you keep avoiding our questions. It does raise doubts. I'm starting to think you don't believe us. B, go switch the open sign to closed. I'm going to go and make sure the surveillance isn't watching. When I give the signal, J, show him how serious we are.

"That's music to my ears," Jeremy said, a feral grin plastered on his face as his eyes never left Wayne.

Ben marched over to the door and flipped the open sign to closed.

Rachel meanwhile circled around the counter and went

into the back room. She spotted the security apparatus and sat down at the desktop. She navigated to the security feed and turned it off. She deleted that day's recordings before getting up and going back the way she came. She opened the door. "Go ahead. Show him we mean business. It's all taken care of." She watched Jeremy reach across the counter and grab Wayne's collar while she adjusted her own tie.

"All you had to do was answer some questions, you stupid bastard," Jeremy growled through his teeth. He dragged him around the obstruction and over toward the lines of shelves. He hurled Wayne toward the nearest, causing him to crash into it and knock it over into another shelf causing shelves to topple over like dominos. The sound of falling shelves echoed in the small store along with the surprised yell of Wayne as he fell on top of the nearest.

"That's going to suck to clean up." Rachel took a step forward. She listened to Wayne laying on top of the recently knocked over shelf moaning. "You wanted to give us the run around earlier. Do you feel like being talkative yet? If not, we have other means of forcing you. See, I'm not the boss, but I can give you an introduction to the boss if you'd like. He's not nearly as polite as us though."

"What do you want to know?" Wayne said between moans.

"He finally sees some sense," Rachel said. "Good. Did the cartel give you a number to call them?"

"They did." Wayne attempted to get up from the mess only to find Jeremy's dress shoes clad foot keeping him in place on his chest.

"Would you be so kind as to give us said number?"

"It's in my front pocket."

Ben kneeled and reached into said pocket. He retrieved a folded piece of paper and stood up. He unfolded it and nodded. "It is indeed a phone number." He got up and walked over to Rachel, handing over the note.

"Very good." She inspected the crumpled paper and stuffed it into her coat pocket. "Now let's just have you come with us, and you'll be back here cleaning this up by morning." She snapped her fingers. "Pick him up."

Jeremy and Ben hurried over and grabbed an arm each, dragging him to his feet.

"You, sir," Rachel swaggered forward toward Wayne, "are coming with us tonight to meet the boss."

Wayne lifted his head with wide eyes. "Don't hurt me," he begged with wide eyes.

"He just wants to talk," Rachel said. "I'll let him know of your cooperation. Since you were so accommodating, I won't even tell him you stalled us. Like I said before, you'll be back here by tomorrow morning cleaning this up."

"Alright, fine. I'll go meet him," Wayne said with determination in his voice. "I know what you types are capable of if I refuse."

"No need to throw shade right when we were being so nice," Rachel said, a fake look of indignation on her face. She took a step forward and threw a fist into Wayne's stomach. She nodded toward the back door. "Take him out the back, and put him in the trunk. The cameras in here are taken care of. We can't let the street cameras see him getting carried out." She called out to the retreating three men once they started moving. "Good thing you didn't spring for cameras out back too." She smirked and looked at their handiwork, the now messy store and fallen shelves covering most of the floor. She walked over to the only visible light switch and flicked it to the off position, cloaking her in darkness. She remembered where the obstructions on the floor were and navigated her way around them in the pitch black until she came to the back door. She opened it and saw the pair of men slam the trunk shut. "Let's get him out of here and back to father." She ran around the car and jumped in the driver's seat after slamming the door to the shop shut.

Ben and everybody else took off their masks once they were in the car. "Good job, everybody," Ben said from the passenger seat. He looked back at the scowling Jeremy. "You got him talking with your show of force back there. Nice job."

"Thanks." Jeremy spared a momentary glance at Ben before returning his attention to the window at his side. He crossed his arms and kicked back in the seat.

"Father will be pleased with our work. We should get some useful intelligence off him. If we're lucky, we can hit them where it hurts. No one saw us. I got the ancient vhs tapes of the surveillance system right. We're home free."

"Let's hope the son of a bitch talks," Jeremy said from the backseat. "I want more targets to take my aggression out on."

"If I know anything about my father," Rachel looked up into the rearview mirror, "it's that he'll give you targets. You don't have to worry about that. I just want a full night's sleep." She blinked rapidly after bringing the car to a stop at a stop sign. She rubbed her eyes with the back of her hand before hitting the gas again.

"Do you think the poor bastard will survive the questioning?" Ben asked, leaning his head back against the seat's headrest.

"I don't think Father will want to bury a body for nothing. My guess is he'll be back tending that little store tomorrow morning. That's assuming he manages to convince Dad he won't inform the cartel about what's happened. If he thinks he will, then some grunt will have an even busier night than we did."

"The guy's an idiot," Jeremy said from the back. "He'll talk freely. He did earlier. Why wouldn't he when he's surrounded by men under threat of torture? I can make him talk if he gets brave. I proved that earlier."

"Just don't get in Dad's way. He has, shall we say, an affinity for questioning prisoners," Rachel said with a sly grin.

"Noted," Jeremy said.

5

—————

Daniel opened the creaky sturdy door. The stairwell led down into the cold cellar. He could see three people there already. He smirked as he descended. "I see you brought him back. Good to see."

"Who are you?" Wayne asked. His arms were behind him, wrapped around a metal beam, tied together with rope. He angled his blindfolded eyes every which way in an attempt to look at Daniel. "Why did you send them after me?"

"You've got a lot of sack to address me like that." Daniel reached the bottom of the stairs and hopped down to the concrete below. "My name is not important. What is important is that you tell us everything I want to know. If you do that, you get to go back to your mundane little life of tending to your store." He sidled up to a few feet in front of Wayne and stared down his nose at his prisoner.

Ben backed away until he felt a table pressing against his lower back. "He was talkative earlier, boss. We figured you'd want a shot at him, just in case."

"Talkative, huh?" Daniel got to a knee and tilted his head. "You are aware of the Crag Cartel, yes?"

"I know of them," Wayne said.

"I should hope so." Daniel laughed in a boisterous tone. "Considering you work for them now. It'd be a little awkward if you didn't. So tell me now, why didn't any of them protect you? I assume they promised such things when they threatened you - that they'd keep you safe from the syndicate and such. Am I wrong? I ask because here you are, and my men tell me they didn't see a single cartel member. It seems they do not treasure your partnership."

"Why am I here?" Wayne asked. "I'll answer as best I can. It's not like they told me all their secret plans though. You may be disappointed."

"You keep that attitude, and things will work out just fine." Daniel got back to a standing position. "My first question is how much are they paying you?"

"Paying me? You got this all wrong." Wayne let loose a genuine laugh. "That's not how they do business. It's not 'We'll pay you such and such and you play ball'. It's more like 'You'll do this, or we'll kill you and your whole family'. They said if I didn't do what they said, that they'd kidnap my wife and child. There was the implied threat of their death hanging too. I didn't have any choice."

"What do they have you doing? Surely they went to all that trouble for you to actually do something. Are they making you pay them for protection?" Daniel asked.

"No protection as your men will attest to. I do have to kick up a payment every couple weeks to stay on their good side though. As far as I see, I don't get anything out of this except to stay breathing. Which I'm starting to doubt since I'm tied up blindfolded."

Daniel looked around at the three other occupants. "Can

you believe they don't even protect the man after taking his money. Some thieves really don't have any honor nowadays. I blame the younger generation." He directed his attention back to Wayne below him. "Calm down, Wayne. We're not savage animals like you're used to. All we want is to talk."

"That's why your boy roughed me up earlier, right?" Wayne asked.

Daniel looked over at Rachel who nodded her head over toward Jeremy. "Wayne here wasn't forthcoming without a little persuasion, and our boy provided just that. Let's be fair now. You aren't hurt from a little shove. Now are you?"

"I'm going to have to clean the entire store now. My back will be killing me by tomorrow night."

"Alright, fine." Daniel shook his head, the faintest hint of a smile on his features. "We won't harm you anymore. I'll even send a man over to help you clean up as a token of our gratitude if you just help us out. Never let it be known that the syndicate is unreasonable."

"Really?"

"Yes. So long as you stay answering our questions. I'll have a man drive you back and clean it up. Now answer me something." Daniel rubbed his chin as he spoke. "Did they leave you a phone or anything to contact them? A phone number or anything would work."

"They did give me a number, but it was only for emergencies. I never called it. I don't even know if it's a real number, or if they gave it to me for peace of mind." Wayne hung his head. "The truth is I never planned on calling them to find out. I was hoping this would all just go away." His voice turned brittle. "It was stupid of me to even imagine such a thing. I knew I'd get dragged into this kind of shit when they turned up."

"A number you say?" Daniel smiled. "I'm going to offer

you a deal, Wayne. I want you to listen carefully. It's not a deal I offer just anybody that ends up in this room. You've not seen our faces. Did they tell you our name?"

"They said something about a syndicate; but no, they never gave me a name if that's what your asking. I just want to go home to my family, sir."

"You will, if you agree." Daniel's voice softened. "You're not fit for this life, it's evident for all to see. All I want from you is to give us that phone number. You do that and never tell the cartel what happened here, and your life will go back to normal. Well, you have to pay them until this war is over, but after that it'll be business as usual if we win."

"We already have the number," Rachel stepped forward and handed the paper from earlier to her father.

"Okay then." Daniel looked down at the number. "Then I only need you to answer my other questions, and we're done."

"Win?" Wayne asked. "What happens otherwise?"

"Then you have worse problems since they're the ones in power then. You'd best hope we win. Is it a deal, Wayne?"

Wayne turned quiet for a full minute contemplating his options before sighing with a nod. "It's a deal. I'm not going to ask why you want my help since I don't want to be any more involved than I already am, but sure. Look in my wallet. I managed to write down how much I have to pay them if that helps."

Daniel used his hand to gesture to Jeremy. "Get it for him."

Jeremy stepped forward and reached into Wayne's back pocket as he angled himself so it could be reached. Jeremy handed the brown leather clad wallet over to his boss. "Here."

Daniel unfolded the container and spotted a torn off,

white piece of paper shoved in front of a picture of a young girl on a swing smiling at the camera. "That's a beautiful girl. Is that your daughter?"

"Yes, sir. It is."

Daniel turned to look at Rachel. "She reminds me a lot of you at that age." He tossed the wallet back on Wayne's lap. "Alright, here's how this is going down. You're keeping that blindfold on. We can't have you knowing where we are. Once you're back at your store, your escort will help you out at the store. Do not try anything stupid. Life is too short and fickle to do foolish things. I truly want you to go home to your daughter."

"Thank you, sir."

"Don't get all mushy now." Daniel snapped his fingers and looked at Ben. "You, go get an escort for the man. Make sure they're physically fit. We want to put our best foot forward with the shop repairs."

"Yes, boss." Ben gave a small bow and trotted up the stairs.

"While he's doing that, let me tell you what they're likely to do if they find out you were here. It'd be smart for you to never reveal this interaction. I know some people would think they're clever by telling them after I let them go. Here's what would happen. They would give you a pat on the back while their associate would be behind you with their finger on the trigger. You're not a part of the gang. Why would they trust someone who talked with the enemy boss. You're compromised. To boot, they really would kill your family. When I said we're your only hope, I meant it."

"With all due respect, Mr.?"

"Call me D. Because if you don't do as I say, you and your whole family will be fucked."

"Right. Mr. D, with all due respect, I'm not stupid. I know not to talk about this."

"You're a smart man, trying to keep your head down. Just know we appreciate you cooperating. You've no idea how many we question who play tough. You made our job easy, so we try and reciprocate."

Ben opened the door and came back down the stairs with a guard trailing behind him. "Sorry it took so long, sir. I have his escort ready. I briefed him on the job and what's expected of him."

Daniel nodded and looked at the man behind Ben. "You know to help this man clean his shop up then?"

"Of course, sir. It will be immaculate by the time I'm done," the grunt said from Ben's side with a bow.

"Good." Daniel turned his attention back to Wayne. "You're going home."

"Already?" Rachel asked from the side. "That was quick and not like every other questioning I've been a part of."

"Sometimes you need the carrot more than the stick, sweetie," Daniel said with a smug grin. "Knowing which is necessary is a skill you will learn in time." He turned and headed back toward the stairs leading up to the main level and spoke as he climbed the stairs. "Get him back to his shop. As for the rest of you, you have the rest of the night off. So relax and get ready for the next time I call."

"Yes, sir," almost everyone said as they watched their boss disappear behind the door.

"You heard Father," Rachel said. "Get on with it. I'm going to my room. You boys have a good night. I have a baby to feed and be a mother to." Without further ado, she followed her father's footsteps, leaving the room full of men to themselves in the basement.

She closed the door behind her and went into the main

living room to see Daniel on the couch with Roger, playing with him with assorted toys she'd bought before. She came up behind the pair. "Where's Lauren?"

"She's in the kitchen preparing his food." Daniel jingled the toy keys in front of Roger's beaming, smiling face. He reached forward and grabbed the ring. Daniel let go as Roger took hold of it. He gave a happy squeal and shook the keys causing a loud clacking noise which caused even more squealing of joy.

Rachel sat on the other side of Roger and focused on the growing child. "I didn't think the boss of the syndicate would want to be seen playing with a baby in the living room. Wouldn't that be seen as soft?"

"That's something my father would have said. I've learned there are exceptions however. If the men see their boss playing with his grandson, what are they going to do? Talk shit behind my back about how I do actually have a heart? Besides, no one's going to stop me from interacting with my grandson."

"Grandson is it?" Rachel asked, looking up at him. "The last I remember you claimed he wasn't."

"I still don't approve of the method or the name you gave him, but he's my grandson, blood or not."

"There's nothing wrong with his name." Rachel's tone temporarily changed to a chilly one.

"Sure." Daniel took the keys Roger was handing back to him. "Whatever you say."

"Sorry for taking so long." Lauren rushed back into the room holding a jar and a plastic spoon. "I had to find out where the boys hid the applesauce variety. It's his favorite."

"Don't worry about it," Daniel said.

Rachel picked up Roger and looked back at Lauren. "Let's head to my room. It'll be quieter there."

"You two girls have fun now. I'm going to relax in here with the boys who go on break. That's like bonding with the employees, right? Even the boss deserves a break every now and then." He brought both of his arms up to the top of the sofa at his sides and reclined his head back with a sigh.

"Yeah, Dad." Rachel hefted her and Roger up, getting to her feet. "Let's go, girl." She led Lauren up the stairs and to her private room. "Here we are. We should have some privacy here. Just wait one moment." She placed Roger on the nearby bed. "Watch him a second."

"Sure thing." Lauren sat down beside Roger and kept him entertained.

Rachel went to a backpack tucked away in the corner of the room, unzipped the main compartment, and retrieved a wand like looking device.

"What even is that thing?" Lauren asked. She watched Rachel run it along walls, behind the bed, nightstand, and anything else she could reach.

"It detects listening devices."

"That's a little overly cautious, isn't it?"

Rachel continued her work as she spoke, running the device over what she could. "I want privacy for the conversation we're about to have."

"Uh oh." Lauren took the lid off of the applesauce after placing Roger in her lap. She placed a towel underneath on her lap and one on the bed. "That doesn't sound like a fun conversation."

"Alright, my room is clean, just as I'd hoped."

"I'd certainly hope your dad wouldn't bug your own room."

"I wouldn't put it past him." Rachel placed the detector back in the backpack before sitting on the other end of the bed. "Now, remember when I told you how I named this little guy?"

"Your uncle figure as I recall. You said he was an ex-gangster that worked with your dad? Didn't you say he got shot in some gang accident?"

"I did say that when father was there if you recall. That's not what really happened though."

"Do go on." Lauren set about feeding Roger as she spoke.

"Look, when I tell you this, you need to know that you can't tell anybody what I'm about to tell you. I need your loyalty. I mean complete loyalty. To me, not my father. If you can't handle that, we'll forget this whole thing. Can I count on you?"

Lauren dipped the spoon into the applesauce and shoveled more into Roger's mouth once he was ready. "Jesus, what the fuck are you about to say? Look, I'm not going to run to anyone and talk. I'm smarter than that."

"My father had the entire thing orchestrated. He killed my uncle."

"What the hell? Why?"

"It's a long ass story. My father believes he betrayed him. I know the truth however. It was petty revenge. Revenge for getting me out of this life. We ran away, and he despised him for that. To be fair, we thought Father was dead. His own sister, my aunt, said he was dead." She shrugged. "So we left and made a new life."

"Okay. I don't mean to be rude, Ms. Morris, but why are you telling me this?"

"Look, he killed the man I viewed as my second father. What I haven't told you yet is he blackmailed me to join this group, saying he wouldn't kill him if I did."

"And he killed him?"

"Yes. He denied it, but he never shed a tear and seemed happy. I can add two and two. I know he killed him." Her voice filled with venom. "He killed him because he knew I loved him, and I was in too deep to leave. He got his petty little revenge and made an enemy out of it in me."

"Christ alive. You know what would happen if anyone heard you say that?" Lauren asked.

"Why do you think I asked if I have your loyalty? If you're having second thoughts, tell me now." Rachel narrowed her eyes at Lauren.

Lauren placed the now empty food container in the nearby trash can and placed Roger to the side. "No, I'm with you, Ms. Morris."

"Good. He killed him after promising me he wouldn't, all because he knew I loved him."

"Loved him how?"

"Excuse me?"

"You told me he wasn't blood related." Lauren gave a sly grin. "So was it platonic, familial, or something more?"

"It was one sided for a long time. Then he got together with another woman, so I gave up. I was more of a daughter to him then."

"So your dad murdered your stepdad basically. That's tough. What do you plan on doing? Screwing him over on a deal or something as payback?"

"Not quite. Did I ever tell you how my grandfather died?"

"Not that I know of."

"He was murdered. Now I have no solid evidence, but I believe that my aunt or father manipulated Roger to kill him for their own gain. I figure, turnabout is fair play. This dirty ass life has taught me as much."

"You don't mean?" Lauren's eyebrows raised with a hand raising in front of her mouth. "Tell me you aren't serious."

"I aim to become leader of this syndicate and avenge a wrongful death all at once. I will lead us to even greater heights."

"Christ."

"Not by raw power, but by cunning, intelligence, and planning. No one will even know it happened. Now if you disagree, then I have bad news." Rachel reached for her firearm and took it out of the holster with one hand. Her other hand snaked around the back of her and extracted her knife. "What's it going to be? I really don't want to, but I need to cover my ass here."

"Jesus!" Lauren gasped and put her hands up in surrender. "I told you, I'm good. I'll go along with you. Just promise me you include me in the planning. I don't want to be in the dark on this coup d'etat. If we want this to work, we need to work together."

"Perfect." Rachel holstered her weapons and showed a beaming smile. "I just had to be sure. You know I love you." She sat down beside Lauren and gave her a hug.

"Yeah." Lauren wiped a bead of sweat off from her brow and returned the hug.

Rachel pulled away from the embrace. "This war will be the perfect smokescreen for us."

"Your dad's not going to go out in the streets for anything to happen though. He'll be holed up here in this nigh impenetrable fortress. I assume that's why he got it."

"An opportunity will present itself. Even if it doesn't, I can use my influence to manipulate my dad to put himself in an unfavorable situation."

"I don't mean to put a damper on you," Lauren said, rubbing her right forearm with her left hand. "You know you're talking about your own father here. Doesn't that fill you with some hesitation? I mean he raised you, didn't he?"

"You know what I remember? Dad being gone and Roger keeping me safe from multiple armed gunmen when I was like seven years old. He got himself shot multiple times and nearly got killed to keep me safe. The fact my father was absent and then years later had the gall to kill the man who did nothing but sacrifice for me solidifies my mind."

"Fair enough, and damn. I didn't know that."

"That and he saved my ass a little more than a year ago. I lied to him about a school project and dragged him to an illegal dog fighting ring. He had to kill someone just to get us home safe. Then he kept me safe while all that shit went down. I was such a spoiled little shit. I had no idea what I had until I lost it."

"You've obviously made up your mind. I just thought I'd try. He sounds like a great guy."

Rachel looked down at the carpeted floor. "He wasn't just great; he was the greatest man I ever met. That's why I named this little guy after him." She placed her palm gently on Roger's head and rubbed, eliciting a happy squeak. "He's the last vestige I have of him, and I'm going to keep him safe. My father will go to war at the drop of a hat. I don't want that for him. I'll rule using more tact instead of raw power." She looked up at Lauren. "Power can work, but always requires men and women to die before it does."

"Alright, so what's our first step?"

"For now? Nothing. It won't do us any good. When the time comes, I'll give you more instructions. Make sure you follow them to a 't'. Do that, and we'll be good."

Lauren looked down to see Roger rolling over, his head on the pillow, and saw his eyes close. She scooped him up only for him to fuss. She got up, walked over to the crib, and laid him down. She covered him with the blankets and moved back to the bed. Her voice was low, barely audible. "I'll be ready. You just be careful. We can't have you getting killed. I assume you're planning on ending this war?"

"Ideally. I'll admit I'm biased against these dicks, but I'm willing to put the past to rest if it means keeping my baby safe." She flexed her prosthetic finger as she spoke. "That's assuming they're willing to see reason. They could assume we're weak if the leader dies. I will not be seen as a weak leader."

"I think we're putting the cart before the horse here. You need to be leader before you focus on that."

"True," Rachel said. "For now, let's get some rest. I'm sure tomorrow won't be any easier and we need to be prepared. Just remember what I said."

"Alright." Lauren pushed herself up to a standing position. "I'm going to head to bed then. Have a good night, Ms. Morris."

"We've known each other for a while. Call me Rachel. Just not in front of any of the others."

"Got it." Lauren ambled over to the door. "I'll see you tomorrow then." She flung open the door and exited, leaving Rachel and Roger alone in the room.

Rachel looked over at the crib and let loose a large exhale. "We'll see how this plays out, but I need help to pull this off. If she talks, I'll have to play innocent. She'll be killed. I know dad wouldn't take her side. It's up to her at this point." She got up and walked over to the crib and stared down at Roger's immobile form. She reached down and pulled the blankets up where he'd kicked them down. "It's all for you, baby. Mama's doing her best for your future. You know Mommy will always do anything for her boy." She gave a heartwarming smile. "Even if it means Grandpa going away. He'll put you in danger. I can't have that."

She stood overlooking her adopted son for a long while before moving to her nearby window and looking out over the forested view. She looked down and saw a group of three men in a group patrolling the perimeter. Chris looked up at her and waved. She put on her best sour look and brought a finger up and wagged it back and forth. The man's eyes went wide and looked away. The others in the group could be seen laughing as they walked. "Morons," she said with a sneer in a quiet voice. "You can't play around when you're the patrol. It's too lax. I'll talk to Dad. He'll whip them in shape. If there's one thing he's good at, it's that. That, and killing," she said, a scowl still on her face.

Eventually after staring at the landscape for a while, she backed off and closed the curtains. She took off her dress suit and pants. She walked over to the nearby closet, clad only in her bra and panties, and opened it. She plucked out her favorite pajamas and put them on before heading to the bed and laying down. "We'll see what tomorrow has in store for us. Good night, sweetie."

Her only response was the sound of Roger rolling over.

6

———

"I'm glad you're up early," Daniel said, sitting at his makeshift office desk in their new lodgings. "Close the door. I have something private I need to discuss with you."

Rachel closed the large wooden double doors behind her and walked forward toward the desk. The small room had bookcases on either side, barren except for only a few books scattered in them. "What is it?" Rachel felt a bead of sweat roll down the side of her head. *That bitch! Don't tell me she ratted me out already,* she thought.

"I have an important job I need you to do. I got a call a few weeks back from your aunt."

"Elizabeth?" Rachel asked. "I'm surprised they let her have phone calls in that supermax prison she's in."

"It wasn't official. She borrowed another inmate's cell phone they smuggled in. Anyway, she told me she's pregnant."

"Uh, she's in a women's prison isn't she?"

"Some guards are male. Now that's not why I'm telling you. Shut up and listen." He cleared his throat before continuing. "She had some very specific instructions for me - which I found hilarious given I'm the boss now."

"I don't like where this is going."

"She said she was going to have her baby soon." Daniel got up from the chair and turned his back on his daughter. He pulled the billowing red curtains to the side, revealing an open window. "Do you want to guess why she told me that?"

"She's going to the hospital, and she wants out."

"In so many words, yes. She wants a rescue."

"In a hospital?"

"Yes. She figures it'd be easier than escaping a supermax facility, and she's probably right."

"You decided I'd be the best for that job?" Rachel asked. "She knows I went along with Roger. She'd kill me."

"As far as she knows he dragged you along. You never testified. Only Roger and Ana did. She'll probably pull rank on you, but nothing can be done about that."

"Can't it?" Rachel asked. "I'm the number two here, not her."

Daniel turned around a smirk on his face. "That's my girl. You're right. She's not in the syndicate yet. I'm just telling you she'll try and pull rank as the elder criminal. Be prepared for that, and don't lose your head. Let her think that if it comes down to it. Now I'm sending you, Lee, and you can pick the last member. I'd leave Jeremy here. He'll be useful in the war while you're gone. He and Davis are off limits. They have their own assignments I need done."

"So that means Ben, Lauren, or one of the newer people. Ben it is."

"I can watch Roger if you want her with you. I don't mind."

"I appreciate that, but you're a busy man. He needs a

full-time babysitter. Ben will do fine. He's effective, follows orders, and keeps me in line when needed."

"Good." Daniel's voice turned deadly serious. "Just don't get too close to him. You hear me?"

Rachel rolled her eyes. "You're saying to not fuck him."

Daniel winced. "Yes. I've seen the way he looks at you when he thinks nobody's looking. He's not half as slick as he thinks he is. He's too respectful to try anything, but be careful; and don't do anything that could be misunderstood."

"Looking at me huh?" Rachel waggled her eyebrows. "I'll have to keep that in mind."

"I am serious," Daniel said. "I've seen what happens when powerful women fall for men in this business."

"I'm sure Aunty would testify it was the most fun time in her life."

"And look where she's spent the last year because of him."

"I'll be careful."

"You'd better. I don't need to be a blood related grandfather at my age." Daniel sat back down, leaving the window open, natural light flooding in behind him. "Now as for the job itself - she gave me a laundry list of items you'd need to be successful." He reached down behind the desk and hefted a large brown cardboard box up onto the desk with a grunt. "Here. It has everything you'll need."

Rachel grabbed the box and slid it toward her. "What's in here?"

Daniel counted on his fingers as he rattled items. "Two nurses' uniforms, two forged identifications from the hospital they're taking her to, another fake identification for my sister, a digital camera, a new laptop, the keys to the car you'll all be taking, and three syringes filled with anesthetics. Oh, I forgot one. I also threw in a new license plate in the back just in case. She claimed she'd be there tomorrow. How she knows is a mystery. I'm pretty sure they don't take pregnant females out of prison until their water breaks."

"Really? You can't guess? She's probably going to lie and tell them her water broke even if it didn't. Think about it. She knows a breakout is there. She'll get there. They have to take her if her water breaks. Besides, labor can be delayed up to a day, so it will be fine if we're there on the right day."

"Thank God you know about that stuff. So that's your job. Get her out of there."

"You want me to waltz into a hospital, take out two or more guards, get a notorious crime lord, and just walk out? Police will lock down the state after they find out she's gone."

"So make sure they don't find out until you're out of there. I'm sending the best electronic expert we have. Cameras won't be a problem. The guards and any personnel like nurses will be your biggest hurdles, but I have faith my little girl can figure it out. You always were good at creative problem solving. Now math was a different story."

"Thanks, Dad."

"Now go gather your team and get going. You need to be in Missouri by tomorrow. That's like a twelve hour drive, so get going. We can't have you all late."

"What about the baby?"

"What about it? Unless she really does go into labor on the day she lies, she'll still be pregnant. We can get a midwife or someone to deliver it."

"If she does deliver it there?"

Daniel paused for a long while before answering. "Your mission is to get my sister out. The baby is a secondary concern."

"Alright, but may I ask something?"

"Go ahead."

"Why are we going to all this trouble to get her out? She's going to jockey for your leadership role. You know that."

Daniel let out a loud laugh. "She may try, but her time as leader is over. I'll take care of her. Besides, she's been getting real friendly with a shot caller of the Crag cartel. She claims she can end this war if we get her out."

"In a women's prison?"

"The prison does have a male wing and a female wing. Passing messages behind bars is not a great feat. It checks out too. I had Lee check to see if any of their big wigs were there, and he confirmed there are three. The name she even dropped matched exactly. She's telling the truth."

"Alright. It will be done. Just don't expect me to give up my spot as number two to her. I won't."

"I would expect you to fight. If you didn't, you'd look weak. We won't have that."

"Exactly."

"Good, then get going and assemble your team. I expect you all to leave here by tonight at the latest. You have a few good hours to prepare, so use your time wisely."

"I'll get on that. We'll be there by tonight. We'll have plenty of time."

"Always treat it as if something will go wrong, because odds are something will," Daniel said. "Never forget that. Don't get overconfident because you've got a few jobs under your belt. I was the same way when I was your age. I nearly got men killed because of it, so listen when I say this."

"I understand. I just wanted to display an aura of confidence." She picked up the large box.

"Which is great for the rank and file, but leadership needs to be cautious. Now get going. I have things to work on, and I know you have work to do. Be careful out there. I don't want you ending up in prison. This is probably the most high-profile, difficult job I've ever assigned or seen. I trust you can do this. Do not prove me wrong. Now get out."

"Yes, sir," Rachel said. Without further word she turned around and exited the room. She wandered the hallway until she spotted Ben talking to a few men on the couch in the living room. "You." She pointed at Ben. "You're with me. We have an important job. By the way, have any of you seen our resident tech guy? You'd know him. He's a big guy with glasses and thinning hair."

"I saw him go down that hallway, I assume to his computer room."

"Okay, come with me then. He's coming with us."

"Interesting." Ben hopped up and moved over toward Rachel around the couch. "I'm anxious to hear this job." He offered his hands. "I'll carry that for you."

"Thanks." Rachel handed the box over.

The pair left the room and went in search of Lee. Rachel went through the door mentioned by Ben. "Have you been to the computer room yet?" Rachel asked. "Because I haven't."

"It's right up here around the corner on the left." Ben pointed further down the red carpet covered hallway. The large windows to their left showed the tree covered view they had come to get used to. "That guy's a little creepy. Don't tell him I said that," Ben said in a quiet voice. "He stays in that room all day, only coming out to eat. He never comes out to talk to anyone."

"He's an introvert. He's fine. He's reliable. My father would never have hired him if he wasn't. Besides, he's going to save our asses on this hell of a job."

"I don't like the sound of that." The pair turned the

corner and saw a room with a taped piece of paper hanging on it that read 'Computer Lab'.

"I guess this is it." Rachel pushed open the door to see Lee packing a suitcase.

"I'm almost ready. Give me just a second."

"I'm guessing Father already told you what we're doing then," Rachel said, watching the big man pack his suitcase, putting his personal laptop in last.

"He informed me of my duties on this little job. It's a small hospital in Missouri. It won't be nearly so hard as some of the jobs I've done. The hard part will be on you guys' part. All I have to do is loop the cameras and make sure you get out clean. You all have to actually get her out."

"Get her out? Get who out of where?" Ben asked.

"I'll explain later," Rachel said, watching Lee finish closing his suitcase. "Do you know where this car is?"

"It's outside. I'm going to go load my luggage up." Lee hefted the large item off the bed and looked at the two. "I'd suggest you pack a bag too. It could be two or three days down there depending." He walked up to the pair and let them split, allowing him passage past them.

The two looked back at the now open doorway. "You heard the man," Rachel said. "Pack a bag and meet us outside. I'll do the same. When we're ready, we're going on a road trip."

"I guess that's that," Ben said.

9 hours later...

"Finally," Rachel said while parking the car. "We're here. That took long enough. It wouldn't have felt so long if we all had taken shifts." She opened the car door and delivered a glare in Lee's direction.

Lee hefted his suitcase out of the car and held it at his side. "I never got a license, so sue me. I always lived in big cities, so I just take the bus or a taxi or something. The last thing we needed was to get pulled over."

"Right," Ben said. "Let's just get a room and get set up. If we're going to break a most wanted criminal out of custody, we'll need to be well rested."

"We may not have the luxury of time," Lee said, leaning against the front of the car. "We'll have to see once I get an internet connection." He looked over at Ben. "Make sure we get a room with internet. I need it."

"Right, I'll go get one then, shall I?" Ben exhaled and walked off in the direction of the motel's office.

"What do you propose for this mess?" Rachel asked, crossing her arms.

"I'm going to check hospital check-in and see if she's there already. You never know if something happened. If she's not, we get a good night's sleep. If she is, someone pays a visit in there and plants the camera. I can then watch and listen for the best time to go in."

"Intel is never bad to have, true. We can plan our approach easier that way."

"My thoughts exactly. Extraction will be the hardest part. Getting out of the state will be paramount. Subtlety will be needed in the hospital to make that a reality."

Rachel walked a few paces forward, toward the well-kept motel before turning back and facing the computer expert. "Well, no time like the present." She pointed toward the office with Ben coming out. "We have our room."

"Let's get settled in then." Ben held up the key he was given. He opened the front-seat passenger door and took out the bag below the seat.

"Don't get too comfortable," Rachel said, following suit. "Now lead on. Where's our room?"

"Right over this way," Ben said with his free hand pointing toward the building. "It's not a suite, so don't expect much." He led the group over to their room and unlocked it before entering first. "Oh, this is worse than I thought."

They entered a dimly lit, visibly dusty, cramped room with two beds. A small television was mounted directly opposite the beds.

"Fantastic," Rachel said. "Looks like you two are bunking together, or one of you is on the floor. I don't care which way, but I'm sleeping alone. We'll figure that out later. For now, let's focus on our first step." She threw her bag on her designated bed. "Lee? You're up."

Lee plopped down on the opposite bed and dug out the laptop Daniel left in the box. "I'm connecting to our wi-fi as we speak." His fingers danced across the keyboard, filling the silence in the room with the clattering of mechanical keyboard presses. "I found their website. Now let me get set up, then I can access their sign in records."

"You can access that?" Ben asked.

"Every hospital has online records nowadays," Lee said, not looking up. "Accessing it's a lot easier than some of the other jobs I've had. I'm just setting up my precautions. Give me a minute. Better safe than sorry as they say."

"I read somewhere once she has the kid, they give her two days before they haul her back to prison," Rachel said.

"Why are we doing this anyway?" Ben asked, still standing between the two beds.

"I can't tell you that. Suffice it to say it's worth it, assuming she's telling the truth. Which is a big assumption with her. If she is, this war will be over before you know it. That's all I'll say."

"I'm in," Lee said. "An Elizabeth Morris was checked in officially today at three pm. She's on the third floor in room 304. She checked in earlier today."

"Perfect. Then before we bed down for the night we need to pay a visit to the hospital." She pushed herself off the bed.

Ben gave her a quizzical look. "They're not going to allow her visitors. She's probably got guards posted outside and inside the room."

"We're not going to visit her, dummy." Rachel tapped the side of her head with her index finger. "We're going to plant the camera that father left us. We can gauge when the guards go on bathroom breaks or possibly even influence it. Using that knowledge will allow us to make our move at the best possible time."

"Alright, I'm following along," Ben said. "Does it say she's had the kid already?"

Lee looked back down at the artificial light of the screen. "Yes. She did."

"What are our orders about the kid?"

Rachel put on a stern face. "I asked father about this, and he said, 'Elizabeth is our priority, not the kid.' It sucks, but that's our orders."

"Which is good," Lee said, placing the laptop to the side, still powered on. "Getting a baby out of a hospital would be another level of difficult. They've cracked down on that in recent decades. We can thank all the people who've kidnapped kids from the nursery for that."

"People do that?" Rachel asked. "It just goes to show, we're not the worst out there by a long shot. Now, I can't be the one going inside to plant the camera."

"I'm not going inside," Lee said, sneering. "I have to check if the camera is working when it's placed."

"Fine," Ben said, rolling his eyes. "I'll do that too."

"You're a doll." Rachel reached over and pinched his cheek, eliciting a groan from him.

"Just curious," Ben said. "Why can't you go in, boss?"

Rachel released her hold on Ben's face. "I'm the one going in pretending to be a nurse. I can't be seen in there anymore than need be."

"Fine. I'm just placing a digital camera. How hard can that be? I'll go up to the third floor, place the thing in a subtle position, and then get out of there."

"Not quite," Rachel said, shaking her head. "Subtlety will be needed. Go to the toilets, duck into a room for a few minutes and then get out. You're just another guy who's visiting their poor family. Lee," she snapped her fingers, "get the man a reason to go in there. Who's in the nearby rooms that could get visitors?"

"Let me look," Lee said, the taps of the keyboard replacing human voice in the cramped motel room. "There are a few rooms nearby that he could wander into. There's a Fitser in 301, Maynard in 302, and Orson in 303, surrounding her room. He could duck in any of them for a few minutes, explain he has the wrong room, and get out. Nobody would bat an eye."

"Nobody in a coma he could visit?"

Lee looked up at her and back down at the screen, all while shaking his head. "It's a maternity ward. Take a guess who her neighbors would be."

"Well, surely they have a guest waiting area then. He could go sit down there. They usually have a plant he could use for its concealment. So long as the door is visible, we'd be good."

"You do have a point. According to these floor plans, her room is near a waiting room of sorts. Even if it doesn't have fake plants, he could plant it on top of a vending machine or somewhere inconspicuous."

Ben got to his feet. "Let's go plant this camera. I want to get back here and get some shut eye."

"It said she got here today, so we have all day tomorrow to get it done," Rachel said. "Let's go then." She clapped her hands and the group got ready.

A half hour later...

"Now just be subtle in there. You know where her room is. What was the number again?" Rachel asked, looking at Ben beside her.

It was 304 I believe," he answered. "It's right by the waiting room, and I can plant it there. I just wait there for a bit, plant it, and then come out."

"Let's hope it's that easy. If anyone gets suspicious, this will be infinitely harder. You're just a visitor so far as anyone knows."

"Wish me luck." Ben grabbed the handle and pulled it down, pushing the door open. He marched toward the multi-story building amidst the packed parking lot. Rows of cars were on either side of him as the heat of the day pounded down on him from the sun above. He wiped his brow as he walked toward the air-conditioned building. He pushed the front door open and saw the information counter in front of him with the elevators further down the hall.

He walked by the desk. The receptionist gave him a passing glance before returning her attention to the work at hand. He made for the elevators and pushed the up arrow. He tapped his feet and crossed his arms, staring up at the indicator above. A pleasant ding alerted him that it had arrived. He saw a crowd of people inside, so he stepped back allowing them to exit first before ducking inside once they were all out. He turned around and pressed the three among all the other numbers representing floors.

He looked around the cramped space, leaning against the wall behind him. "Good old elevator music. It never gets old." The familiar ding indicated another stop. He looked up to see he had arrived at his destination. He took a deep breath and exhaled just before the door opened.

He could see a desk of sorts and a small resting area at the end of the hallway filled with vending machines, seats, and a glass table with piles of magazines sitting atop it. He passed the desk and moved toward the vending machines at the end of the hallway. He bought himself a bottle of water and sat down near the only plant. He could see down the hallway to his right and saw the ultimate prize. A room with a guard outside, looking back and forth. He could see the nearer door. The number three oh three was on the front of it.

He grabbed a magazine and opened it, crossing his legs in front of him. His right hand dug into his pocket, hit the little button on top of the device, and placed it as subtle as he could in the plant container. He angled it toward the door and flipped the page. He took a swig of the water bottle he'd bought and passed a bit of time before getting up and retracing his steps toward the elevator. On the way, he ducked into the nearby male bathroom. He tossed the spent water bottle in the trash can on the near pristine tiled floor. He got into an empty stall and pulled out his phone when it vibrated.

He read the text to himself in a whisper. "Camera's good. Get out of there as low key as you can. Also remember to destroy this phone before we leave the place."

"Did you say something?" A booming masculine voice asked from the stall over.

"Sorry, man." Ben filed the phone away in his pocket, got up from the toilet, and flushed it. He opened the stall and walked over to the sinks to wash his hands. As he did, the stall where the voice came from opened to reveal a large man with a smile plastered on his face. He stared into the large mirror in front of him. "You look happy. I'm guessing your kid's on the way."

"She's already here, good sir." The man took the sink next to him and got busy sanitizing his hands with soap and water. "I am now Mr. Fitser with a baby girl of my own."

"Hey, man, congratulations," Ben said with a warm genuine smile. "It's the biggest day of your life I bet. I wish you all nothing but the best. I'm just in here to visit someone."

"No special lady for you yet?" Mr. Fitser asked.

"I may have my eye on one, but no, we're nowhere near that stage yet," Ben said, looking back to the mirror, his cheeks flushed red. "I don't think she'd be interested in me anyway."

"Now don't take that attitude, son," the older man said. "Women love confidence. That's how I hooked my wife." Mr. Fitser reached over to the roll of brown paper towels and dried off his hands. "Regardless, I have to get back in the room with my wife. I get to hold my kid after my wife feeds her."

"Enjoy it," Ben said, following suit, drying his hands. "I'm going to head out soon after a quick visit."

"You remember what I said," Mr. Fitser said, pointing at Ben. "Be confident, and a nice young man like you will have no problems with the ladies. Trust me." He bumped open the door with his waist and exited the room.

"Guess it's time I visited who I'm here for," he whispered to himself. He exited the bathroom and stopped in front of the nurse's station.

The young man looked up from the desk with a subdued smile. His right hand ran down the green attire as he spoke. "How can I help you, sir? Who are you here to visit tonight?"

"I'm looking for the Orson family. I'm a friend. I heard they had their kid recently."

"You heard correctly," the nurse said with a friendly smile. He looked down toward the monitor and looked back at Ben. "They're in room 303. You may not have much time in there. I believe she's about to go to sleep, but if you hurry you might make it before lights out."

"Thank you very much for your help. I should hurry then to not interrupt her sleep. Have a nice night."

"You too, sir." The nurse turned his attention back to his work as Ben walked off toward his newfound destination. He mentally ran through the awkward conversation he was about to have. *Oh, I'm sorry. I must have the wrong room. Yeah, that will work. Then I exit the room and walk out. If the nurse says anything, I act like she was ready to go to bed. No big deal, right?*

He stopped in front the door labeled 303 and inhaled sharply. He gripped the handle and opened it, stepping inside.

"Is it time already, nurse?" a female voice asked. "It seems like you were just in here not too long ago."

Ben turned to face the woman lying in the hospital bed. "Oh, I'm sorry," he said. "I think I have the wrong room. I'll just leave. I don't want to disturb you."

"You're not a nurse?" the brunette woman asked, sitting up as best she could. "You don't have to leave."

"You're sure?" Ben turned to face her.

"I've been in here alone for hours now. Other than the occasional feeding for my new baby girl, I've been just sitting in here watching television. I'd welcome a little conversation if that's alright. I'm Ellie Orson. Nice to meet you."

"If you don't mind, neither do I. I'm Ben." Ben saw the child in the hospital's crib on the other side of the room and smiled. "Your little girl is beautiful," he said before approaching the bed and sitting down.

"That's nice of you to say." The woman looked at her baby across the room as she spoke. "It's the one good thing I got out of dating my ex. He can't take that away from me." She turned to Ben, now sitting in the chair nearby. "I'm sorry. You don't want to hear about my problems."

"I don't mind," Ben said with a warm smile.

"You're quite polite. That's rare nowadays. It's also under-appreciated by a large amount of the population, men and women alike." She gave a hollow smile and stared off toward the foot of her bed. "I don't know what I'm going to do, Ben."

"I'm sorry?"

"I'm a single mother if you hadn't put it together yet. I don't mean to start a whine fest in here, but it's all that's on my mind. Don't get me wrong, I love my baby. I'm just worried I'll screw her up accidentally."

Ben scratched his nose. "I think that's natural."

"Really?"

"I'd be more worried if you weren't thinking of that to be honest. Can I tell you something?"

She nodded, now turning to look him in the eye.

"I don't mean to change the subject, but a woman I have my eye on is a single mother as well."

"Seriously?" Ellie asked. "Aren't men supposed to not

want to go anywhere near a single mother? That's what everyone acts like."

"I guess some guys may be like that, but it never really factored into my mind. Mind you she adopted, but who cares about that anyway? She's still the same person, kid or no kid. She's still the charming, strong, caring woman I've come to know."

"You really love her, don't you?" Ellie gave a knowing smile. "Damn, and here I was hoping I had a shot. I'm joking about my part in that, but you care for her. I can tell."

"Well, it's a little complicated."

"It always is," Ellie said, a sad smile now adorning her features. "I haven't heard of a single relationship that was simple."

"True enough. It's a little awkward when she's my boss though."

"Ooh, that's rough."

"You don't know the half of it in our line of work," Ben said, looking down at the tiled floor in the dimly lit room.

"What's your work if you don't mind my asking?" Ellie leaned her head back on the pillow and pulled the blanket higher up over her shoulders.

"I'm in sales." Ben looked away from her. "She's my, and a lot of others, supervisor."

"Is she a real hard-ass then?"

"The farthest from it. Yeah, she's a little feisty sometimes, but she's under a lot of pressure from corporate. When it comes to crunch time, she makes sure we're focused. But I wouldn't say she's mean or wrong about how she goes about it."

"Let me give you a little advice, Ben," Ellie said. "She's not going to notice. Are you picking up what I'm putting down?"

"Not really." Ben scratched his head.

"Such a typical guy." Ellie shook her head. "She's a working woman. She's not going to pick up on your feelings unless you let her know directly."

"Won't that just piss her off or get me fired?"

"It would depend on if she shares the same feelings. Worst case is you get fired and rejected. Just think of the best case though. She accepts, you two become an item, and you get married. I don't know about you, but that sounds like an acceptable risk to me. Especially since I can see you're head over heels for her even from here," Ellie said, sitting up as best she could and fluffing her pillow.

"Let me help with that." Ben adjusted the pillow and let her rest back on it. "Just confess to her? That's your advice? That's easier said than done."

"So is everything else in life. I'm just saying that you're going to regret not going for it if you don't tell her. Maybe she'll find some bad boy and get married to him. I've seen it entirely too many times."

"Like Warren," Ben said loud enough to be heard.

"Oh, you've already got a rival huh?"

"Yeah, and he fits the description of bad boy to a 't'. He has been known to flirt with her, but she always shoots him down. It still pisses me off though."

"That's why you haven't I assume. You don't want to get rejected also. I did notice you didn't say he was fired though."

"What about it?" Ben tilted his head.

Ellie chuckled. "Then odds are she won't fire you. I am betting you act like you are now. If a cute, nice guy confessed, I'd say yes. Just don't do it at work and you'd be fine. Do it in a private setting. That will give you the best chance of success. She won't want to be seen as inappropriate in the workplace. Other than that, just go for it."

"Just go for it she says." Ben raised a hand to his face, muffling his voice as he looked up at the ceiling.

"In the immortal words of some guy, don't be a pussy. Be a man. Nothing ventured, nothing gained. Right?"

"You might be right."

"I am right. You'll learn that with women too. We're usually right."

"Citation needed on that one. I think ya'll just like to think that."

"Don't ever say that to her. Just be the bigger man and play along. Trust me. Even if you are right, don't do that."

"We'll have to agree to disagree. Honesty is important in a relationship." Ben stood up from the chair.

"Leaving already?"

"You're probably drained, I should let you get some rest." A high-pitched crying emanated from the cradle across the room that escalated into screaming as he finished the sentence. "I'm sorry. I seem to have woke her up."

"She hasn't eaten in a while. Can you pick her up and bring her over before you head out?"

"No problem." Ben made his way over to the cradle and ever so carefully placed one hand under the baby girl's neck while his other snaked under her body and cradled her in his arms. He walked back to the hospital bed and handed her off. "There you two are. Have a good night."

"Good luck, playboy," Ellie said. "You'll need it."

7

"What the hell took so long in there?" Lee asked as Ben got back in the car. "It's been like half an hour."

"I visited someone."

"Really?"

"Yeah," Ben said, slamming the car door shut. "We had a lovely conversation. I figured it'd look more natural if I really did visit someone. I'd say it worked wonderfully. No one gave me a second look."

"So long as you're good, we have to get back to the room and plan tomorrow out." Rachel started the car and pulled out onto the road.

"Her room looked like it had one guard out front," Ben said.

"There's another inside," Lee said. "It's standard procedure to have two." He leaned his head back on the seat behind him, his thin hair shifting, showing a bald spot on the top of his head.

"I can get inside by dressing up as a nurse. We even have the fake ids if they get curious," Rachel said. "Then Ben will

77

wait outside, under the guise of visiting whoever the hell he visited today. We'll all be on call," she said, turning the wheel. "When I give the signal, you make your way over. I'll get the guard in the room. From there, we'll use the remaining sedative and stuff one of them in the bed under the covers. The other can be put in the bathroom. If all goes well, the guards will be out of the picture. Elizabeth will then dress up as a nurse, and we'll walk out back to the car. We'll be gone before they even notice anything is wrong."

"We should have contingencies in place just in case," Ben said.

"We do," Lee spoke up. "I'll loop the cameras in the stairwells and hallways. Did you see any clocks in there?"

"Not in the hallways. I did see one in the patient's room."

"What about the stair wells?"

"I took the stairs on the way out," Ben said. "There was a camera in the one I was in."

"We're not taking the elevator, so, Lee, it's up to you to keep us off the cctv."

"If there are no clocks, I doubt they'll notice anything's up. Even if they are staring at the screen like a damned zombie. There's nothing to notice in a static picture."

The car pulled into the motel's parking lot. Rachel parked the car and took the keys out. "Then let's get inside and go over specifics. I will not have anybody winging it tomorrow."

The group exited the car and collectively moved back into the shared motel room.

Rachel led the way, waiting until the door was closed before she reached down toward the large brown box her father sent along with them. She plopped it down on the nearest bed close to the door and opened it. "If we're to be successful, we need to know the tools we have." She pulled out the two nurses' uniforms and matching identifications. One had Rachel's likeness on it, while the other had Elizabeth's face on it. "I will use one of these to get into her room."

"Do you think they'll buy that?" Ben asked. "You're a new face."

"They've been there like one day, dude," Rachel said. "For all they know, I had today off or took a different shift than they were on. It'll be fine. That's the easy part. There will be at least two guards. You said you saw one guard outside the door?"

"That's what I saw."

"Then that works out. I can take care of the one inside. When you see me go in, stay close to the room."

"How close?"

"Close enough to get in there within a few seconds. You don't have to be outside the door since that'd be suspicious, but close enough to help when I distract the outside guard to come inside. We can't have him fall over out in the hallway."

"How are you two going to incapacitate two guards anyway?" Lee asked, sitting on the other bed.

"Good question," Rachel said. "This is how." With great care, she pulled out a capped syringe full of medication.

"What even is that stuff?"

"Dad said it's a strong-ass sedative. What that means, I have no clue; but he sprung for the expensive stuff, so I trust it'll work. I'll administer this to the guard inside, then somehow get the other guard inside the room. Ben, when you see the guard coming inside, you follow suit as soon as you can. You'll have one of these to stick him with. You do know how to stick someone with a needle, right? I mean, it's not exactly brain surgery."

"I think I can figure it out," Ben said, looking at Rachel and then avoiding her gaze. He looked down at the floor, a slight crimson hue adorning his cheeks.

"Don't tell me you're exhausted after just talking to someone earlier," Rachel teased him, a smile on her face.

"I'm fine." Ben cleared his throat and returned his attention to Rachel. "You said we're putting one in the bed and one in the room's bathroom?"

"I figure it'd be our best bet for remaining undetected as long as we can. By the time they'd realize what happened we'd already be long gone, probably out of the state. Before that, we need to focus. We take out the guards, set them up, and then you," she pointed to Ben, "will head out to the car and pull it around to the exit around the back of the hospital."

"The back?" Ben asked.

"I have the floor plans here." Lee turned the laptop around to face the pair and pointed toward the screen from above with his pointer finger. "Elizabeth's room is here. Am I correct?"

Ben leaned forward, squinting his eyes for a moment. "I believe that is correct from the mental map I made."

"Good. So if you all take this stairwell here..." He moved his finger a bit and tapped. "You remember this stairwell?"

"Yeah, I remember it."

"That leads to this." He clicked, changing the floor plan's view to the first floor, and pointed. "The exit leads to the back parking lot. You'll need to move the car here after you're done inside."

"Why can't you just move the damned car? I have to hurry outside while our target's changing and drive clear around the building? Don't you even start on the I don't have a license bullshit. It's a parking lot, not the autobahn."

"Would it surprise you if I said I never learned how to drive a car at all?" Lee asked, avoiding Ben's piercing gaze.

"How a man your age never learns such a crucial life skill is fucking beyond me." Ben rolled his eyes with a shake of his head.

"I never had reason to, alright?" Lee fired back.

"So you keep saying," Ben said. "Fine. I guess I'll do that too."

"You're a doll," Rachel said, sitting down beside Ben and patting him on the shoulder. "I knew I could count on you."

"Yeah," Ben said, awkwardly looking around the small room. "You just make sure you two get there on time. We're not going to have a lot of time before they find the guards sleeping."

"You think so?" Rachel asked.

"Nurses would probably go in there every few hours. Not to mention if your nurse charade has any chance of working, it'd have to be timed very well. Say, an hour after the last nurse visit. So, we'd have less time than the whole two hour interval."

"Good point. Lee," she said, snapping her attention to said pudgy man. "Have you timed how often the nurses go in there?"

"Uh, no. We just got the camera up and running."

"Well since you can't drive, you're going to time nurse shifts tonight. You only need to time two shifts, so you'll still get some sleep tonight. We need to know our timings tomorrow morning so no bitching. I don't want to hear it."

Lee let loose a loud sigh. "Fine, I get it. I'll clock two rounds of nurses going in and see how long the gap is. Then I need some sleep if I'm going to mess with their cctv feed."

"That works. Also, don't forget to use this." She dug

around in the large box and furrowed her brow after a few minutes before Lee interrupted her.

"I already got it out of the box. This is the new laptop. It will be destroyed after this operation." He gently patted the top of the laptop's screen. "Such a shame too. This is a pretty nice model for a throwaway."

"Just remember to destroy it," Rachel said. "Did I forget anything about tomorrow?"

"We've got the cameras planned for. We have a plan for the guards and how everyone will slip out tomorrow. Our last item on the docket should be getting back home," Ben said. "Once they find she's gone, you realize not just state police but the FBI are going to be on a manhunt? They'll put checkpoints on every major highway out of the state."

"They can't shut down every highway across the country," Rachel said. "They're going to hope we're still in the state. We won't be hopefully. To be safe, after almost an hour after we leave, we'll take smaller roads if that will make you feel better. Better safe than sorry after all."

"Then I think we're good to go."

"Good, then I'll take this bed," Rachel said, patting the bed she sat on. "Lee, move so Ben can sleep there. You're on watch duty for two rotations before you can sleep, remember?"

"I got it." He carried the laptop over to the small table against the wall and sat in the cheap chair beside it.

Ben moved to his allocated bed and stretched his arms above his head with a yawn. "Wake me up when you're done watching the shifts. I'll move to the floor and sleep there."

"Afraid of a little male bonding?" Rachel asked, laying down.

"Sure, let's go with that."

"Could also be I want our overwatch to at least not be

dead on his feet tomorrow. Also, this is a double bed. I'm not sleeping with another guy on a double bed. No thank you."

"I will never get men and their fear of being close to other men."

"No, you won't. It's a guy code thing."

"Fine then. Just don't bitch to me when you're still tired tomorrow morning. I expect you two to be alert and ready."

Ben took his shirt off, revealing his toned abdomen. "I'll get us coffee tomorrow morning. We'll be fine."

"Good." Rachel rolled over when she caught herself staring at Ben's chiseled lean frame. "Then go to sleep already."

The next morning in the hospital parking lot...

"Are we ready?" Rachel asked from behind the wheel, nurse outfit already donned. "Once I go in there, we're committed." She scratched her dyed black hair and donned fake glasses.

"I don't want to mess with their cameras now. If they notice, our cover would be blown," Lee said, laptop perched on his lap. "I'm ready to whenever. I'm already in their network and they haven't noticed."

"I'll head in before you do and stay close to the room," Ben said from the passenger seat. "It'd look less suspicious if I'm visiting the same person I did last night. Her room's right next to Elizabeth's anyway."

"Everybody on the call?" Rachel tapped her ear.

"I am," Ben said.

"Obviously," Lee said.

"Fine, pay attention. Ben, when I say 'Could you help me out?' or something like that, that's your cue to come in. You'll need to be there quickly, so don't get too comfortable in there. I'd start moving once you hear me get into the room to be safe. Timing will be paramount. Don't forget your package. You're just bringing a present, but she will need those shoes, so don't delay."

"I understand." Ben patted the bag in his lap. "I'll be quick. Just let me go in first, you follow me in. You have your props all ready?"

"Got my ID's, disguises, and my syringes. You have yours?"

"I do." Ben reached into his jacket pocket and pulled out the covered needle. He dropped it back inside.

"Good, then get going. We'll be back home by tonight if we do this right."

"I'm on my way," Ben said as he opened the door, walked toward the hospital, and disappeared within.

"I'll give him a few minutes and head in."

"Their network doesn't look too sophisticated. There's a little security, but nothing I can't handle," Lee said, typing from behind her.

"Then it'll be the human element that's the decider."

"From me?"

"You, the camera security guy, me, and Ben going inside. Never count out humans in stressful situations to make it harder than it first appears," Rachel said. "With that said, stay ready. I'm heading inside now."

"Good luck."

Rachel exited the car and made her approach toward the hospital. She entered the doors, made a beeline toward the elevators, and pressed the third floor button once inside. The elevator stopped before her desired floor, and she watched as a male nurse stepped in. He looked at her before turning around and pressing his desired floor.

He stood next to her with crossed arms and leaned back

against the wall. "You must be a new hire. I don't remember seeing you around."

"You can tell?" Rachel asked. "I'm a little nervous."

"You'll be fine. Don't let Nancy push you around, and do your job. You'll be fine."

The elevator dinged as the number three above them lit up. "This is my stop," Rachel said. "I'll see you around."

The doors shut behind her as she surveyed her surroundings. The long narrow hallway and nurses' station could be seen in the distance. She spotted the lounge area she'd seen before on the camera footage. Using that knowledge, she ascertained her objective and strode forward. She saw the guard standing outside the room and moved forward with confidence toward the middle-aged man with a mustache.

He looked up from his chair and stood up. "Were you briefed on rules regarding the prisoner?"

"Yes."

"Good. Just to be safe, don't talk to the prisoner, don't get close enough to be grabbed, and don't give her anything besides medication. I'm only saying this to cover all our butts, miss. I don't mean to hold you up. You can go in." He opened the door and held it open for her.

She stepped forward. The first thing she saw was Elizabeth laying in the hospital bed. She could make out the handcuffs around her nearest wrist attached to the bed. The baby laid near the guard in a cradle across from the bed. The guard sitting across from the bed nodded at Rachel. "It's that time already?"

"You know how it is." Rachel sidled forward and approached the bed. She reached down and grabbed the chained appendage.

Elizabeth watched Rachel, all the while staying quiet.

Rachel's voice was quiet, almost imperceptible. "I need a distraction." Her voice raised. "Your pulse is fine. Now let's see about your blood pressure."

"Get off of me." Elizabeth yanked on the chains, causing a creak from the bed below.

"Whoa." Rachel backed off. She saw the guard in the room get up and run over. "Easy now. Don't fight me. I'm just here to help."

"Fuck off and go die." Elizabeth kept struggling.

"Why are you always like this?" The guard got in front of Rachel and grabbed hold of Elizabeth's hand.

Rachel reached inside of her nurse's pants pocket and extracted one of the needles. She took the cover off the syringe. "I've got something to calm her down. Just try and keep her still if you would, sir."

"Thank God," the guard said. "I was just getting tired."

"Now," Rachel said.

"What was that?"

"Nothing." Rachel stepped forward and stuck the end of the syringe into the guard's neck and pushed the plunger down.

"What the hell?" The guard dropped Elizabeth's hand and covered the puncture site with his hand. "I feel weird." The guard stumbled side to side until Rachel caught him with a grunt. She raised her voice. "Help! Guard, come in here!" She gently lowered the guard to the tiled floor as the door behind her opened.

"What the hell's going on in here?" his angry voice asked.

Before Rachel could answer, Ben appeared through the now open door and shut it behind him. He dropped the bag on the ground and a needle could be seen in his right hand already prepared. He thrust it into the oblivious guard's neck and followed suit. He wrapped his left arm around the guard's throat and the other around his chest.

Ben whispered in the guard's ear. "Just go to sleep. It'll all be over once you wake up."

This guard put up a little longer fight than the first, but within a minute or two he was out on his feet.

"Alright," Rachel said. "Ben, you search your man for the key. I'll search this one and get her free."

"Finally. It took you all long enough," Elizabeth said from the bed.

Rachel ignored the jab and frisked the man at her feet. "I got the key. Now, help me drag this one to the chair. He'll look like he fell asleep on the job." Rachel looped her arms under the guy's arms as Ben got to the other side and grabbed the legs. They maneuvered around until they managed to get the guard into the chair. Rachel angled his head back.

"There. Now drag that one onto the bed once I get her out. We'll cover him up and you can go get the car ready." She took the key and unlocked the handcuffs as she spoke. "Get up, girl. We need the bed."

"Don't presume to give me orders."

"Auntie, with all due respect, shut the hell up and do what I say if you want to get out of here and not go back to prison. Now," she reached up the front of her shirt and removed the folded up nurse's uniform and pants and pointed at her aunt. "Put those on. We're walking right out of here."

Elizabeth did not answer but instead glared at Rachel as she got out of the bed.

Ben kicked the bag over to Elizabeth, hefted the man into the bed, and covered the asleep man with the covers. He made for the door. "I'll move the car since that idiot can't drive. We'll be ready when you two make your way down."

"You couldn't find a better hiding space than your shirt?" Elizabeth asked.

"You're lucky I could even smuggle that in here. You're lucky they thought I must have been a little chubby."

"Nice dye job." Elizabeth took off the patient gown, giving Rachel a full view of the aging, but still attractive gangster boss from the front.

"No shame I see."

"Why would I?" Elizabeth put on the pants first. "You're my niece. I assume Danny sent you."

"Correct."

Elizabeth hoisted the scrubs over her head with a wince and put it on. "You've changed since the last time I saw you."

"That's a long ass story I'll tell you later. Blame your brother for that. He gave me no choice in this shit."

"If he did what I think he did, I'll have to slap some sense into him. Tanya, your mother, would have done the same." She pulled the shoes out of the bag and donned the ID that Rachel gave to her. "Now let's get Bernard and get out of here."

"Bernard?"

"My baby." Elizabeth took a step toward the cradle before Rachel grabbed her hand.

"Father's orders were to leave him. It's hard enough to smuggle you out, never mind a potentially loud infant. Blame him, not me. Orders are orders. You know how it is. Besides, you can always get him back later. We have a guy that can track him."

"Are you fucking serious?"

"Deadly. Now come on. We're on a tight time window here." She pulled Elizabeth away from the cooing baby toward the door. "We'll get you your kid back. Trust me. Real talk though, girl to girl, we need to move. Take it up with your brother when we get back."

"Fine already." Elizabeth kept looking at her baby as she walked until she passed through the doorway. The door swung shut, obscuring her view. She turned around and took her hand back from Rachel as they walked down the hallway. "This is it?" she quietly asked, a smile on her face.

"We're just two nurses on break is all," she said with a beaming smile on her face as she led Elizabeth toward the stairwell they'd planned on earlier. They walked past a doctor who nodded at them as they passed in the hallway, with the pair returning the gesture.

They reached the stairwell and ducked inside.

"Hold on." Elizabeth grabbed Rachel's hand as she looked further down the stairwell. "There's a camera."

"It's taken care of," Rachel said, pulling out of the grasp. "It's on a loop. Now let's go. It's only a matter of time before someone notices something."

"You've thought of everything, haven't you?" Elizabeth asked.

"I sure hope so. If not, I'll be joining you in maximum security prison for the rest of my life. I can't let that happen with Roger."

"Excuse me? You're still with him?"

"Yes and no. It's a long story. I'll explain once we're on the way back home. It'll be a nine hour drive. We'll have time then." The pair had made it down one flight of stairs when Elizabeth visibly slowed her pace.

"Are you alright?" Rachel asked, leaning forward. A lock of dyed black hair fell in front of her face. She brushed it aside and reached out toward her aunt.

"I'm just tired is all."

"You did just give birth and all. Just keep moving and suck it up."

"Easy for you to say." Elizabeth grit her teeth and kept putting one foot in front of the other.

Somewhere else, not too far away at that very moment...

"What the hell?" A man in a security uniform stared at the static images of the stairwell. "Did they finally fix that? I never heard about it if they did." He stared at the image of the bottom floor stairwell for a full minute before reaching to his side and picking up the phone beside him. The phone rang once before it was picked up. "Hey, I'm noticing something odd on the camera in the east stairwell, bottom floor. I'm not sure what it is. Did they finally fix the exit sign at the bottom? Well, I ask because it's not flickering like it usually is. Yeah, it's just dandy now it looks like. Can you just check it out? Fine, I'll get you a damned coffee next time I see you. Thanks, buddy." He hung up the phone and returned his gaze to the monitors in front of him.

Back with the girls in the stairwell....

"We're almost there," Rachel said, leading the pair down the last flight of stairs before they reached the ground floor. "Just keep going."

"Easier said than done." Elizabeth said through her teeth.

"Just stand up straight when we see anyone. You're a nurse, not a woman who just gave birth, and our freedom depends on your ass acting like it."

Their conversation was interrupted by the door below

opening and a man stepping through. The pair continued down the stairs.

The man closed the door behind him and turned to see them. "Hello," he said, a friendly smile on his face.

"Hey," Rachel said, trying her best to force a believable smile.

Elizabeth hopped down off the last stair and elbowed Rachel in the side. "He's cute. You were just telling me you were single. Go for it, girl."

"Oh come on." Rachel looked away and toward the floor.

"Sorry, ladies. I'm just here to check on something. If you'll excuse me."

"Ah poo," Elizabeth said. "I guess he's already married. All the good men are. I'll find you one yet."

"Come on already." Rachel stepped past the man toward the door. "I just want to go to lunch already. I hope you find whatever you're looking for, sir."

"I'm coming, I'm coming." Elizabeth followed after her.

"Sorry about her," Rachel called out over her shoulder. "She's incorrigible when she gets like this."

"Don't worry about it!" the guy said before turning back toward the stairwell. "Now let's get to seeing about this sign and camera..."

The two women exited the stairwell and immediately saw the back exit to the hospital. Another man stepped through it before they could get there. This time he was carrying a ladder with him. "Oh, excuse me, you two," he said angling the climbing tool so it wouldn't hit them as he passed by.

"You all must be busy today. We just saw another maintenance guy a minute ago," Elizabeth said.

"Ah," the man passed them, still talking. "It's just one guy being a worrywart, but it's his job. You know how it is.

It's nothing compared to the work you two put in day in and day out. Have a good one," he called out as he approached the door the pair just left.

"That's our cue," Rachel said, pushing the door leading outside open.

Their car pulled up in front of them. A noticeable scar was visible near the taillights. The near back door was thrown open. Elizabeth climbed in while Rachel ran around it and jumped in the front passenger seat. They slammed the doors shut, and the car immediately started moving again.

"You're going to love this story I have for you, boss," Ben said with a quick glare into the rearview mirror directed at Lee.

Elizabeth followed the look over to Lee. "What's that?"

"What is it, Ben?" Rachel asked. She watched the passing traffic go by.

"We have a situation here because of 'Mr. I can't drive' back there."

Rachel turned around, putting her elbow on the top of her seat and looked at Lee. "What did he do?"

"Imagine my surprise when I get outside and see the car already moving."

"So?"

"So, I saw it scrape another car on the way out of the parking spot. I don't think anybody was in the car, but they're going to know the license plate number with the cameras around, so we'll need to fix this. We have a minor dent on the side of the car now."

"How do you propose we do that?"

"It's rather simple, but we're in a hurry. We need some spackle, some spray paint, a screwdriver and a spare license plate."

"We have a license plate in the trunk. Dad thought ahead, thank God, in case the plates were caught on camera. As for the other shit, a quick visit to a hardware store should solve it. We'll just have to get somewhere away from prying eyes before we switch them. It won't take more than half an hour."

"Half an hour," Elizabeth shook her head. "We should be making as much distance as we can." Elizabeth reached over and slapped Lee across the face hard with the palm of her hand. "I'm not going back to prison because of a fat fuck like you."

"Sorry, ma'am."

"I don't want to hear sorry." Elizabeth looked away, out the window to her side. "I just want to be in a safe place, and your ass just complicated that."

Rachel looked away from Elizabeth and back at Lee. "Why would you do that?"

"I figured driving around a parking lot wouldn't be hard, and I was sitting in here anyway. I thought I'd make myself useful."

"You certainly did something," Ben said, sarcasm tinting his voice heavily. "We have like an hour before the FBI is aware she's missing. God damn it all. There's a hardware store. I'm going to get what we need."

"I'll stay here and make sure nobody else does anything stupid as hell," Rachel said, still looking at Lee. "You have enough cash on you?"

"It should only be like fifty dollars. I'll be fine," Ben said, putting the car in park right in front of the store.

"We should be on our way home now," Rachel said, staring with narrow eyes at Lee. "Father will hear about this complication."

"Please no," Lee said, his voice soft.

"You damn near compromise this whole thing, and now you're going to beg?" Rachel asked. She looked to his side to see her aunt watching the exchange with interest. "What would you do, Auntie?"

"You're asking me?" Elizabeth asked, bringing a hand to her chest. She looked at the fat computer expert beside her with a smirk. "I'd wait until we got home, and then I'd give him a time honored test."

"Meaning?" Rachel asked. "Is this what Uncle Roger told me about with Ana that one time?"

"That's the one." Elizabeth's face contorted into one of anger. "I still can't believe that duplicitous bitch turned on me."

"Did she ever tell you why?"

"No. What did she tell you?"

Rachel turned back to face the windshield. "She said it was because of exactly what you suggested. She only found out later your little trick with it."

"Are you shitting me?" Elizabeth leaned forward in her seat. "She turned because of that show?"

"Apparently people don't like thinking their life is being driven by chance," Rachel said. "He did say it was a damned good show though."

"Of course it was," Elizabeth huffed. "It was me after all. You have to show the rank and file who's boss. Did Roger ever say why he betrayed us?"

Rachel's mood darkened and looked down at her lap for a full minute before answering. "You're not going to like it you know."

"I need to know the truth."

Rachel raised her head and saw Elizabeth staring straight into her eyes. "Fine. He got an encrypted email from her professing how she wanted out. He went to meet her of course, and she played the helpless maiden in trouble."

"With his attitude I can see how that would work. He always did think he was some hero."

"He was a hero," Rachel said back immediately. "Just not to you that time."

Elizabeth let loose a breath. "True."

"Anyway, she convinced him to help her get out of the life, like he had."

"How does that lead to me going to prison along with the whole family exactly?"

"I'm back." Ben threw open the door and handed a white bag over to Rachel before getting back in the driver's seat. He looked at Elizabeth to his right. "Sorry, did I interrupt something?"

"No." Elizabeth fell back in the seat and blew a stray strand of black hair out of her face. "It's fine. Let's just get moving and get back to home. We're still in Chicago, right?"

"Not quite," Ben said, turning the key in the ignition. He backed out of the parking space and pulled up to the light, leading out of the parking lot. He waited for the tell-tale green arrow as he spoke. "We're in Ohio now."

"What the fuck's in Ohio?" Elizabeth asked. "Isn't that whole place farms and forest?"

"Most of it," Rachel snickered. "We're in a big metropolis called Toledo though. Plenty of space for a syndicate to operate."

"After we cross state line, we'll drive for an hour," Ben said. "Then when we get to an area that's desolate, we'll do the repairs and continue. We can't be near Missouri when they find out she's missing."

"They'll lock down the local tri-state area once they find out," Lee said from the back. "It's a good idea."

Ben pulled out into traffic, heading east. "You don't say? Did the camera thing at least work?"

"Nobody gave us any problems," Rachel said. "So I suppose so."

"At least he did his one job right then," Ben said with a roll of his eyes.

8

"How long will this take?" Rachel asked, taking the white bag out of the car.

Ben got out and took the plastic bag. "The longest part will be the painting but if everybody takes a spray can, it won't take more than twenty or thirty minutes. We're over fifty miles away from the hospital, so they won't pin us in."

"Hey," Rachel banged on the window. "Turn the radio on."

"Why?" Lee asked from inside.

"Just do it. That's an order."

Elizabeth got out from the back seat and stretched. "It'd be nice to know when they're aware, you idiot."

"Right," Lee leaned forward and reached for the radio. He turned it on.

"Now get out here and help." She turned to Ben. "What are we doing first?"

"We have bottles of water, right?" Ben asked.

Rachel peeked inside the car. "Yeah."

"Get one for me if you would, boss. We need to mix this spackle with water and then we fill the scrape with that. We spray paint over that, and switch license plates. It's not hard. The only problem we might run into is if it rains. On the other hand, the wind from driving will help the paint dry faster."

Elizabeth looked up into the overcast sky. "Hard to say if it'll rain or not."

"We don't have a choice." Rachel threw open the door and retrieved a bottle of water before handing it over to Ben. "Here, work your magic. I'll get the spray paint ready for everybody." She pulled out the multiple cans and lined them up on the car's hood.

"Let's see how well this works then." Ben opened the container and put some spackle on the trowel. He used said trowel to apply the gooey mixture onto the obvious scratch on the side of the car. "I always hate working with this stuff."

"What?" Rachel asked. "Is it sticky or something?"

"I mean it's spackle. It's paste, so yes it is. It just gets everywhere."

"Stop your bitching in front of your superiors." Elizabeth leaned against the car and raised her nose up with her arms crossed. "It's unsightly."

"Yes, ma'am," Ben said.

"I still can't believe we just left my baby back there. Who knows where he's going to end up?"

"The same place he would have gone if you'd went back to prison," Rachel said.

Elizabeth narrowed her eyes at Rachel. "No kidding. You know something?" She uncrossed her arms and took a few steps toward Rachel. "I remember you being a lot nicer before."

"Things change, people change. You'd do well to remember that."

"Roger taught me that lesson. Right about when he testified in open court. Come to think of it," she eyed Rachel up and down, "I don't remember seeing you there. No wonder Danny wanted you to work for him. He knew you wouldn't betray him."

"Right, Auntie." Rachel stepped up to Elizabeth until they were nose to nose. "Let's get one thing straight. You're not part of this syndicate. I am the second in command. You are here because you're blood related, and you can help stop this war we're stuck in. Do you understand me?"

"Why you little cunt." Elizabeth reared back and winded up a slap, only to have Rachel catch the strike before it landed.

"Ah, ah, ah. Didn't your dad ever teach you not to assault your superiors?"

"You little brat!" Elizabeth's face was flushing, becoming more crimson by the moment. "I've been a criminal since before you were a twinkle in your daddy's eye, and you're going to treat me like this?"

"I'm just setting the ground rules here. If you don't like it," Rachel pointed at the dirt road they rode in on, "then there's the road. Besides, I never heard a thank you." She reached down and patted Ben on the shoulder. "Did you hear one?"

"No, ma'am." Ben said, still hard at work filling in the scrape. "It was quite rude."

"You kiss ass." Elizabeth backed up and turned away from Rachel with a huff. "Fine. Just don't think I'm going to forget this."

"Yes, yes." Rachel waved the thinly veiled threat away. She knocked on the window. "Get your dumbass out here."

Lee got out of the car, leaving his laptop inside.

"Is that the same laptop from before?"

"Maybe."

"Fucking get rid of it. You said you'd destroy it."

"Yes. Just so you know, they can't track this; but it is good operational security, so I will."

Rachel spoke through her teeth. "Do it now, jackass. I've had enough of your bullshit today. We'd be another twenty minutes closer to home if it wasn't thanks to you."

"How should I do it exactly?"

"Oh for fuck's sake." Rachel nabbed the electronic device and threw it to the ground. She placed it in front of the car's front tire. "There. Now when we leave, it'll be destroyed."

"You're telling me you couldn't think of that yourself?" Ben asked with a chuckle. "Some smart guy you are."

"I've just about had enough of you."

"Lee," Rachel said in a tone that brooked no argument. "Do not start with this. You're on thin ice as it is. Everybody just calm the hell down. The other reason I got you out of the car is you, along with everybody else, are going to help spray paint this car. Yes, it'll look a little janky, but the faster we're on the move, the better."

"Agreed," Elizabeth said. She turned around to see Rachel looking at her, an eyebrow raised. "Look, I'm not in charge, granted. I'm just agreeing that we need to get moving, your highness."

"You almost had me in the first half, not going to lie," Rachel laughed. "Fine." She grabbed a can and tossed it underhanded to Elizabeth, Lee, and finally grabbed one for herself. She moved the rest of the spray paint cans to the grass below. She looked down at Ben. "How much longer?"

"I'm almost done. I'm just trying to make sure it's even." Ben leaned closer to the spackle filled scratch. He stood up after one final adjustment. "Alright. Let's get this thing painted. You three start with that, while I switch the license plate to the spare. Pop the trunk, would you, boss?" He moved to the trunk area as he talked.

"Just a second." Rachel opened the driver's side door and did as he asked. "Now let's all get started. Start with the front, and by time we get to the back he should be nearly done. She shook the can in her hand and unlocked the nozzle. "Let's get to work, people. I don't know about you, but I'm tired of standing around just off a damned highway when we should be running." She circled around to the direct front of the car and started spraying the black paint all over the hood. "Start work on the sides," she said over the sound of the hissing.

Lee took one side while Elizabeth took the other. The trio worked on the newfound project in relative silence other than the hissing of the compressed paint being sprayed.

Ben unscrewed the two screws in the upper middle of the license plate and removed it. He tossed the old to the side and grabbed the new plate. He aligned it as best he could, used his magnetic screwdriver to hold the screw on the end, and screwed it in. Once done, he got up to admire his work, his hands on his hips. "There. It's done." He moved around the vehicle. "How's this part going?" He looked on their work. "Passable." He bent down to the grass and picked one up for himself. He moved back to the trunk area and got to work alongside them...

Around half an hour later...

The group threw down their respective spray cans onto the grass below. Their prior green car, now a dark black.

"Alright, people," Rachel clapped. "Now's no time to admire our work. Everybody get inside."

"Finally." Elizabeth was the first to throw open the back door and get inside. She looked back outside. "Get in already, fat ass."

"Right away." Lee hurried inside and sat beside Elizabeth.

Rachel threw open the driver's door as Ben did the same with the passenger side.

They both climbed inside. She immediately started the engine and turned the car around on the small dirt path they found themselves on. The trees passed by with every second, growing sparser. She reached for the radio and turned it up.

"It's the moment of truth," Ben said. "Have they found out yet?"

The car pulled out onto the highway as the radio commercial faded. A male voice took over the airwaves. "Welcome back, everybody. Before we get back to the music we all love, we have some breaking news. Elizabeth Morris, the head of the former Morris crime family, has escaped custody from the local Queen's Son Hospital today. Federal forces are rallying in the local tri-state area. If you see or hear anything that could be of help, please call this toll free number with any information." He rattled off a phone number. "We beg you not to try anything yourself. She is to be considered armed and extremely dangerous. Please folks, leave it for the professionals."

Rachel turned the radio off. "I'd say they found out about fifteen minutes ago then. It'd take them that long to alert the news agencies and radio stations. We're out of the state, but we'll take smaller roads. We can't run the risk of checkpoints. They'll be deploying those on the main high-ways if they have any sense in the surrounding one hundred miles."

"We'd already be clear of our hunters if we didn't have to stop," Ben said, glaring up into the rear- view mirror toward Lee who was busy on his laptop.

The artificial light from his laptop screen lit up his face. "I'm going to ignore the childish poke and inform you that we want to take the next right. The boss is correct. I was scouting our route and see they did set up a checkpoint about ten miles ahead. If we take the exit, we'll go right around them."

"You're making up for it at least," Elizabeth said.

"Are you feeling alright back there?" Rachel asked.

Elizabeth didn't bother facing the young woman and continued staring out at the passing scenery. "Other than not having Bernard here with me, I guess so. I can't believe you just dragged me away from my baby. That's some spartan shit right there."

"What?"

"Did you learn nothing in history class? If a baby was deformed or deemed unworthy, they chucked it off a cliff to die."

"I don't think that was remotely the same thing, considering I said we'd get him back later."

"It sure felt like that," Elizabeth grumbled. "I now know why women get so uppity about their kids. I never understood before. It only took seeing my baby disappear as I left the room to trigger those instincts in me. I have you and my brother to thank for that."

"I didn't expect that, honestly," Rachel said.

Immediately after Ben looked at her with wide eyes but kept quiet.

"What's that supposed to mean?" Elizabeth asked, eyes narrowing.

"I chose my words carefully. When I was growing up,

you were all cool, collected, and never let anything phase you."

"Flattery will get you nowhere in this business, dear niece. Especially when it's easily found out. It ends up being quite insulting. I don't like being insulted."

"I don't like the new you bitching about this either, so let's drop it. This isn't productive."

"Fine." Elizabeth crossed her arms and closed her eyes, leaning her head against the glass to her right.

"It looks like the roadblocks are situated around Missouri, Arkansas, and Illinois. We should veer toward Kentucky and take that way."

"Noted," Rachel said. "They probably think we're headed back to New York or Chicago. Those were your home bases, yes?"

"You know they were," Elizabeth said, her voice tense.

"They're trying to anticipate where you're going. They have no real way of knowing Ohio is our goal. We'll be good even if we have to swing further south than we thought."

"Shouldn't be an issue. They've went all in on the northern roads," Lee said, typing away.

"You are sure they won't notice your monitoring?" Ben turned around in his seat. "Isn't that something they'd notice?"

"Utilizing online live maps isn't exactly illegal. All I'm doing is following the highways and seeing them form. It's not like I'm in their database and watching their orders being sent around."

"You don't like him, do you?" Elizabeth asked, now showing interest with a grin. "You've been on his case this whole time."

"He's annoyed is all," Rachel said. "Normally he's a

regular sweetheart. Well, as close to one as you can get in this line of work."

"You'd better watch him then," Elizabeth said. "Those are the real troublemakers. Trust me on that one. Your uncle was the same way. Just don't make the same mistake I did."

"The jury's still out on whether your interest in him was a mistake."

"I'd say the verdict was pretty damned clear. He sent me to prison with a life sentence. The ones with a conscience, as you make your man out to be," she pointed at Ben, "those always catch up to them. If you know what's good for you, heed my warning."

"Did I miss something?" Ben asked.

"You're not a rat, are you?" Elizabeth asked.

"Hell no I'm not. I just helped break you out of federal custody. I thought that was pretty clear already."

"Roger was a killer too. Do you fancy yourself a good man, Ben was it?"

"I'd like to, Ms. Morris, but I know better than to think that after what I've done."

"Do you believe in God, Ben?"

"Yes."

"Yeah." Elizabeth turned to Rachel. "You'd best watch out for him then. Roger was the same way. That guilt will catch up to him."

"With all due respect, you don't know who the hell I am yet, Ms. Morris," Ben said, turning back in his seat to face the windshield.

"I know enough, young man." Elizabeth leaned forward and placed a hand on his headrest. "You remind me entirely too much of a young man I knew all too long ago." She turned her attention to Rachel. "You remind me entirely too much of myself too."

"No need to insult me now," Rachel muttered under her breath.

"What was that?"

"Nothing, Auntie. It was nothing."

"It sounded like something to me."

"Perish the thought."

9

"You're finally back." Daniel kicked back in the chair, cigar hanging in the corner of his mouth. "I see my sister is here. I could use some good news after another of our men went down while you were gone. At least Jeremy's with his brother now."

"What the hell happened?" Rachel asked.

"He went on an unsanctioned hit-job on his brother's killer again. He succeeded, but he didn't escape with his life." Daniel spoke softer. "It's a shame too. The kid had great potential."

Rachel stood in the middle of the line of people in front of the large desk with her hands behind her back. "Sorry it took so long. There was a complication that we had to take care of on the way back."

"What was that pray tell?"

Ben glared at his right toward Lee but stayed silent.

Daniel followed Ben's stare and went back to his daughter. "Well?"

"Our resident tech specialist tried to prove himself,"

Rachel said slowly and carefully. "It did not work out that well."

"Elaborate." Daniel said with a frown. He looked back to Lee to see him sweating profusely and fidgeting in place, staring at the carpeted floor. "Now."

"On the way it came to our attention that Lee here couldn't drive."

"Seriously?"

"We found it hard to believe ourselves," Rachel said. "Well, we had a plan that Ben would exit the hospital and bring the car around to pick us up behind. When he got out there, he saw Lee hit another car in the parking lot." Rachel shook her head and tried not to smile as she spoke. "Thank God you gave us another license plate, because we used it. We knew they had to have seen us on the cameras because of that."

"You tried to operate a motor vehicle knowing damned well you didn't know how?" Daniel got to his feet and moved around the desk. He stopped directly in front of Lee and stared down his nose at him. "In the middle of a sensitive fucking operation?"

"Father."

"Be quiet." He held out his right hand toward his daughter with only the index finger up. "You answer me, Lee."

"I did."

"You dumb bastard. How the hell do you not know how to drive? Not only that, but you jeopardized the entire operation to, what? Earn brownie points with me or my daughter?" He ceased his verbal lashing and looked back at Rachel. "What were you going to say?"

"He guided us around the police checkpoints afterward, making sure we never even encountered a patrol car. While we did have to stop for spray paint and then repaint the car, he did get us home safe."

Daniel stared Lee down again. "Don't you ever pull a stupid ass stunt like that again. Do you understand me? For that matter, we're getting you some driver's ed or something. We can't have someone with the practical skills of a small child. You find a course and enroll yourself. Do I make myself clear?"

"Crystal clear, sir. I just have one question."

"This had better be good." Anger seeped into Daniel's voice through gritted teeth.

"How am I to get there?"

Daniel snapped and laid a punch into Lee's sizable breadbasket, causing the nerdy man to double over gasping for breath.

"Call a fucking taxi or whatever that new service they offer on your phone is. It's some app I've heard of. You're the tech savvy guy. Figure it out."

Once Lee gathered his breath he stood up and remained quiet, assuming his previous stance.

"Now get out of here." He laid a hand on Lee's chest and pushed him backward toward the double doors.

Lee quickly exited the room leaving Daniel, Rachel, Ben, and Elizabeth.

"I could have sworn he'd never do something so monumentally stupid." Daniel shook his head, staring at the now unmoving door. "I watched that man break into the damned FBI database, and he can't even drive. Christ alive." He moved back to the desk and sat on it.

"Aside from that incident, it went as well as expected," Rachel said.

"So I see." Daniel smiled at his sister. "Did you enjoy the dike lodge, Sis?"

Elizabeth rolled her eyes. "I'd rather shit in my hand and clap than ever go back to those cunts."

"You still have as colorful a vocabulary as I remember." Daniel chuckled. "Now you know why I risked my daughter's freedom to get you out? You do remember I trust?"

"Because I saved your ass when you were bleeding out."

Daniel was not amused with this answer, and he gave her a blank stare. "Try again."

"Yeah, I know the old lady of one of the higher ups of the cartel. We used to throw in commissary items toward communal meals together. It's amazing how much you can bond over cooking in the joint."

"That, or she liked leeching off your commissary budget," Daniel said. "For all our sakes, let's hope you're telling the truth."

"Of course I am, dear Brother." Elizabeth's tone took an indignant edge. "Who do you think I am?"

"What's your plan to end this war then?"

"I just know his wife. That's all."

"You're shitting me," Rachel said at her side. "You have to be joking."

Daniel quieted his daughter with a wave of his hand before standing up and standing toe-to-toe with his sister. "That's not what you let me know when you were using her phone to call me. You said you could stop this war."

"It got me out of there, didn't it? I'd say it worked from my point of view." She gave him a shit eating grin."

"You're lucky you're my aunt or I'd kick the shit out of you myself." Rachel sent a hateful look toward Elizabeth.

"Why you little..." Elizabeth was interrupted as Daniel reached forward and grabbed Elizabeth by the throat. "Huh?"

"I do not appreciate being lied to, dear Sister. Nor do I

like that you endangered my right-hand woman under false pretenses. You are going to make yourself useful or else."

"Or else what?"

"There are worse things than prison. Know this, the only reason you're alive and well is because of your family here. You will treat us with the proper respect. You are not head of the family anymore. You are not affiliated with the syndicate. Do not act above your station, and show the proper respect."

Elizabeth choked out a few words. "Dear Brother, I do believe you've let the power go to your head."

Daniel released the choke hold on his sister. "I'm looking after my men and women is what I'm doing. Now, if you want to join, that can be arranged; but you will not be getting preferential treatment. You're lucky you even got out of that hospital."

"Speaking of which, my niece said it was your idea that we had to leave my Bernard there all by himself."

"That's right. It was dangerous enough getting you out, never mind a screaming infant. What about it? Don't tell me you're ungrateful for our aid? I know Dad didn't raise such a woman."

Elizabeth's cool demeanor changed to one of thinly veiled anger. "You need to watch yourself."

"No, I don't," Daniel said with a laugh. "That's what being the boss means. So long as I watch out for the group, I can do anything within reason. You know that better than I do. Now if you truly want that kid back, we can help with that. You need to play nice though. We'd also have to wait a few months. They're hot on your trail. Who cares anyway? All you'll be missing is the kid waking you up in the middle of the night. You should be thanking me. It's not like the kid will remember whatever foster parents are with him for the next few months."

"Fine," Elizabeth said. "I'll be nice so long as you help me get my baby back."

"Wonderful. Now seeing as our golden goose was a bust, we have more business to attend to this evening. You are excused, Sister."

"Be that way why don't you," Elizabeth grumbled and exited the room.

"Father, what is this job?" Rachel yawned.

"Tired?"

"I had the last driving shift. I've been driving the last five hours."

"I can do it, sir," Ben said with a bow of his head. "I managed to catch a nap after my last driving shift."

Daniel smirked at Ben and looked back to his daughter. "It's just overseeing a weapons deal with Oleg's men. I already have the grunts picked out. We just need a leader. Do you trust Ben here to oversee it?"

"He'll be fine."

"Alright then, you're dismissed. Go see your boy."

"Thank you." She left the two men alone in the room.

Daniel gestured for Ben to follow him. He led him behind the desk and grabbed one half of the huge billowing red window drapes, yanking it to the side. He quickly did the same for the other side. "Come here, son."

Ben did as he was instructed and stood at Daniel's left, staring out the gargantuan window behind the desk. "Yes, sir?"

"You did a good job. I saw your glare toward Lee earlier. You were the one who had to clean that up I assume?"

Ben kept his focus on the dark forest looming outside

the window as he spoke. "Oh no, sir. Miss Rachel did a fine job of that herself."

Daniel chuckled and put an arm around Ben's shoulders. "I know my daughter, Adams. She is not the type to refit a car with a new paint job and switch out the plates. You did that, right?"

"Yes, sir."

"I figured as much. Now you've overseen gun deals over the past month, yes?"

"Of course, sir."

"Good. Now be careful out there. We are in the middle of a war. The flow of money cannot stop however. If we are to win, we need the cash flow." Daniel watched the patrol down on the grass below as he spoke. "Look at them. You'd think they'd learn eventually." He sighed. "Anyway, the van is ready at the warehouse. Now remember they know where it is, but it is heavily defended. Warren's there, but watch your back when you leave."

"I'll be extra careful, sir. May I ask a question?"

"Go ahead." Daniel extricated his arm from Ben and turned back to the table. He picked up a shot glass half full of amber liquid and took a quick swig.

Ben paused and finally spoke. "After I finish this deal and get everything squared away, is it alright if I go home? I need to fix something for my parents."

"Sure thing," Daniel said. "So long as I am counting bills by tomorrow morning, you can head home. All I ask is for you to be careful out there. Now all you have to do is call the number Oleg gave us. The other team is already at the site waiting."

"Thank you, sir. I'll get it done immediately. If you'll excuse me." He said nothing further as Daniel nodded. Ben made for the door and exited.

Daniel stared at the door. "See that you do. We need that cash," Daniel's voice grew lower, "in a bad way."

Meanwhile in Rachel's room...

"Hello, baby. Mommy's back." She took Roger from Lauren and cradled him in her arms.

Lauren watched the mother and adopted son. "I take it the job went well, since you're in one piece and not in prison."

"Oh Lord, don't get me started on that shitshow. The actual job went off mostly without a hitch except for that one idiot - Lee. Aside from that, the whole premise of the job was under false pretenses."

Lauren sat down on the bed and laid back. "I don't understand."

"My aunt said she could help stop this gang war bullshit. It turns out, she admitted to father and me that the only reason she lied and said she could stop it was for us to break her out of custody." She placed a hand on Roger's blonde head, causing him to coo and reach up to her hand. "I have to say, I kind of expected it too. You want to know how I knew?"

"How?"

"She has always been self-serving ever since I was a small child. People think I never noticed, but I had to stay with her for days at one point. I noticed immediately how she treated her hired help. I could tell what kind of a woman she was. Either way, I don't think we're on good terms anymore."

"Why's that?" Lauren asked. "Did you proverbially swing your dick around or something?"

"Exactly that. She always loved to show off her power.

Now she has none. She tried to assume the same role, and I wasn't having any of it. Long story short, I bitched at her and she complained at me. Dad tried to look like he was on my side, but I could tell he was happy to have his sister out."

Lauren sat up. "You think he knew she couldn't do anything to stop the Crag Cartel?"

Rachel paused for a few moments and rocked Roger in her arms. "Quite possibly. That's not what's important right now though." She got up, moved Roger to his crib, and laid him inside before moving back to the bed. She sat down and lowered her voice. "How's it been here?"

"Here? There's not been any attacks if that's what you're asking. Your dad's been running Warren ragged. He only trusts a few people to oversee the gun deals. That kid Jeremy went off halfcocked and got himself killed I hear. So far the cartel hasn't gone after our revenue, but if I was going to guess, I'd say they're due. We went after their money, they'll return the favor if I know how criminal enterprises work. I like to think I do anyway."

Rachel put her legs on the bed and leaned back against the headboard. "Did Dad ask you to do much?"

"He'll sometimes ask me to come to his business room to play with Roger, but other than that he's been leaving us alone. I am the de facto babysitter it seems."

"That's good for you. You don't want to be going outside now I assume."

Lauren brushed a stray lock of black hair back, revealing her beautiful face. "It would be nice to see my parents again, but I'd rather wait until the heat dies down. I don't want to be followed and have them get hurt."

"True that. I'm still in the planning stages of our other agenda. I'll let you know more when I come up with something."

"God help us," Lauren said. "Why did you pick me anyway?"

"Logistics. If you'd said no, I'd have had you reassigned. I know I can see you every day. I know my father doesn't like doing the day-to-day baby care, so it's also privacy from prying eyes so long as we sweep the room every time."

"Alright, moving on from that. I have a question for you," Lauren said with a mischievous grin.

"I'm going to regret this, but go ahead."

"You've been hanging out with that Ben Adams guy a lot since I've known you."

"Are we really going to have this conversation? I thought the high school community was just a lie Uncle told me." She rolled her eyes. "I see it's true."

"Do you know how dreadfully boring it is staying in this house babysitting all day every day?" Lauren asked. "Let a girl have some entertainment."

Rachel rolled her eyes. "Look, I'm not in love with the guy if that's what you're implying."

"I see something there though."

"He's a nice enough guy for this line of work, fine. Does that make you happy?"

Lauren leaned toward her, a mischievous smile on her face. "So you wouldn't mind if I went after him then?"

"Go ahead if you like."

Lauren got up from the bed and moved to the front of it. "Now to just figure out my approach. Is he into the helpless maiden schtick or the new age woman?"

"How should I know? It's not like I've ever thought of that before."

"You're so boring. You need something besides work."

A slight smile appeared on Rachel's face. "Or what? I'll become a dull woman? I'm having a hard enough time as it is without adding complex relationship dynamics into the mix."

"Variety is the spice of life as they say. Besides, admit it." She held her arms at her sides and looked up at the roof. "This is our life now." She returned her gaze to her boss. "Who's to say we can't have a partner?"

"My father, chief among them. He warned me about getting involved with any of the men. My aunt also warned me, specifically about Ben funny enough. Now that you mention it, I wonder why she did. She claimed he reminded her of my uncle figure - Roger."

"To name that bundle of joy after him, he must have been a huge part of your life."

"He saved my life multiple times and became a stand in father once I realized my childish crush would lead nowhere. He always saw me as his little sister if you ask me, since his died."

"Damn. Well now's your chance to date a man like him then."

Rachel laid down on the bed and put her hands behind her head as she spoke. "What part of Dad doesn't want me dating any of the guys don't you understand? He'd kill them."

"Not if he's gone. I'm just saying."

Rachel stared at the ceiling and blinked slowly. "Huh, I never thought of that."

"You could even use it to your advantage if you play it right."

Rachel sat upright and beckoned Lauren over beside her. "Do go on..."

10

B en sat in the passenger seat of the van and watched the trees go by in the window beside him. The rapidly dying light painted everything in a golden hue. "Is this your first real job?" Ben asked the driver.

"It's my first time going out of the warehouse, yes, sir," the male driver said.

"It's just a delivery," Ben said and yawned. "Keep your eyes open and your mouth shut, and we'll be fine. I can handle Oleg's men." His voice raised so the men and women in the back could hear. "Mind your surroundings, let me do the talking, and we'll all go home tonight."

"Yes, sir," the remainder of the cabin answered.

The van pulled off the main road and onto a dirt road splitting the tree line. Another black van could be seen farther ahead.

"It looks like they're already here," Ben said, straightening up in his seat. Everybody look alive. As soon as we stop, we're getting out. Remember to keep your hands where they can see them, and no sudden movements."

Their van came to a stop beside the other and everyone

filed out. Ben waved at the men leaving the other vehicle before speaking up. "You guys been waiting for long?"

"Maybe five minutes," the large man in a suit said with a Russian accent. "Do you have everything we need?"

Ben snapped his finger. "Get the men their product, boys."

Ben's newfound underlings threw open the back door of the van and unloaded the crates stacked in the back. "There, it's everything Mr. Morris promised." He looked over at his men and women. "Help them get it wherever they want. Let's all get home quicker tonight." He looked back at their apparent leader. "How long have you worked for Mr. Oleg?"

"Me?" The Russian man asked, watching his own men supervise the loading. "I've been with Mr. Oleg for over ten years at this point. He wanted me to tell you the money is being handed over." A chirping from his pocket interrupted his words. He fished it out and smiled. "Right now actually. What about you and Mr. Morris?"

"I'm a fairly new guy, but since we're new, that's not exactly special. I've been with the syndicate for a month now, but we're only a month old."

"New does not necessarily mean bad. Have you been tested?"

"Battle tested, finesse tested, and every other test they've thrown at me. I've passed with flying colors."

"So I see. What was your name again? I only remember Mr. Morris himself and what was her name? Rachel I believe it was when they visited Mr. Oleg last month. Your boss knows how to stir up trouble from what I remember. We had a shooting at one of our old hangouts because of him."

"That's above my paygrade, man." Ben gave him an unsteady smile. "I do what the boss man says and make sure everybody stays alive as best I can. The planning I leave to the higher ups."

"As it should be. Grunts do not decide the path of the army, but do their duty." He took off his black sunglasses and rubbed them before putting them back on. "Or how do you Americans say it? Too many chefs, not enough servers? Is that right?"

"You got the saying right. You know, don't answer if you want, but what is your name anyway? I'd like to know the name of the man I'm doing business with if it's alright."

"You are polite. My name is Artyom."

"Oh, like that video game character?"

"It's a very popular name in Russia right now. I don't know about any video games as I don't do that."

"Fair enough, Artyom. You and your boys be careful on the way back, yeah?"

Artyom smiled and extended his hand to Ben. "You too, what was it?"

"It's Ben Adams. Just call me Ben." He took the hand extended and squeezed as hard as was appropriate, which turned out to be quite stiff given his partner.

Without warning Artyom put a few fingers in his mouth before a piercing whistle broke the silence and he spoke in his mother tongue. Without delay his workers filed into the vehicle they had entered in. "Until next time, Mr. Adams. You be careful." With that, Artyom got into the back of his vehicle. As soon as the door slammed shut, it was already moving down the dirt road back to civilization a whole lot better armed.

"Sir?" a male voice said to Ben's left. "Who is that?"

"Who is who?" Ben looked over at the man and saw him pointing down the road Artyom and his men had left via. "Did they forget something?" Amid the dying light of the day he could recognize it as a van, but it was not the same color. "Something's not right." He raised his voice. "Get to cover now."

"What?" one of his men asked.

"Do what I say if you want to live!" He yelled back at him, running over to the far side tree line. He got behind the biggest nearby tree and peeked around, seeing his men make a dash for their own personal cover.

As the last of his men reached relative safety, the unknown van was nearly to where their parked van was. It stopped beside it. Ben held his breath as the driver's side door opened. A petite woman stepped out of the driver's door. "Hello?" she called out. "I saw a bunch of you just now. Please don't hurt us. We're just camping here. We can leave if you'd like and find a different site."

Ben stepped out from his cover. "You're just here to camp?"

"That's right," the woman said. "I won't ask what you were doing. All I'm asking is if you're staying here?"

"No, we were about to leave. We just weren't sure who you were, Miss," Ben said. He snapped his fingers and all his people stepped out from behind their covers, weapons in hand. "Seeing as you mean us no harm, we will leave you to your camping. We hope you have a nice night," he said with a slight bow and a warm smile. "Everybody back in the van, now."

He watched as those he commanded kept their weapons at the ready, eyeing the newfound interlopers all the way to their van before climbing inside, until eventually he was the only one left still outside. He approached the van. "Sorry if we scared you. Be careful out here. You never know who you'll meet. You're just lucky it was us and not another group."

"I'll keep that in mind." The woman turned around and beckoned toward the person still sitting in the passenger seat who had wide eyes all the while. He did not follow her orders, choosing instead to simply shake his head.

"I'll take my leave then and leave you two to it." Ben threw open the front passenger side door and climbed inside. As soon as he'd secured his safety belt he looked at the driver. "Get us out of here. I don't want to scare civilians any more than we already have."

"Yes, sir." The man did as he was told and started down the dirt path. "Sir, can I say something?"

"Go for it." Ben relaxed in his seat a little.

"I thought that was the cartel. I think we all did."

The men and women in the back made it known they agreed with the driver in a chorus of "Yeah, me too."

"That is why we do not shoot first and ask questions later, boys and girls. We don't want innocent people hurt. Even if they do sometimes scare the shit out of us with their inopportune timing." He laughed.

The van pulled out onto the main road, heading back toward their warehouse in town.

The folks in the back could be heard murmuring amidst the sound of the engine as Ben reached forward, turning the radio on.

"The search continues for the infamous Elizabeth Morris. The crime family leader has baffled police so far in her elusiveness. Police suspect she had help escaping from the hospital where she gave birth to a son." The news reporter prattled on before Ben turned off the radio and leaned back in his seat. He shut his eyes as a smile appeared on his face.

Surprise is not something unfamiliar to Ben, but a hail of what sounded like gunfire coming from beside them was entirely new. He immediately hunched forward, covering his head with his hands. He angled his head to look left and saw the driver's now blank eyes staring at him, his head resting on the steering wheel. His brain vaguely noted the brain matter on the floor in front of him.

His examination of his surroundings ended prematurely when his body was flung forward, his arms crashing ahead into the small leg space below as his eyes instinctively closed at the impact. When he next opened his eyes, everything was blurry. His head rang. He brought his right hand up to his head, groaning in pain. "Is anybody else alive?" he asked as loud as he could manage. The smell of gasoline wafted into his nostrils.

He tried to unbuckle his seatbelt only to find it jammed. "Fuck." He looked left toward the mangled remains of his driver. The man's body leaned against the wheel as twisted metal was bent at unnatural angles all around it. His eyes trailed down until he saw a knife holster on the dead body's hip. He grabbed the knife handle and managed to extricate it and cut his seat belt. He turned around and saw a scene of carnage behind him. Among the blood, bullet holes, and assorted smells, he did make out one of their chests moving. "Shit."

Grabbing the door, he pushed it open and fell outside onto the grass below. He got to his knees with a grunt and pushed himself back to his feet. He opened the back door and reached inside. He undid the man's seatbelt and grabbed his arm.

He braced his right foot on the van's damaged frame and pulled as hard as he could muster. He got ready to pull again. "Wake up!" he screamed at the unconscious man, his voice shaking.

"Hmm?" The man in the back stirred. "What happened?"

"You need to get out of there. Get over here now. That's an order."

The man didn't answer verbally, choosing instead to attempt to move. "It's my foot. It's stuck."

A faint light from the front of the car sprung to life. A small bit of smoke wafted upward.

Ben kept his voice calm. "Try to slip it free. We need to move, now." He stuck his head into the cabin again and got closer, inspecting the offending appendage. "It looks like you can get it out. Just twist around and pull as hard as you can."

The light from the front was noticeably brighter. The smell of burning leather was apparent in the small space. Smoke was now visible and thick.

"You don't think I'm trying?" Panic was audibly seeping into the man's voice.

Ben backed out and looked toward the front of the car. "Oh no," he said, barely above a whisper. "We're out of time." Ben pulled out his pistol. "Are you out?"

"No. Call the services!"

"Not an option," Ben said, his eyes watering. More smoke seeped into the cabin, obscuring the view inside.

"Oh God, not like this."

"I'm sorry."

"Please, don't leave me to die like this." He reached out to Ben.

Ben's lip quivered. He lifted the firearm up, aiming carefully at the man's head. "I can only make it quick."

Flames made their way into the back of the cabin. Smoke threatened to completely obscure the view of the inside now.

"God, I'm so sorry." He squeezed the trigger three times in quick succession before holstering the weapon and taking off into a sprint in the direction they were heading before.

Once he was clear of the crash site, he ducked off the road and followed it from inside the tree line.

He reached into his jacket and got his phone. He dialed Rachel's number and brought the phone up to his head with a moan of pain. His free hand made its way to his head, nursing the growing knot on the side of his temple.

She answered with an audible squeak of a yawn. "Yeah? I was almost asleep, Ben. This better be good."

"We were attacked. I need," he paused, his vision swimming in front of him. He grabbed for the nearby aged oak beside him and leaned his weight on its sturdy frame. "I feel dizzy. I need extraction. I'm near the deal location, just off the road heading toward the city," he hissed, then stopped speaking.

"Oh Christ." Rachel's sleepy demeanor switched to panicked on a dime. "Hold on." A clatter was heard over the line. "Shit that hurt. I'm going to get someone there to pick you up. God damn it. Now you tell me what happened right now."

"We were on the ride home." Ben stopped walking and leaned back on a tree. He stayed on his feet. He felt pain all over his torso and legs. "Oh fuck. I heard a gunshot and immediately fell forward trying to get low. I looked over and saw my driver dead. Next thing I know I wake up to the smell of gas. I tried, Rachel. I tried so hard." His voice grew weak.

"Okay, I get the picture. Now shut up and stay awake. I'm going to disconnect and get someone out there. You do some first aid if you can manage. Just do not go to sleep. I'm going to call you back, and you'd better not leave me hanging."

"I wouldn't dream of it."

Ben hung up, keeping the phone in his hands. He tried to walk forward again. "It hurts worse than it did before. Come on brain chemicals, don't leave me quite yet." The phone in his hand broke his irreverent idle chatter. "Yeah, boss?"

"I sent Chris to go get you. You'll be fine. It's going to be a little while. Are you hurt anywhere? Is anything broken? Can you last until helps gets there?" Rachel asked in rapid fire.

"I don't feel like I'm going to die, if that helps. Can I ask you something I've wondered for a while?"

Rachel sighed over the line. "Yeah, what is it?"

"How did you bear managing the pain of having your finger cut off? Was it really blind hatred and spite? Or was that all talk?"

He could hear Rachel laugh and sniffle on the end. He pictured her blinking away tears. "I lied."

"Really?"

"Yeah. It wasn't out of anger. It was out of a survival instinct. My own fear told me to show no weakness. Not a voice or anything like that, but I knew that if I showed him pain, they'd kill us right then. I had to stall for time, and so I tried to peak his sick mind's fancy. Does that make sense?"

"In some twisted way, yes," Ben said, finding his back slamming against a nearby tree.

"Not as fun of a story as the boss's daughter going full badass and goading the enemy though. I prefer it the way the men tell it. You are to never tell them about what I just said." She paused, waiting for a response. "Ben!"

Ben's back slid down the bark until his chin was digging into his chest as his head slumped. "What?"

"Stay awake, you idiot."

"Sorry. I'm so tired."

"I don't care. Now you listen to me and focus. The men have to only be a few miles away at this point. Try to get toward the road now, but do not approach too closely - just close enough to be seen. I do not want you accidentally falling into the damned road." Her voice was tense. "Do you understand me?"

No answer was forthcoming.

"Ben? You had better answer me right now." She waited another moment. "Don't do this to me." Her voice was softer now, almost brittle. "Answer me..."

11

Rachel barged through the double doors to her father's work den.

"This better be important," Daniel said, looking up from the paper he was filling in with the nearby pen.

"We were hit."

"At the gun deal?" Daniel asked, placing the writing implement aside.

Rachel stopped in front of the desk and placed her hands on it. "Yes, near the selling site to be more specific. On their way back to the warehouse they were hit. There was a car crash, so I sent someone to pick them up right away."

"Did they deliver the guns?" Daniel asked, looking up at his daughter, the stale scent of tobacco lingering in the room.

"What?"

"Did the Russians get the hardware or not? It's a simple question."

"Yes. Jesus, Dad. Aren't you worried about the men and women who were on that job? All but one are dead. Do you hear me?"

"Of course I'm worried about their wellbeing, princess. What kind of boss do you think I am? I just needed to know if I had another phone call to make before I deal with this blemish." Daniel stood up. "Now who survived?"

"It's Ben, Dad. He managed to survive the car crash. He was a little incoherent, but he got his location to me."

"At least he got the job done," Daniel said. "I can't say the man has impressed me with his track record, but he does get the job done every single time."

"What is that supposed to mean? What's wrong with his record?"

"Well, I seem to remember the one time I sent him with you to protect you, and you came home one finger lighter," Daniel said. "A father does not forget such things. Even if they aren't entirely his fault."

"He helped get Aunt Elizabeth out of prison. Doesn't that count for anything? He's helped us break and enter, assault, murder, and evade federal police. Do I need to continue?"

"Aren't you paying a little too much attention to this guy?" Daniel asked. "Yeah, it sucks he got hurt; but why do I sense such an attachment? I deliberately told you not to get too involved with this guy."

"I'm sure that works for all the dads everywhere when they tell their daughter the same thing." Sarcasm laced Rachel's voice. "What if I just care about the men under my command?"

"That better be all that it is." Daniel pointed at his daughter. "For his sake you'd better not let me find out anything different."

"He's my best soldier, Dad. Forgive the hell out of me for wanting him to be alright," Rachel huffed, looking away.

"Besides, it's not like you ever made those official rules when we initiate people you know."

"Rachel, I don't want you involved with him, or any of the men here. It's not him specifically."

"Why? Are you going to come up with a real reason or blame Uncle Roger some more?" Rachel held her ground until her eyes widened and looked down at her dress shoes.

"Look," Daniel rubbed one of his eyes. "I just know the kind of men who work for us. Hell, I used to be one myself and yes, even that man. I know how men here operate. It's very few and far between that one actually cares."

"You cared for Mom. Look, I get it. Just how about you trust me to make my own decisions? I won't force the guy into it or anything if that's what you're worried about."

"The answer is still no," Daniel said. "Now was that all you had to talk about? Your little crush is going to be bedridden for a little while. I get it. I need to focus on helping the families of all the men and women who died tonight, so if you'll excuse me."

Rachel stood there and shook her head.

"That means get out," Daniel said, tapping his finger. "Now."

"Fine then. I need to prepare his room for him anyway," she said, a smug grin replacing the previous sheepishness.

"You'd better be getting your little friend to take care of that and not yourself. I don't want the men to see that," he called out after his daughter between the closing doors. "I'll have to nip this in the bud before it grows out of control," he mumbled to himself, picking up the phone.

Half an hour later...

"This looks bad." Rachel and Lauren stood at the bed.

They just watched a group of men carry him in and plop him down in the bed. "This nasty bump on the head scares me the most." She reached toward the large knot and poked it gently with her prosthetic finger before pulling away. "Not to mention he has bruises all along his rib cage and legs.

"He looks like he was in a car crash," Lauren said in a deadpan voice.

"He was."

"Seriously?"

"Yeah. Weren't you paying attention to me earlier?"

Lauren licked her lips looking down at the shirtless unconscious male in front of them. "I lost my train of thought there. Sorry."

"Down, girl. Damn," Rachel said, turning back to Ben. "Do you think he'll wake up? The men said he was passed out when they found him."

"You did call a doctor to come take a look at him, yeah? Because it looks like he may need one."

"Hmm." A small moan of sorts came from Ben below them in the quiet dim room. "Where am I?" Ben's exhausted voice asked. "The last thing I remember I was in that forest."

"I told you I sent Chris, the new guy, to pick you up, you dummy," Rachel said, pulling up a spare chair from the nearby table over toward the bed. "I also remember telling you explicitly not to fall asleep."

"I didn't mean to, boss." Ben looked up at his blonde boss and the black-haired woman standing beside her.

"I know. Car crashes tend to take it out of you I'd imagine. Especially ones accompanying a hail of gunfire."

Ben stared into the drab gray ceiling as he spoke. "I'll never forget that scene so long as I live."

"What scene?" Lauren asked, sitting down beside Ben's feet lower on the bed. "That is, if you don't mind my asking."

"I'm very sorry. Who are you?" Ben asked.

"Oh, that's right," Rachel said with a chuckle. "I guess I never introduced you two. Ben," she gestured toward her glasses wearing friend. "This is Lauren, my babysitter and friend. You can trust her as you would me."

"If I tell you this, you would have to promise to never tell anyone, ever."

"Why?" Lauren asked.

"Do you promise?"

Rachel elbowed Lauren in the ribs. "I promise."

"I won't tell a living soul."

Ben let out a breath. "Fine. When I woke up from the crash, I managed to get out. I noticed one person still alive. Naturally I tried to get him out..."

"I see where this is going," Rachel said, her voice quiet.

"...only to find out his foot was stuck," Ben said, looking to his left away from the women. "Next thing I knew fire was spreading toward him. I didn't know what to do. He was begging me to not leave him to die like that. So I didn't."

"You don't mean?"

"I put him out of his misery," Ben said, his voice full of dismay. "I figured it was better than burning alive. I figured it was the least I could do. There was no time."

"I'm," Lauren paused, "sorry for asking such an insensitive question."

Ben didn't elect to answer but instead chose to redirect his gaze back toward the girls. "It's something I'll live with, somehow."

"I didn't mean to make you feel worse. I just..." Lauren sighed and gestured to the room around them. "Just imagine being cooped up in here all day every day. You tend to get curious and ask questions to those still going out. It doesn't excuse my asking, but that's why."

"It's fine," Ben said, making eye contact with Lauren.

"Alright. Well, I'm glad you made it out, Ben. I'll leave you two alone. I need to go feed Roger. He's probably driving the boss nuts. He's babysitting while I'm here."

"I'm surprised he let you go in here."

Lauren laughed. "I'll have you know he had a job for me regarding you specifically, Boss." She poked Rachel in the shoulder with her finger. "You already can guess what it was. What you do when I leave is totally out of my control though." She backed up toward the door. "I hope you feel better soon, Mr. Adams. I'll see you around."

"Goodbye," was all Ben could muster in a quiet voice.

"Don't pay her any mind. She's just too curious for her own good." Her tone turned somber when she still saw Ben's downcast features. "Look, I know it's hard losing men and women under your command. I've been there myself. Hell, once I had to put down one of our own when he turned on me in the middle of an op. I know the pain you're going through here." She reached out for his hand and grasped it in her own, causing him to turn to her.

"Miss Morris?"

"Shh." Her voice became quiet, smoother, barely above a whisper. "Just listen and rest." Her thumb freed itself from their hands' embrace and traced patterns on the top of his hand. "I thought you had died on the other end of that phone you know. One minute you were answering and the next, nothing but silence met my ears."

"I'm..." Ben started.

Rachel raised a lone finger and pressed it up against Ben's lips, quieting him as she shook her head. Her tone stayed soothing as she continued. "It was at that point something occurred to me. Do you want to know what that was?"

Ben knew better than to verbally respond, still feeling

the warm skin of her index finger pressing against his lips. He shook his head yes, his eyes widening.

Her pink lipstick clad lips curled into a smile. "It was because I realized I might never see you alive again. Don't make me say such embarrassing things. Now, let me check your head really quick. It's quite the nasty knot you have there. It's almost as big as a golf ball." She stood up from the seat and leaned forward above Ben. His eyes naturally wandered down as he noticed the overly large sized shirt Rachel wore was keen to fall under gravity's pull granting him an eyeful. He averted his eyes away before she could pull back.

"You're still awake, so that's a good sign I suppose." Rachel bit her lip, still looking at the wound. "Does your head hurt?"

"It's so far the worst head pain I've ever felt, but I've never suffered from migraines or anything of the like so I wouldn't know."

"I know something that'll make it feel better." She looked down with a dangerous glint in her eye. "If you ever, and I mean ever, tell anybody I did this, I'll kill you myself. Close your eyes."

Ben did as he was instructed.

Rachel bent down and planted a chaste brief kiss on the protrusion. She immediately backed off and looked away, a brilliant crimson blush adorning her cheeks. She cleared her throat, the red slowly exiting her face. "There. Did that work?"

"Uh, I think so." Ben opened his eyes and saw his boss mostly composed standing at his bedside.

"You'd better count your blessings." She leaned back down as he heard a noise. His eyes moved toward the door and saw Daniel in the doorframe watching his daughter.

Ben could hear Rachel's voice directly in his ear, her voice a breathy whisper. "You need to get your rest. So get some sleep." She pulled away and turned around with a jolt. "Oh, Father. I didn't expect you here so quickly."

"So I see." He gave a dirty glare toward his daughter and briefly toward Ben before his features turned to a happier one. "I'm glad to see you're awake, son. You are dismissed."

"Yes, Father," She stopped as she passed by. "Be nice, Dad." She left without further word, closing the door behind her.

"She's always been impulsive. What about you?"

"Sir, I've always tried to have a plan. I've found wandering in unprepared to have horrific consequences."

Daniel sat in the chair Rachel had recently abandoned. "I know this is hard to talk about right now, but I need answers about what went down."

"Of course. I'll answer to the best of my ability." Ben tried to sit up with a grunt only to involuntarily end up where he began.

"Calm down. Was it the cartel? Could you tell?"

"All I remember was talking with the men, then I heard gunshots. I was in the passenger seat and I immediately fell as far forward as I could. It was there I saw the driver's brains splattered on the floor. Then it all went black. I assume that was when it collided with the tree."

"They didn't finish you off. That tells us they either were lazy or they're efficient."

"Quite."

"That means they sent the big boys, not just lowly junkies and debtors."

Ben shuffled under the covers with a wince. "I have no idea, sir. I just know they were effective with their automatic weapons. They're also good at ambushing tactics. They waited until after the delivery. I have the feeling they could have interrupted it before."

"Why would they though?" Daniel scratched his stubble covered chin. "Could it really be so simple as a power play? To show they can hit us anywhere, anytime? I don't think they'd let us do business, son. I think they showed up late. Regardless, they showed us that they're after us. Now, tell me about the crash. Leave no details out, that's an order."

"Yes, sir. I managed to crawl out of the crash. I had noticed one other person in the back alive, so I opened the back door. I pulled on him when he woke up, and we noticed his foot was caught. I tried, sir. We both did. Before I knew it, fire was coming from the front. He panicked and started begging me not to leave him to die like that. I did the only thing I could think of for the man."

Daniel frowned. "It was better than having him burn to death. Thanks for giving him a painless death. Now I'm guessing that's when you called my daughter?"

"That's correct."

"Which leads to you laying here," Daniel said. "I get the picture. Look, shooting him took a lot out of you. Right?"

Ben looked down into his lap. "I don't know if I'll forgive myself anytime soon, sir."

A brief look of understanding passed Daniel's features before returning to his stone-cold demeanor. "We don't need forgiveness, Adams. You remember that." He stood up with a groan. He arched his back, pressing his hands into his lower back. "Oh, and there's one more thing."

"Yes, sir?"

"I appreciate that you tried saving our man's life and all. Here's the thing." Daniel cleared his throat. His voice turned to hardened steel. "Word to the wise. If you know what's good for you, you shouldn't get involved with my daughter.

Now I saw earlier. You didn't initiate that. That's good. You just remember what I said. Alright?"

"I understand, boss. She's off limits."

"Exactly." Daniel flashed a grin. "You've always been quick to understand. That's what I like about you. I'm heading out." He walked to the door. "Goodnight."

"Goodnight, sir," Ben said, his voice detached as Daniel slammed the door hard. "Was Miss Morris doing what I think? If she was, I'm in trouble in more ways than one...

12

"How are you doing this morning, sleepyhead?" Rachel shut the door to Ben's room behind her. "Did Dad scare the bejesus out of you yesterday?"

"In so many words. He was quite adamant."

"I have a feeling I know about what." Rachel sat in the nearby chair beside the bed. "Was it about me?"

Ben looked her in the eyes. "Do you want the whole quote? It was something along the lines of if I know what's good for me, I won't get involved with you. I chalked it up to fatherly things honestly. I wasn't offended. Don't worry."

"That sounds like something he'd say. Let me tell you something. I don't care what he says."

"You mean?"

"Don't make me say it out loud after yesterday. I made it obvious then. I'm not the type to give up just because someone says to. Are you?"

"Generally, no. But when it's a guy that can have you killed since he's the boss, I was a little more concerned."

"You leave him to me. Now, I'm not going to force you seeing as I'm your superior and all."

"Far be it from me to say no to you."

"At least you know what a girl wants to hear some of the time. Like I said, leave Dad to me. I'll handle him. You just focus on getting better quick. We'll need you back soon."

"Oh, I hate to ask this, but I need a favor," Ben said.

"Provided I don't have a job, I'll do it. What's the problem?" Rachel said, leaning back into the chair.

"I don't think I'll be getting out of bed today, and it's the day I usually give my parents my rent money."

"Your parents charge you rent money?"

"No. My dad's in some dead-end job. He's a custodian in some big shot office. Anyway, I barely even got them to take my money. I had to threaten to move out unless they took it. My father is a prideful man you see. My mother, bless her soul, has been a housewife; so I give them five hundred a week."

"How old are your parents anyway?"

"My father just turned sixty. My mother's fifty-eight."

Rachel looked upward for a moment. "They must have had you late if my mental math is correct.

"They also don't know who I work for. If you do go, I'd appreciate you keeping that a secret. I don't want to worry them."

Rachel shrugged. "Fine by me. What am I going to say when they ask why their baby boy isn't the one making the delivery? I assume you don't want me saying you were injured on the job."

"Just say I got back and immediately was sent on another job. They'd believe that," Ben said. "They think I work in some big office job. I assume it's because of the formal wear we are required to have on." His right hand disappeared beneath the sheets as he dug around in his pocket. "At least you all didn't completely strip me when I got here." He pulled out five one-hundred-dollar bills and handed them over to Rachel.

"I'll get it there. Is there anything else I should know about your parents?"

"Dad's probably there until midafternoon. His job's a graveyard shift. They're easygoing. Don't be a jerk, and you'll be fine."

"Are you implying I sometimes am a jerk?" Rachel asked him with a serious face.

"No?"

"I'm joking. There's no need to take everything so seriously all the time. I'll get it done this morning." She got up and bent over at the waist, this time not giving Ben a show. He felt her hand barely touching the bump on the side of his head. "At least this is getting smaller now. I think that's a good sign."

"I feel better today." Ben tried to sit up in the bed only for her petit hand to land squarely on his chest, gently keeping him down on the mattress.

"What is it with you men? You know it's alright to be injured and to be taken care of, right? If you are about to disagree, squash that right now and realize I'm correct."

"Uh, alright then."

"Good boy." Rachel slid the hand across his chest, grabbed his hand, and squeezed. "Now I'm going to be back tonight. Do you think you can survive the boredom with only television?" she gestured toward the thirty-inch television across from the bed sitting atop the dresser. "God knows I wouldn't be able to."

"I'll manage somehow, Miss,"

"Call me Rachel. Cut the miss bullshit. It makes me sound like I'm old. Besides, we're closer than mere work acquaintances at this point."

"I'll manage, Rachel."

"You learn fast. I like that. Now, I'll be back tonight. I'll make sure to send Lauren in every so often to make sure you have enough water and food and such. You'll also probably need help getting to the bathroom with all those bruises."

"How do you know I have bruises all over?" Ben asked. "Wait, did you and this Lauren look at me while I was half naked?"

Rachel turned around and didn't answer.

"You did, didn't you?"

"We had to ascertain the extent of your injuries."

"I guess I can't get married now."

Rachel didn't verbally answer only deigning fit to burst into uncontrollable laughter at the remark. "That's something the woman's supposed to say when she's seen naked. Good Lord."

"It got you to stop being embarrassed, yeah? Besides, it's not like I mind if a cute woman wanted to see me naked. Oh wait, I didn't."

"Do not take back what you mean. Did you mean it?" Rachel asked, turning to face him again.

"Yes," he said in a quiet voice.

She leaned down closer to his face, staring him in the eyes. "I like honesty. You've earned this before I go." She closed the gap and delivered a feather light kiss to the lips before pulling back. "I'll be back later. Don't worry about your parents. It'll be taken care of. Just recuperate as best you can. See you later."

"Goodbye," Ben said, staring at Rachel's now retreating form near the door. His mind was going a million miles an hour as he tried to force the words out of his mouth.

He watched her exit the room. He reached over to the nearby night table beside the bed and grabbed the remote.

He pushed the power button when he heard multiple female voices outside of his door. One of them clearly belonged to Rachel, the other he couldn't recognize. He couldn't understand what was being said, only that as soon as the argument started, it ended.

He was about to change the channel when the door opened again. This time Elizabeth entered the room. "Hello, Miss Morris."

"Quiet," she said, closing the door behind her. She eyed him up and down on the bed. She pushed a stray rogue white hair back, a cocky smirk pasted on her face. "You were part of the crew who got me out. You were the guy who got mad at that moron for jeopardizing the entire operation. Ben, I think it was."

"I still think Lee is an idiot in all honesty, Miss Morris."

"An idiot? Maybe I was wrong about you."

"Ma'am?

Elizabeth moved closer to the end of the bed and sat down beside Ben's feet. "I wasn't lying in the car you know. You do remind me of Roger. Do you know who that is?"

"When we were being held prisoner, she told me about him. She said he was an old gangster friend of her fathers. She was sure he was going to come rescue her, and he did too."

"That sounds like him alright. I heard he died not too long ago."

"I wouldn't know too much about that, Miss Morris. I only technically met the man once. The boss hung him out to dry on that rescue. I felt bad about it once I realized what happened."

"Danny told me how it happened, don't worry. I'm just wondering what my niece sees in you. You do seem to be a kind of nice guy. It's obvious as daylight she likes you even if she herself doesn't realize it yet. Is that all it boils down to?" She squinted her eyes as she asked her next question. "You two haven't hooked up yet, have you?"

Ben's eyes bulged as he stuttered out a response as best as he could manage. "I-I-we-we,"

"That's a no. So, it's not you being able to get her off. Now that I mention it..." She scooted further up the bed, her butt now near Ben's waist. One of her hands graced his chest and slid across his physique. "You are quite adorable in how you react." Her voice became distant. "Just like him." She shook her head. "You've got a nice body from what I can feel."

Ben jumped as her hand reached lower than he was expecting.

"It's a nice size too." She removed her hand from where it shouldn't have been and moved it up to his head. She caressed the knot on his head. "How'd you get all this?"

"We were riding home from a gun deal. We were ambushed. I was in the passenger seat. As soon as I heard gunfire, I ducked down as far as I could. I saw the driver catch one to the head, and we crashed. These bruises and injuries are from the crash. I wasn't hit or anything. Don't worry."

"Poor thing." Elizabeth put on her best caring voice. "You've been through so much. Mama can't let her young man suffer like this." Her hand rubbed the side of his face, eliciting a blush from the young man. "Tell me something. What is it you do here for the family?"

"The syndicate?"

"Danny really went with that name?" She rolled her eyes. "Yes, what do you do with this syndicate?"

"I oversee the rank and file, occasionally doing bigger jobs as you saw at the hospital."

"Of course you do," Elizabeth said, a sad smile on her face all the while. "How would you feel about a promotion?"

"Ma'am?"

"Call me Elizabeth, sweetie," she cooed, sliding ever higher up the bed. "If you're mine, we should be on closer terms."

"I wouldn't turn one down. It's not my main concern though."

Elizabeth moved her hand from his face to his ear, gently playing with it as she spoke. "I'd love to get you out of harm's way. I know you had to watch us argue in the car, but keep in mind I'm Daniel's sister. To think I won't be a part of the leadership would be stupid. You don't strike me as stupid, sweetheart."

"I'd like to think not." Ben gave her a shy smile.

Elizabeth leaned down, close to his face. "You let mama make you feel better." She pressed forward until their lips met. She sat back up and looked down at Ben's crimson form with a knowing smile. "You don't have much experience with women do you, young man?"

"Not especially," Ben said, his face still red.

"I wouldn't tell your coworkers that. They'll give you shit for years." Her index finger poked him in the nose with a playful smirk. "You don't want that, believe me. I've seen that happen. It'd be such a shame if it happened to you. Don't worry. I can keep a secret."

"I'll keep that in mind." Ben's eyes wandered a little further down than was appropriate.

Elizabeth followed his line of sight, the same playful smirk appearing. "Oh that's right. My niece is rather flat. She always did take after her mom. I won't hold it against you. If there's one thing that prison's good for, it's that you'll be in great shape by the time you get out." She pulled up her shirt, revealing a toned belly. "Don't you agree?"

"It's very attractive for sure," Ben said. "It's just your brother was in here last night and he was rather insistent that I not get involved with -"

"I can handle Danny. Do not worry about him." Her voice was reassuring and soothing. "Don't go trying to use that as an excuse. Say it straight out."

"Not at all. I was just under the impression he didn't mean just his daughter."

"Well..." Elizabeth looked away toward the open window across the room with natural sunlight pouring in. "Even if you don't always say the right thing, you are fun to play around with. I'll see you around, handsome." She made her way to the door before turning around and blowing a kiss along with a wink, closing the door behind her.

Ben looked down at the controller still in his hands before changing the channel. "What the hell's going on? I was screwed before, now I'm beyond fucked." He closed his eyes as the sound from the television continued unabated. "And not even in a good way yet."

A short while later in front of Ben's house...

"I think this is the place." She looked down at the printed-out piece of paper with the address written on it. She glanced at the clock in her car to see it was just after nine thirty a.m. "It's not too early, right?" She checked her coat pocket to find the letter stuffed with the five hundred dollars Ben gave her. Now sure of her cargo she got out of the car and strode with confidence over the modest but well-kept front yard. She climbed the stairs, adjusting the sunglasses in front of her eyes before pressing the doorbell.

She looked at the exterior of the house that she could see. The trimmed lawn was immaculate. "They keep their place looking good," she said to herself. She returned her attention back to the door right before it flung open.

A short lady opened the door and greeted her with a smile. "Hello there."

"Hello. I'm sorry for the inconvenience, but I'm here because of your son, Ben Adams."

"Did something happen to him?" she asked, her voice changing to one of concern. "He didn't come home last night."

"I'm sorry, Mrs. Adams, it's nothing of the sort. I probably don't need to tell you this, but your son is one of the hardest workers we have. I'm his coworker. I was talking to him at the office this morning when he handed me this before he rushed off to the next city they sent him to." She reached inside her coat pocket and retrieved the plain white envelope before handing it over with a smile.

"He trusted you with this?" she asked, eyes wide.

"We've grown to be good friends over the last month. It's nice to meet you. I'm Tanya Jones."

"Tanya? I've heard that name before. Oh, my goodness. You're that girl Ben's talked about. Come on inside. I insist." She stepped back, beckoning Rachel forward.

Rachel obliged and followed her inside before closing the door behind her.

"It's an honor to meet you, dear. I'm Patricia Adams. You can just call me Pattie. Follow me if you would." She led the pair through the first floor living room and into the kitchen around the corner. "Can I get you something to drink, Tanya?"

"A glass of water would be heavenly if it wouldn't be too much trouble. I've been in a rush since this morning."

"It's no problem at all, dear. Any friend of my boy is a friend of mine." She set about getting a glass of water. "You know, as his mother a part of me is happy to hear you say he's one of your hardest workers." She placed the glass of water down on the table in front of Rachel. "Another part is worried. I hardly ever see him anymore, and he always looks worn out."

"It is demanding work. He's never shown any strain that I've ever seen. He always just accepts the work we're given with a smile and gets it done right away. It's quite admirable if I might say," Rachel said before taking a drink from the glass.

"May I ask you a potentially impolite question?" Patricia asked.

"It's the hand, isn't it?" Rachel politely laughed.

"It is the gloves."

"I knew it. I had an accident a month ago. Do you mind if I take my glove off?"

Pamela sat down in the nearby chair. "Go right ahead."

"I just recently got the prosthetic." She looked down at the table between them, showing Patricia her hand with the prosthetic finger. "I'm still not used to it. Leave it to me to pay this much and still not show it off, right?"

"You don't need those gloves, sweetheart."

Rachel looked up and saw Patricia giving a warm, wide smile.

"They are perfectly fine as they are. They are nothing to be embarrassed about. Especially not when they're on such a delightful, cute, young woman like you. Tell me something." Pamela leaned forward, her elbow on the table. "Are you a natural blonde?"

"I am."

"God, I am so jealous. I always wanted blonde hair growing up." She referenced to her own pure black hair.

"I got it from my mother I am told," Rachel said, looking back up at her host.

The sound of footsteps from the second floor interrupted the conversation as they audibly moved from above them toward the steps she saw when she entered the house. A thin framed older gentleman with a pair of glasses came down in uniform and stopped. He smiled and raised his hand. "Why hello there."

"This is my husband, Virgil." Patricia nodded toward her husband.

"Virgil Adams, ma'am." A country accent bled into his voice. He reached a hand toward her and shook Rachel's hand with a firm grip. "It's a pleasure to meet you finally."

"You've heard of me?"

"Sure. I've heard our son talk about you more times than I can remember. Remember, sweetie? There was that time he told us about the cute blon-"

"Excuse my husband and his lack of tact," Patricia said. "We don't want to make it awkward between you two or anything. We just want our boy to be happy is all. You understand?"

"Don't worry about it." Rachel waved off the concern.

"Is he alright though?" Virgil asked, sitting down in the remaining seat next to his wife at the table. "He didn't come home."

"He's off on another job again, honey," Patricia said. "Which reminds me - why are you in uniform? You're on nightshift, aren't you?"

"In a manner of speaking," Virgil said. "I just got a call on the cell. They need a double shift today. Now I'm sorry, but I need to head out now." He got up with a loud grunt.

"What about breakfast? You haven't eaten anything today. You know you need to watch your blood sugar."

"I'll get something on the way to work, sweetie. I'll see you soon," he said over his shoulder as he made his exit.

"That man is insufferable." Patricia sighed, looking genuinely worried.

"He's a hardworking man," Rachel said.

"Indeed he is. Too bad the only job he could find after his injury was being a janitor. Or what was the word he said he is officially? I think it was custodian. It's a fancy word for janitor. Don't get me wrong. It's good honest work, but we both know it's not where he wanted to be at sixty years old. He's the best kind of husband you can have though for an old housewife like me. Oh listen to me prattling on and on complaining. I don't mean to subject you to all my insecurities."

"It's quite alright." She finished the glass and stood up. "Unfortunately, I do have to head back to work myself. I'll be taking my leave. Thank you for your hospitality."

"You're far too polite." Patricia stood up and walked her back to the door. She opened the door for Rachel. "You should come over for dinner at some point. I'm sure Ben would love that."

"We'll have to see if that's something he wants, but I think it sounds fun." Rachel opened the screen door and exited. "I'll see you later." She turned mid stride and waved goodbye before returning to the driver's seat of her car.

As soon as she closed the door, she pulled the phone from her back pants pocket. "Yeah, Lauren?" She held the phone up to her ear. "Tell Ben his parents got the package."

"Your father has sent word that nobody is to go out alone, so get back here quickly. It's urgent."

"Understood. I'm on my way home."

13

"What's happened?" Rachel asked.

Daniel cleared his throat from behind the desk. He looked at Rachel, Warren, and Elizabeth in front of him. "Good, you're back. I called this meeting and updated protocols because of last night. You all know what we have to do since we were attacked again."

"We fire back," Warren said. "Harder and better than they did."

"If there was such a thing as a textbook answer in our line of work, that would be it," Daniel said with a wry grin. "You're not wrong, but we're going to be sophisticated in how we do it. Davis, you're taking lead on this. I want you going with Lauren. What's her last name?" he asked Rachel.

"It's Taylor, Dad. Lauren Taylor. Shouldn't we be sending someone else?"

"She joined the syndicate. She knew what she signed up for. Besides, you wanted the damn kid so badly, you should watch it occasionally yourself. You know, be a good mother."

"Fine," Rachel acquiesced with her father. "How are we going to strike back at these jerkoffs? I want to be involved."

"The closest you're going to get involved is telling Lee his job. We need the ability to control a car. Now I know you have the means to do just that."

"She does?" Warren looked to his side at Rachel.

Daniel nodded. "I was there and saw it in action. Albeit I think that bitch ended up pressing the button, but I know the tech still works. I also know Roger wouldn't have let you have it without teaching you how to use it. You need to brief Lee on this program." He looked over to Warren. "Davis, you're also taking Lee with you. He'll be your way of ending them."

"Sir?"

"You'll understand more when you see it in action. Basically, you and Taylor are going to be his chauffeur and protection."

"Brother," Elizabeth spoke up, "may I ask a question?"

"You're lucky you're even in the room, Liz." Daniel directed his attention toward her. "Go ahead."

"You never did strike me as the sophisticated type. Why not go about this quick and dirty like you always did when you were working your way up?"

"People live and learn, Sis. Besides, you were boss once. You know it's a numbers game. We don't have nearly as many men and women as this cartel who also has a street gang at their beck and call. Now, Davis, we would like this to look like an accident. I don't care how you have Lee do this. You can have him run their car off the road into a tree, drive them into the Maumee River, or anything else the lot of you can come up with. Get creative. We don't want the authorities getting wise to the heat going down while still making our point. If you can't find a shot caller, go after the highest-ranking officer or individual you can find. We need to take out their bigger players. They're the ones kicking up money to the higher-ups."

"How do we set about finding them, sir? We've been looking for a month now."

"Lee told me, after his little misadventure rescuing my sister here, that he was getting close to something. In fact, right before I had him send that mass email out, he told me he'd found something. I don't think you'll have a problem finding a target."

"You'll probably want to take a directional microphone just to be safe," Rachel suggested. "It'd make it a lot easier to know just who's the leader."

"Good idea," Daniel said.

"You should send more than three people, dear Brother. Take it from me." Elizabeth circled around the desk and stood to Daniel's right. "It's always better safe than sorry."

"The syndicate isn't quite as populated as the family was. We need to take care of what manpower we have. This is the safest course of action while still retaliating. You will respect my decision in this manner and never second guess me again." He gave her a withering sideways glance. "Is that understood, Sister?"

"Crystal clear. You inherited Dad's penchant for believing wholeheartedly in his plans. Confidence is nice, but realize when you should take advice."

Daniel did not answer, but merely delivered a longer glare that shut his sister up. He returned his attention to Warren. "Now go make this happen." He shifted his gaze to his daughter. "You, go take care of your son."

"Son? I've not heard anything of this? Who's the father? Wait, don't tell me…" Elizabeth covered her mouth with her hand.

"No, thank Christ above. It wasn't your old flame. It's a

long story. Stay here after, and I'll explain in full. The rest of you are dismissed. Now go get it done."

Rachel and Warren turned and exited the door, leaving the siblings.

Warren shut the door behind them. "Guess we're both heading to the same place then."

"Let us hope he can make a copy of my program. I will not hand him the original flash drive."

"Is there a reason?" Warren asked, walking side by side with her through the mansion.

Rachel led them toward Lee's room as she spoke. "Yeah. My mother made the program." She reached up and flicked her platinum blonde hair. "It and this hair are all I have left to remember her. I am not handing over the last of her accomplishments to Mr. I can't drive in there."

"Excuse me? Who can't drive?"

"Lee. You know, the computer tech wizard. He can't drive."

"He can't?"

"Hell no he can't. Have the men not passed around that story yet?" Rachel tried to hide her laugh.

"It's the first I've heard of it."

"Long story short, he tried to prove he could on a job. He couldn't of course and damned near got us all busted. So give him all the shit you want for that. He deserves it. Just don't let him know I told you to. It'll be funnier that way. Ah," the pair stopped in front of a door with a taped sign on it saying 'Tech Lounge', "here we are."

She knocked and opened the door once she heard Lee welcome them in from the other side. She pushed the door open. "You just keep the door unlocked?" she asked as they entered the messy room.

"Why wouldn't I?" Lee said from the desk across the

room in front of multiple monitors. "If I may ask," he said, turning his rotating chair around to face the door, "why are you two here today?"

"You're up first," Rachel said to Warren.

"We need you for a job." Warren took a step forward over a stray wire running across the floor. "You'll be going along with me and one other."

"I'm surprised they want me anywhere near this," Lee said.

"Thankfully," Rachel said, "you're not being asked to drive this time. Or they'd really be screwed. Anyway, my part in this is to show you how to use a program my mother made."

"No offense, but I don't need -"

"Quiet." Rachel shut him up. She plugged the flash drive into the nearest computer's usb slot. "Now, I made a copy of this program. It's a little old by today's standards, but it still works. I want to hear what you think of it."

Lee swiveled the chair back around as the gui for the program appeared on screen. He leaned forward. "The Ui is ancient, but it gets a pass. It's intuitive, yet sophisticated. The code is ancient, but is immaculate. Where did you get this from?"

"That's a secret. What you need to know is the car tab here." She grabbed the nearby mouse and navigated to the tab with a car icon on it. "Do you see this dot?"

"Looks like it's right outside."

"It is. It's my car. Warren, go to the window and tell me what you see."

"Sure, why not?" Warren moved over to the other side of the room next to the only window and looked outside. "Yeah, that is a car alright. A nice one I might add."

"Watch what I do, Lee." She remembered Roger's teachings and did exactly what he told her.

"Holy crap, that car moved back."

"I see." Lee rubbed his chin, a small smile spreading across his face. "It's ingenious. Is this because of the onboard computer in all cars nowadays?"

"Bingo. This was designed when that trend was just beginning. Thankfully cyber security in cars hasn't progressed much."

"I see how it works. I can make this work," Lee said.

"Prove it," Warren said. "Make her car go back to where it was."

"I swear if you ding my car I will beat the shit out of you. I do not want a repeat of the hospital parking lot," Rachel said.

"Oh ye of little faith." Lee did exactly as she instructed.

"He did it."

"Then my part in this is over. It's up to you two now. I'll go and send Lauren over. Make sure you three get along now." She walked back to the door.

"Now get your shit ready," Warren said. "We're going as soon as this Lauren gets here."

"Got it."

In the middle of town in a van an hour later...

"Now what was this important information that the boss said you have?" Warren asked from the driver's seat.

Lee had his trusty laptop at the ready. "See that establishment ahead? The one with the cars parked around the block."

"The restaurant?"

"My informant says that is where a meeting between the

cartel and their little gang underlings is taking place." He reached down and handed a black device resembling the shape of a gun. He raised the cord and passed the headphones connected to it. "Use this toward that little table."

Lauren took it and donned the headphones before turning the device on and pointing it toward the umbrella covered table

"We're sitting ducks out here," Warren said, keeping a steady eye on their surroundings. "I don't like this."

"We must get close enough to hear. We don't have a choice," Lee said.

"Quiet," Lauren said, bringing a hand up to the earphone. "I hear them talking. This is the group we're looking for. We just need to find out who's the big man on campus."

"I can tell you from here who that is if that group is the men we're looking for," Warren said. He showed a cocky grin. "It's the guy with his back to us."

"How could you know that?" Lee asked. "You can't even see them well from back here."

"I can see how every man there is looking at him."

"He is the only one speaking," Lauren said.

"Of course he is," Warren said. "The Stingers always show due deference to the higher ups. You were given a beat down if you didn't. Dollars to doughnuts that guy's their liaison for the higher ups."

Lauren took off the headset and passed the devices back to Lee. "Now that we know who it is, what's our play?"

"We wait." Lee donned the gear and took her place in listening, occasionally typing bits and pieces of the conversation. "When they leave, we make our move. I have a number of options that we have, depending on which way they go."

"They'll probably go toward Stinger territory. No doubt they've holed up there. It's safe after all," Warren said, tapping his finger on the steering wheel.

"In that case, we'd have two options."

"So, while we're waiting," Warren looked over at Lauren, "tell us a little about yourself."

"What? Me?" Lauren asked, placing a hand on her chest.

"You're not new, that I remember."

"I was in the first wave of recruits. I just was picked up to be Miss Morris' babysitter. As a result I haven't been out on ops."

Warren chuckled. "Don't tell me you're soft."

"I passed my entrance test. I can take a life if I need to."

"Fine. What about before you joined the syndicate?"

Lauren gave him a sideways glance, her tone even yet firm. "I killed a man before I joined. That's as much as you're getting out of me. Suffice it to say, I can handle my own shit."

"Easy there, girl. I just like to know who I'm trusting with my life is all. I wanted to know if you were the type to bitch about actually having to do what the rest of us do and not sitting in the villa all day."

"You can try me if you want, big man," Lauren said.

"You're so touchy," Warren said, laughing. "It's enough to make a man curious. Fine. I'll drop it."

"They're moving," Lee said from the back.

"It's showtime, boys and girls." Warren started the engine and fell in line behind the car the old man entered.

"They are moving the way you predicted."

"What's your options then?" Lauren asked.

Lee answered amidst several clicks on his laptop. "It depends if the train timing is with us or not."

"Train huh?" Warren asked. "It looks like we may be in luck." He pointed to the left as they approached the railroad crossing. The bar blocking access to the other side ahead of them had lowered amid the ringing.

"Let's get it done then," Lee said. He directed the cursor over the correct car, infiltrated the car's computer system with a click. "I'm in control."

"Let's hope your remote-control driving is better than your actual driving," Warren said, watching the car ahead jut forward awkwardly with unsteady movements.

The roar of the rapidly approaching train drowned out much more dialogue.

Lee managed to plant the car directly on the tracks. He raised his attention toward the soon to be accident zone and saw a lone man in a blue uniform banging his firearm against the window. The telltale signs of red and blue lights behind him illuminated the surreal event unfolding.

"He's not going to make it," Lauren said, barely audible over the nigh deafening horn of the train now naught but one hundred feet away.

The window finally cracked, shattered, and the man reached inside, desperately attempting to pull out the occupants of the vehicle.

Midway through the attempt however the train finally reached the site and crashed into the car, along with the policeman, and swept the wreck further down the way. The mangled body of the officer was flung to their right out of view from where they were.

"We need to leave," Warren said, pulling out of the backed-up traffic and performing an illegal U-turn. "What are the fucking odds of a patrol car being right there? Are they following us?"

Lauren turned around in her seat. "I think he's more concerned with getting an ambulance and a unit down here than chasing us. Besides, he's still on the other side of the slowing train."

"Let's hope so."

"This is a double blessing when you think about it," Lauren said. "Except for the dead innocent part."

"Explain," Warren said.

"Think it through," Lauren started. "They're going to find out who that was in the car. If they bother trying to find out who it is, what happens? They'll see it was a bunch of illegal aliens. In today's climate? They'll get a sob story along with the cop for being a hero. If they do put it together, it brings attention to the cartel. Maybe not necessarily leading to arrests, but they can't lay low as easily then. The FBI will catch wind and send someone out."

"Sounds like a double-edged sword to me. If the FBI comes here, then we're liable to be caught in the crossfire."

"It is possible. It also opens options for us," Lauren said. "Try to be positive and think outside the box. We can use this. Every negative has a positive side if you examine it."

"If the boss gives the go ahead, sure."

"It's already done," Lee said from the back. "Let's just get back and see what the boss says. Is this what you guys felt like when you first killed someone? I feel weird."

"It happens to everybody the first time," Lauren said.

"Normally we don't see bodies flying through the air though," Warren said in a jovial tone. "Your first was stylish. I'll give you that."

"I don't think you're helping," Lauren turned around in her seat and saw a downcast Lee, glowing screen sitting at his side. She could just barely make out restrained tears threatening to fall forth. "Let's just keep it together until we get back."

14

"That wasn't exactly what I'd call subtle. I saw on the news earlier about a train colliding with a car," Daniel said, standing in front of the trio. "Just answer me one thing. Why was a policeman killed?"

"He was trying to get them out of the car and played hero," Warren said.

"I had locked the door and blocked them from unlocking," Lee said. "I also had control of the vehicle. They weren't getting out in time. My timing was immaculate."

"If you proved anything, it's that," Daniel sighed. "Now we have to hope they don't get suspicious and start investigations. Let us hope they just treat that badge as a hero, and label it a freak accident with a bunch of - what was it they call them on the news? Undocumented immigrants I think it was. If they piece together that it was Crag Cartel members in that car, we could have a real problem later. Anyway, the news said there were no survivors."

"I don't see how there could have been, sir," Warren said. "I saw it with my own eyes. It was brutal."

"You got the job done. I just wish there hadn't been any

complications. Who am I kidding? There are always complications. It's the nature of the business. Good job everybody. You did exactly as I asked. With any luck, the cartel won't even realize we were behind it. If they're smart, they probably guess it's us though. It's not like they need proof. We need a more permanent way of ending this shit. You are all dismissed. That is except you, Lee. I want to see you for a few minutes."

Lauren and Warren excused themselves and left the older man with the technologically gifted younger one.

Daniel cleared his throat. "I'm not one much for this kind of crap, Lee, but I can see that look in your eyes. Tonight was your first kill, wasn't it?"

"Yes, boss," Lee answered with as much conviction in his voice as he could muster.

"Look, I'm not going to tell you to be happy. You did your job. Make your peace with it. Did you ever sign up for a driver's ed course?"

"I did, sir," Lee's voice was almost robotic in how quickly he answered. "I start next Monday at three pm."

"Good. That'll take your mind off things. Just don't forget one thing before you go. Never hold onto bad memories. Leave that shit behind you. It doesn't ever take you anywhere you want to go. Now you're dismissed. Go get some sleep for Christ's sake. You look like you're about to bawl your eyes out. Don't let the men or women see that if you know what's good for you."

Lee politely excused himself.

"That boy's a wreck," Daniel said under his breath once he saw the door close. "Where is that sister of mine anyhow?" He hefted himself out of his executive chair and left the room. He wandered the halls until he came to the main living room where he spotted his sister lounging around watching television. "There she is." He sat down in a nearby recliner. "I was worried you might be straining yourself," he said with a sarcastic edge. "I see that was unfounded."

"You ever pushed over seven pounds out of you? No? Shut the hell up."

"Do you remember when we were sixteen?" Daniel asked.

Elizabeth muted the show with the nearby remote control before turning to her brother. "I thought we agreed to never talk about that field trip."

"Not that, you idiot," Daniel said. "I was talking about when Dad taught us that we need to make ourselves valuable."

"You're not serious. I'm in no condition to work, and I'm nuclear. I can't go on jobs."

"I don't want you out there," Daniel pointed over his shoulder. "I do however want you to make yourself useful."

"What the fuck's that mean?" Elizabeth asked, crossing her arms under her chest with a huff.

A few of the men in the living room looked at the pair arguing. They tried to look like they weren't, but they weren't very successful due to their ogling and quiet whispers.

Daniel continued. "All I've seen you do is sit around. Well, except for that one wild rumor that you were flirting with that boy. I knew that was bullshit though."

"I see people still talk. It's not much better than prison in that regard," Elizabeth said. "What do you want me to do exactly? It's not like I'm able to say no. It's not like I can just leave."

"Your daily job will be to clean the bathrooms and kitchen, for now. I may or may not have other things for you later. Be thankful that's all. I need every available man and woman out on the streets. Ergo, I need someone to help take care of this place. You get me?"

Elizabeth didn't bother answering verbally.

"Do you understand?"

"I get it," Elizabeth hissed.

"Good." Daniel reclined. "Then we can keep the men from talking. They were starting to you know. I won't have them talk like you're some freeloader."

"Oh, so this is for my benefit? I see."

"It's a win for everybody. I get more bodies for the war, and you don't look lazy. I'm a genius. I know."

Elizabeth got up without saying anything to her brother.

"Getting an early jump on work? Good. Do you know where the cleaning supplies are?"

She did not answer verbally, but instead replied with a middle finger aimed back at him as she turned the corner. She made her way through the halls until she turned a corner and saw Rachel outside an open Ben's door. She saw Ben hobble his way forward. She could hear Rachel as she approached.

"That's good. Does it hurt too bad?"

"I'm fine," Ben said. "I need to get up and around again as soon as I can."

"There's no need to baby him." Elizabeth stopped a few feet away from the young pair.

Rachel looked over at her aunt. "I just didn't want him to hurt himself if he was playing the tough guy."

"Aw, poor young man," Elizabeth cooed. "Your own boss doesn't even treat you like a man. She's treating you like a child. We both know how grown up you are, don't we?" She turned her attention toward the now visibly annoyed Rachel. "You're still too young to know how to treat a man I see. Well, I'm not arguing. Now why don't you go see how your baby's doing? I'll take care of getting him settled."

"We're fine." Rachel stepped in front of Ben and looked up into Elizabeth's eyes with unbreakable will. "Why don't you go clean the toilets? You know, like Dad asked you to."

"What?" Elizabeth took a step back.

"Did you really think Dad would let you live here without doing anything? I was going to go watch that show when he told me his plan, but I was the bigger person and decided to help," She backed up and placed a hand on Ben's shoulder.

Elizabeth grit her teeth but quickly regained her composure with a demure laugh. "Mature women do not gloat, dear. It's unbecoming. There is nothing wrong with hard work. Rubbing it in someone's face is unladylike. Aww," she stepped forward, placing a hand on Ben's cheek. "I feel sorry for Ben here having a little girl as a boss and not a woman. She doesn't know how to please a young man. Not like me. Isn't that right, sweet thing?" She stepped back and took her hands off him when she heard a quiet growl coming from Rachel. "I'll take my leave. I know when a woman's jealous. She should be." She winked at Ben and continued past the duo. "I'll see you later."

Rachel watched her aunt walk past them and through a nearby door before returning her attention to Ben. "I swear that woman is insufferable. I'm sorry that you have to deal with a fifty-year-old woman putting the moves on you. Just play along with her. You don't want to piss her off, even if she is powerless right now."

"I'm not trying to piss her off," Ben said. "I've just never really had to deal with that kind of attention before."

"Now let's get you back inside before she comes back." Rachel guided Ben back through the door and to the bed.

"You should be up and around before you know it if you can walk that easily."

Ben sat on the side of the bed. "Between your dad threatening me and everything else that's happened recently, I've been trying to make sense of everything."

"Dad threatened you, did he?" Rachel asked, sitting beside him. "What did he say exactly?"

"Essentially that if I knew what was good for me, I wouldn't get involved with you if you know what I mean."

Rachel exhaled and fell back on the bed, looking up at the ceiling. She blew a stray platinum lock of hair out of her face. "That sounds like him alright. What about you though?"

"Excuse me?"

"Be honest with me now. What do you want? I'm not going to force you into a relationship with me or anything. I'd never do something like that. However, I'd be lying if I said I wasn't interested."

"I don't feel like it's a matter of what I want," Ben said. "The boss said if we got together I'd be put down. It's what I got out of it anyway."

"I know a way we can be together, and Dad won't mind. It'll take a little while to implement, but I won't get you in trouble in the meantime. Tell me now though. Would you be interested in that?"

"I would be interested in seeing where this goes honestly. You know, just without the looming threat of death hanging over my head. There's also the whole your aunt telling me I'm hers thing. That makes it awkward."

"She said that?"

Ben gingerly changed position. "She sure did. I didn't know what to do. I didn't want to piss her off, especially right after the boss told me what he did. As a result, I kind of went along with it."

"That would be awkward."

"Tell me about it. What the hell do I do now?"

"Play along with her."

"Seriously?" Ben asked.

"Seriously," Rachel said. "Denying her won't accomplish anything but putting you back on her and probably Dad's radar. We don't want that. Besides, I know why she wants you. You remind her of someone she used to know and love. It's not real love, don't worry. I don't even know if she's capable of real love."

"Ouch," Ben said. "Now that's a way to talk about your aunt." He turned, showing her a small smile.

"I'm just telling the truth." Rachel got up off the bed and helped Ben lay down and get comfortable. "Don't you worry about Father or my aunt. I have a plan. You trust me, right?"

"More than anyone else here."

"Good. Remember, keep a low profile, play along with grandma in there, and do what I say when I say it. We'll be together before you know it. Try and relax. I have it all under control." She pulled the blanket up over him.

"Thank God you have a plan. I was driving myself crazy thinking about what I was going to do."

A knock at the door interrupted the pair. Rachel answered the door and took a step back to let Lauren enter the room.

"Hey," she greeted Ben. "You feeling any better yet?"

"As well as can be expected."

"That's good." She turned her attention to Rachel. "You need to hear this news. The boss has your aunt cleaning the toilets and the kitchen. I just saw her cleaning before I came in here."

"Oh shit. He was serious when he said that." Rachel let loose a genuine laugh. "Then what I said must have really pissed her off."

"You bluffed?" Ben asked.

"Sure did. I didn't think Dad would really do it."

"I don't mean to interrupt you two," Lauren said, readjusting her glasses. "I need to talk to you in private, boss." She looked back at Ben. "If that's alright?"

"By all means," Ben said.

"Let's head to my room then..."

Rachel's room a few minutes later...

"What's so important you had to drag me away from Ben?"

"Sorry about that. There's something I need to tell you though. The last operation reminded me of it in the worst way."

"Go ahead," Rachel said, leaning against the wall.

"You know I undertook the same as everybody else."

"Get to the point."

"It wasn't the first time I'd put someone down," Lauren said, looking side to side. "I killed someone before I joined the syndicate."

"You're saying you're a wanted woman?" Rachel asked. "You should have said that shit before. Father would have never sent you out. If your face got caught on a camera, we're fucked."

"No," Lauren tried to calm Rachel down in a soothing voice. "It's not like that. I got away clean. It's classified as an unsolved mystery right now. I'm just sure there's going to be wild rumors flying around about me now since I didn't exactly explain it."

Rachel simply stared at Lauren with a blank look on her face before rolling her eyes. "That's what you're so worried about? Jesus Christ. Who did you even kill anyway?"

"It was my father."

"Your dad? What the hell? Why?" Rachel asked.

"He used to beat me and my mother. A few months ago I snapped and moved here from Oregon."

"Enthralling. So long as it doesn't affect us now, we're fine. Sorry to hear about your messed up childhood, sincerely, but we have things to work on now."

"Wait," Lauren reached out toward Rachel.

"It better be good. I'm making good progress with Ben. I don't have time to comfort you about a few rumors flying around. Just own it. If anything, the rank and file will treat you with more respect if that story flies around."

"It's not just that," Lauren said. "I think something's wrong with Lee. He seemed really off after our last job."

"Define 'off'," Rachel said. "He's always been weird."

"I don't think he'd ever killed anyone before. He had this faraway look after the policeman and cartel died on that railroad track.

"If you're so worried about him, then go talk to him. I'm not his keeper or even his direct boss. Dude's got his own set of problems. I don't have the time to solve them for him. Now, is there anything else?"

"Now when you said progress, what did that mean?"

"I meant I've never seduced someone successfully before. I think I'm doing well. Aunt's doing the whole domi-nant mommy thing. I'm going for the more conventional method. You know, being nice, helping him out, and being his friend in this mad house. I think he trusts me."

"A good basis for any romantic relationship. Tell me something. Do you actually have feelings for him?"

Rachel looked away. "Possibly."

"Good. Then it's not an act. He'll fall for you hook, line, and sinker. No man could resist you genuinely going after him. Just watch out for her."

"What's that mean?" Rachel asked

"It means," Lauren said, "that his type generally has a thing for her type. Think about it. He's shy, never had much attention from women. Those types like the dominant mommy thing. It makes them feel wanted. Don't underestimate her. She knows what she's doing, and she's still got the body to make it work."

"He won't fall for her. I know that."

"Hubris is a dangerous thing, boss. Never count your chickens before they hatch. Remember, as nice and sweet as you think he is, he's still a man. Never underestimate a determined older woman when it comes to getting what she wants, especially when she has a body like that. You do not want him working for her, do you? According to the stories I heard, it's how she gained power. She utilized a guy named Roger to kill her father. She reeled him in with her body and antics. With the recent change to her duties, you can bet your bottom dollar she's planning something, and she'll need help. I don't know what yet, but mark my words. Her interest in him is mighty suspicious with this timing."

"Roger was an altogether different man," Rachel said, her eyes looking down at the carpeted floor as she spoke. "Lesson taken though. It's not over until it's over."

15

"Davis, what do you think our next move should be? I've gotten the warehouse secured and had that camera installed so I can see what's happening." Daniel stood shoulder to shoulder with Warren by his desk. The two men looked down on the map of the city. He pointed at the map. "You hit them around here."

"More around here, sir," Warren poked the map a little further away. "The restaurant we found them at is where you're pointing to. The railroad tracks were here. From what I have seen, the police chalked up the crash to illegal immigrants and a hero cop. It seems the worst we'll have to deal with is a parade of sorts for the cop, and a sob story filled news cycle for the cartel boys."

"That means we're unaffected for the time being. We need to plan a way to end this war once and for all. How do we go about winning against an organization with thousands of bodies, deep pockets, and even more weapons than we have?"

"Make it unprofitable to fuck with us," Warren said. "We took out a lieutenant of sorts who gives kickbacks. We're talking either an assassination south of the border, or we keep taking out the people who send the money south of the border. That's how I'd do it. Money is the only thing these types listen to. If it was me, we need to utilize our computer division to see where all that money's going. We can plan based on where it's flowing."

"It's a good idea, but wouldn't he need bank account numbers, names, or at least something to go off of?" Daniel placed both palms on the desk and leaned forward as he looked sideways at Warren.

"I know the perfect place he can start looking."

"Do tell, Davis."

"I know a lot of the OG's in the Stingers still by name. I'll bet you anything, boss, that they're kicking up money to someone higher up the line. Whether they're using fiat currency or crypto, you can be sure they're paying. He can follow those accounts and get us a name. It's simple back tracing logic. Then we can systematically dismantle them, force them to leave our city, and establish dominance to every group out there. If we make the Crag Cartel back off, that's major street cred right there."

The door flung open to reveal Rachel. "Sorry I'm late." In her right hand she held a baby monitor.

"Right. I suppose I did have you babysitting," Daniel said. "I have something new for you as well. You're to go to the computer room and learn everything you can from Lee. Make it your mission to learn as much as you can."

"Understood. May I ask why?"

"This doesn't leave this room. Lee looked broken up after the train incident."

"Oh yeah," Warren said. "He hadn't killed anyone before, had he?"

"Negative," Daniel said. "All I made him do was prove his

technical skill, which he did with flying colors. If he asks why, tell him it's so you can be the one to go along on those kinds of jobs in the future."

"I mean I was the one who taught him how to do that."

"Then tell him you'll be going on those jobs in the future and need varied skills. I don't care. I can't have him break. We're shorthanded right now. When things settle down, we can recruit a dedicated field division of the tech department. For now, you're the closest thing we've got since we can't send him out anymore for fear of him flying off the handle."

"It's awfully nice of you," Rachel said.

"I'm always nice," Daniel said. "Now beyond that, we should expect retaliation soon. They have to know we're the ones who killed their men. Davis, how's the warehouse's defenses?"

"I left four men fully armed there, taking rotations on watching the cameras and patrolling. If they're attacked, they'll know beforehand."

"The place is empty of guns anyway after our last deal. Keep a skeleton crew there to keep it secure."

"Will do. Also, I have good news, sir."

"I could use a little after all this shit. Out with it, Davis," Daniel said.

Warren pulled his phone out and dialed a number before putting it to his ear. "He showed up earlier than I anticipated. He's been on patrol duty, but I think he could be utilized better. Yeah, come in now." He hung up and gestured to the door. "You know the guy I was telling you about before? He's here and ready for duty. I already initiated him. He's trustworthy."

The door to Daniel's office opened showing a middle-aged man with spots of grey in his stubble and his fading brown hair. He was well built and strode forward with confidence.

"Christopher Bristol, I assume?" Daniel asked, extending a hand across the table.

"Yes, sir," Christopher said, shaking Daniel's hand. "I am at your disposal."

"Well, if it isn't the new guy I met recently. Was security not thrilling enough for you?" Rachel asked. "Where did you find this guy?" Rachel looked up at the taller man.

"Oleg sent him our way. Apparently they knew each other."

"I made my way in some uncouth circles in Europe over the past decade. I met him one night in a bar in St. Petersburg before he came here to America," Chris said. "I saved his ass that night on a gun deal gone wrong. We were all lucky we didn't end up in Siberia for that shit. There were a lot of dead Russian cops by the end of the night."

"It's good you can take care of yourself. I'm sorry for the immediate rush, but we need a job done and I can think of no one better," Daniel said. "As of now, you're promoted from patrol and security to operations. Davis, take Bristol and go kidnap one of their men. Rachel, go with them to the tech department and help Lee get them the intel they need. That is all. Dismissed, and good luck."

All three gave a small bow and left the room.

"Follow me, boys." Rachel led the trio through the mansion's decadent red carpeted hallways. They passed a marble bust of a head. "If Davis recommended you, I can't wait to see how you perform. What should I call you? Bristol or Christopher?"

Chris gave a lady killer smile. "You can call me Chris, cutie."

"Word of advice, the last guy who flirted with me was threatened by Father. I won't tell him you did such, but word to the wise." Rachel smirked at him. "Besides, I already have my eyes set on someone."

"He's a lucky man then." Chris's eyes wondered further down than would be considered polite, eventually landing squarely on Rachel's butt as she walked in front of them.

Warren looked over to him and followed his line of sight before elbowing him and clearing his throat. He mouthed "Bad idea" to him and continued in his normal voice. "You sure picked a fun time to join us. You are aware of our situation I take it?"

"Why would you assume such?"

"You're not stupid, Bristol," Warren said. "You wouldn't join a family without having an inkling to what's happening."

"It's true." The group entered the hallway where the tech room was. "I figured the pay would be good considering the need for manpower is raised in such times, never mind someone trained in combat."

"Trained are you?" Rachel looked back and followed his eyes down before frowning. "What? Were you army or something?"

"Nothing quite so formal. I learned on the job shall we say. You learn how to shoot accurately or you don't survive the amount of firefights I've been in with other degenerates."

"We'll leave the whole life story for another time," Rachel said, pushing open the door leading to Lee's room.

"What is it now?" Lee spun around in his swivel chair.

"You guys don't even have a cute tech girl," Chris whined. "Here I was hoping for a cute blonde girl or something."

"Then you're in luck." Rachel giggled as she took a spare chair and sat down.

"What?" Lee said, rotating the chair with a squeak.

"I'm your new assistant of sorts. Don't argue with it. It's boss's orders. I won't get in your way. I'm just here to do those jobs like you did last time. We assume you'd rather not be the one every time."

"That's putting it mildly. To what do I owe the pleasure of your company again tonight?" Lee asked.

"You're not going out again, don't worry," Warren said. "We just need you to track down one of the OG's from the Stingers. He's paying the cartel, so we're going to follow him and take him out."

"If that's all, then fine." Lee exhaled and rotated the chair back toward the multiple monitors.

Rachel quickly jumped up from her chair and moved to stand behind Lee's chair, looking at the screen.

"You're excited," Chris said.

"Out of curiosity's sake." Rachel never took her eyes off the monitor. "Do you have any idea who I am? I don't mean that in a fussy way. I'm genuinely curious."

Chris took a step back and leaned against the wall by the door. "The daughter of the boss. I caught that much earlier."

"Any clue what she can do?" Warren asked, locking his gaze on the nearby man. "Trust me when I say I trust her in a warzone as much as I would you. So try and show a little more respect, huh?"

Chris raised his hands, palms out in a surrendering motion. "I get it. I'm sorry. Is that better? It's just the kind of guy I am. I like to joke around."

"Learn the time and place, funny man," Rachel said. Her right arm fell to Lee's, halting the cursor on the screen. "Wait. What is this site?"

"I'll put the address on your flash drive, but to answer your question, it's a background check service."

"Won't they see you running the check?" Rachel asked, releasing her hold on Lee.

"Not if you take the necessary precautions." Lee continued typing and clicking. "I'll teach you that afterward, but all they know is that someone is paying in cryptocurrency to look up a name." He looked over his shoulder. "Speaking of which, what was the name of this mystery target?"

Warren spoke up. "The name is Bert Portman."

"A gangster named Bert?" Chris tried to stifle a laugh by putting a hand in front of his mouth.

"You say that now, but he got made fun of a lot," Warren said.

"Your point being?"

"He's one of the meaner sons of bitches they have as a result," Warren said. "He's also paranoid."

"Meaning?" Rachel asked.

"I'm checking his email account now. From this, it looks like he has an alarm system. He bought it last month according to his confirmation email. I have the model here too," Lee said. "I'm looking up how this one differs from others. This will take a few minutes."

"I don't guess you know if it can be disarmed?" Warren asked.

"I am not a technician. I can't tell you that. Your best bet would be to disarm it remotely. This model is on the cheaper side. It can be disabled remotely by using a remote of the same frequency. Usually they give the home two, but I can make something work." He got up from his swivel chair and moved to the opposite side of the room near his bed. He got a box out from under his bed and opened the cardboard container. "Yes, it looks like I have what we need. I'll just need to make an adjustment." He moved over to his work desk nearby with the box.

"You've done this before?" Rachel asked, getting up and coming over to watch.

"My father used to mix up the garage door opener and the alarm remote all the time. I've done this more times than I can count," Lee said. "It's easy to make a universal remote. Just be sure to be close when you use it. These things' range sucks."

"Good to note," Chris said, his voice mildly sarcastic. "If we can turn the alarm off, we're golden. It all rides on our expert."

"It's done. Like I said, be close to the house and hit this button here." He walked over and showed Warren which button to press. "Just remember arrow up is alarm off. Down is bad. It'll set off the alarm immediately. Don't confuse the two. For you, boss, you use that laptop over on the desk. You can destroy it afterward."

"I think I can remember that much." Warren pocketed the remote control. "Is that all we need for this place?"

"Oh," Rachel interrupted. "You'll probably need a driver if the two of you are going inside. Someone tech savvy enough to watch the camera, which means I'm volunteering myself. Damn it all."

"Why?" Chris asked. "Get this guy to do it."

"I'll tell you why that's not an option once we're in the car," Rachel said. "When were you two going out to do this anyway?"

"It'd be best to do this at night when the neighborhood's asleep," Warren said. "It's in the middle of the Stinger's ghetto. The less people seeing us, the better."

"Then let's get going." Rachel got up, retrieved the laptop, and walked past the two men and out the door.

"Come on, Bristol," Warren said, walking toward the door. "You don't want to keep the boss waiting."

Outside Bert Portman's house in a van...

Rachel put the van in park across the from their target's household in the circular street. "Anyone see someone looking at us?"

Both men in the back put on their masks and gloves before looking out their respective window and out the back before answering.

Chris spoke up first. "It looks like everybody's asleep, boss. No one's up at two in the morning anyway."

"It never hurts to be thorough," Warren said. "Communications check."

Rachel reached over into the passenger seat and picked up the laptop Lee gave her before they left. "I hear you. Let me see what you're walking into."

"Bristol?" Warren asked.

"I hear you. You really do know how to do this crap," Chris leaned forward and looked at the screen as she worked.

"There are no cameras in there other than two cell phones. Let me see what I can do," Rachel tapped the touch pad. "There. Wait, that's just a picture of a dark ceiling and some snoring. Let me try the other phone." The screen changed again, this time all that could be made out was a bright light. "That one's in a lit room. They left their phone on the table. You have at least one person awake in there. Do with that information what you will."

"Everybody get down low!" Christopher's panicked voice spurred everyone into action.

A bright light filled the cabin of the van as everybody got as low as they could manage. The sound of a motor died. A muffled sound of a door opening and incoherent chatter was all that could be made out. Once it all went silent for a good minute, Rachel lifted herself up and peeked out the window. "Was that car there before?"

"What car?" Warren stretched and looked out the window she referred to. "No, it was not. Who the fuck is that?"

"Now that I could maybe help with. Be very quiet. The onboard microphone shouldn't pick up any of our voices, but just to be safe." She finished her order with a final click and voices could be heard coming from the laptop.

"I hope you had a pleasant drive here, sir."

"In this shithole neighborhood?" a Spanish accented voice asked. "You're lucky I even took the time out of my day to see you face to face. Do you have our money or not?"

"Of course I do, sir. It's right here."

"Give it here," the accented voice growled along with the sound of shuffling.

"I think you two need to get out there. We don't want our golden ticket to leave. We need the cartel member. Feel free to kill the original mark. I'll leave the engine running. Be careful now."

"You heard the pretty lady." Chris cocked his handgun with a cocky smirk and opened the back door.

"Don't leave me behind, hotshot." Warren hurried after him.

Rachel watched both men approach the house across the way and turned her attention back to the laptop. "Are you going in the front or the back?"

"Front," Warren said.

"Alright. They just picked up the phone. I have a better view. Go in on my signal, and make sure the alarm is off." Rachel saw the video feed change from bright light to a tanned Hispanic man.

"You dumbass. Is that a cell phone?" The boss stomped up to Bert.

"So? Who the hell cares if it is?" Bert asked. "I always have it on me."

Rachel could see the front door behind the boss's shoulder.

"Go in now."

She saw the front door open and two men duck inside.

"Shit! I told you, man. It's fucking amateur hour around here." The boss man ducked out of frame. The table crashed to the side as the phone viewer fell to it behind cover. She could see both targets behind the improvised cover.

"They're behind the table. They're not firing. Bristol, flank around now. Davis, lay down suppressing fire and do not let them breathe."

Gunshots rang out both outside her car and over the laptop's speakers. Lights turned on in several of the houses around her.

"I'm almost there," Chris said, gunshots in the background of the call. "But they're frisky tonight."

"Hold. I'll tell you when they're reloading, and you can go."

Rachel couldn't see the guns their adversaries were using, but she could hear the clicks.

"They're out and reloading. Go now."

Another two gunshots rang out, the camera fell with a groan and slid across the floor. It still showed the front door, but from around the table now. "I got him." His tone turned steely. "Drop the fucking weapon, or I put it between your eyes, you piece of shit." A clattering was heard on the video feed, signifying the cartel member's weapon hitting the floor.

The video feed showed Warren rushing into the room. He kicked the weapon away from him. He reached into his pocket and produced a pair of zip ties and bound the man before the pair dragged him away from the camera and toward the door.

Rachel jumped out, circled around, and opened the rear doors. She hopped back in the front seat and unlocked all the doors before starting the engine.

By the time she was ready she felt a thud and heard the rear doors slam shut before two other doors opening then slamming shut. She immediately put it into drive and hit the gas.

A woman could be seen through the still open door running down the stairs.

"That's not going to be a fun scene to happen across," Rachel mumbled to herself.

"Forget her," Chris said, taking off his mask. "She made her choice when she married a gangster."

"At least it went better than the last kidnapping job, eh boss?" Warren asked. "She survived. That's an improvement."

The sound of sirens cut him off. "Were we made?"

"I don't think so," Rachel said, slowing the van down.

"There's no fucking way any of them called the police, you stupid ass Morris idiots." Their guest raised his voice from the back.

"You didn't gag him?" Rachel asked.

"I thought we were in a hurry," Chris said. "Do we have any tape in here?"

"Check the glove compartment. There's some in there I'm sure."

Chris leaned forward and opened the glove compartment while the cartel member continued unabated.

"You know your whole organization is going to be wiped out. We have more men, more guns, and more money. Do you really think your little syndicate is going to stop us?"

"Let me shut his ass up," Chris said loud enough to be heard as he pulled out a roll of duct tape. He slammed the glove compartment shut before turning around and climbing over the back seat and tumbling into the back.

"You alright back there?" Warren poked his head up over the divide in the cabin. "Yeah. You're fine I see."

Chris tore off a piece of tape and covered the tied up man's mouth. "Let me take care of your feet too while I'm at it. We can't have you trying anything cute." He moved over and got to work further immobilizing their newfound target.

"Oh shit," Rachel said. "We have to improvise now."

"Why?"

"Look." Rachel pointed out the front window toward their warehouse a few blocks away. Numerous police cars were surrounding it with their red and blue lights flashing away.

"What do you think happened?"

"Who knows? There's only one way to find out. For now, we have to head back."

"With him in tow?" Chris asked, climbing back over the divide and buckling up again.

Rachel turned around and headed for the villa. "It's our only choice, just to be safe. Call Dad. You have a burner, yes?"

"Always," Warren said, pulling out said device. "Yeah, boss, we have a slight problem. There are police at the ware-"

Warren paused, causing Chris to look at him sideways.

"I understand, sir." He hung up. "He said to come back to the villa."

Earlier in Daniel's work room...

"If it's not one thing it's another," Daniel shook his head and hung up the phone. He glanced over at the tiny monitor on the side of his desk and did a double take when he saw his four men in the warehouse taking up defensive positions behind various metal support beams and aiming their rifles at the entrance. "Oh shit, they're attacking."

He watched as the door burst open and bodies fell into the warehouse onto the floor. Body after body attempted to enter, some having a modicum of success but dying a few feet inside. A wide smile appeared on Daniel's face as he cheered at the display, much like a sports fan during their championship of choice.

"Get their asses!" he screamed at the display. "That's right. Show them who they're fucking with. That's my boys."

He watched the carnage ensue until he noticed his men having to take cover and reload. "Take rotations reloading, you simpletons!"

Two cartel members took the opportunity to duck through the door and fired off a salvo as they dashed toward any cover. The shots knocked one of his men to the ground. He couldn't tell if he was dead, but he didn't get back up.

One of the men didn't make it there as, reloading completed, they put him down. The remaining member found cover behind a nearby metal support beam

"Come on. You all don't have that much time. There are no more coming in. You need to finish this, and get out now." Daniel found himself chewing his fingernails as he watched the attack unfold.

He saw two of his men come out from their cover and approach the beam from two different sides. He could see the remaining man throwing down cover fire all the while until they got close.

Both men fired their weapons and the body fell to the ground. The nearest two fired another two shots each into the now limp body on the floor then checked their surroundings.

"Come on. Get the man, and get out of there already. You're cutting it close, depending on how many people called the police."

He watched the men drag the body out the other door of the warehouse, leaving the dead cartel bodies the only thing left on the screen.

He hung his head. "I hope that young man's alright, but it looked like it got him good. They certainly didn't send their best and brightest on that assault. It was like watching fodder running into a blade." He grabbed one of the shot glasses at his desk and the bottle of amber liquid. He filled the glass and took a swig.

"Why only send that many untrained on that kind of an attack?" Daniel swirled the contents of his glass around. "Are they testing us? Could be. It's either that, or they thought they'd catch us unaware at this hour. That's probably what it is." A phone in his pocket chirping interrupted his theorizing.

He answered it. "Yeah?"

"Yeah, boss, we have a slight problem. There's police at the ware-"

"I bet so. We did in fact get hit, Davis. I just watched it myself. Get back here now, and be careful," he said before hanging up the phone. "Is that place ready yet?" Daniel wiped a bead of sweat off his brow. "We need a place to assemble our guns..."

16

Daniel stepped out the front door and watched the van pull into the compound. Two visibly armed men in suits closed the fence behind it. He adjusted his tie and cleared his throat while the van parked nearby.

Rachel put it in park and took the key out before hopping out of the car. "We have an extra tonight, Father."

"What does that mean?" Daniel stepped forward, closer to the back of the van.

"Careful," Warren said, stepping out of the car. "We have a special guest, sir."

"Well go on then," Daniel said. "Don't let me delay it."

Chris opened the van's rear doors from inside and smiled. "You may want to take a step back, sir. He's a feisty one." He hopped down to the gravel. "Mr. Davis, if you'd please."

"Who is this guy?" Daniel asked Rachel, now standing beside her.

"The guy you sent us after's boss. Or rather, the guy he was paying in the cartel. We figured if we found out who his boss was, we can get an even bigger target."

"Or a way to strike at the head of the snake. Good job, everybody." He watched the two men yank their prisoner out and get him to his feet. "Take him to the building out back. Chain him up. I'll be there shortly. If anyone's squeamish, they don't have to go. Now take him away."

"Yes, sir," both men said before dragging him around the house out of view.

"I suppose you've put it together that we were hit while you were out on that job," Daniel said to his daughter as they followed the group toward the makeshift prison he had designed.

"How many casualties?" Rachel asked, her voice sullen.

"Maybe one," Daniel said. "The cartel didn't send their best, which confused me. We put down all of them, but they got one of ours."

"They were testing our capabilities it sounds like," Rachel kicked an especially big rock out into the grass being illuminated by the overhead light attached to the villa. "I wouldn't be surprised if they're planning another attack as we speak." She yawned and covered her mouth with her hand. "They ruined the warehouse with their little test too. I'd call that successful for them."

"If you're tired, you can go to bed. We don't need you for the questioning."

"I may retire early after we get something, but I have a fitting idea for how we can dispose of him."

Daniel pushed the door open to the small concrete building with matching floor. They saw their prisoner standing in front of them shirtless with shackles wrapped around both wrists and ankles, all connected to the wall behind him.

"This is sick, man. Who even designs a room like this?" The man struggled against his bonds.

Daniel took off his dress coat and handed it over to Warren beside him, then did the same for his hat. "That would be me, young man." Daniel rolled his neck side to side, eliciting a crack before stopping and pounding one fist into his other open hand. "Is this going to go the easy way or the hard way? I'd prefer the hard way if I'm honest. Now at least tell us your name. Be polite. I know you had to have had a mama that at least taught you that much."

Jingling met their ears as the chains yanked away from the wall. "Fine," the young man said. "My name is Juan."

"Juan what? Introduce yourself properly."

"It's Juan Martinez, alright?"

Daniel cracked his knuckles. "Now, Juan, you are going to tell us the name of your boss."

"You really think so?"

"I know you will." Daniel leveled him with a hook, causing Juan's head to turn to the side. "Oh look, I've already gone and broken your nose.

Juan looked back at him, his nose crooked with blood pouring out of it. "Is this all you got?"

"Play tough now. It'll only get worse and worse until you realize," Daniel stepped forward again, leveling a punch into Juan's exposed stomach, talking through Juan's coughing and wheezing, "that the quicker you talk, the less bullshit you go through. It's that simple. Isn't that right, Mr. Bristol?"

"Damned right, boss." Chris leaned against the wall and watched the display with a straight face.

"It's not like we necessarily want to maim you," Warren stepped forward, coming shoulder to shoulder with Daniel. "We won't shy away from it though."

"Of course not." Daniel patted Warren's shoulder. He stepped yet closer to Juan and kneed him in the groin.

Warren and Chris winced at the impact as Juan's high-pitched cries of pain filled the enclosed room.

"Just tell us your boss's name." Daniel looked at Juan. He rolled his eyes when he realized he wouldn't be getting an answer. "This," Daniel kicked him in the groin again, "is not ending." He stepped back and took a deep breath.

"Alright," Juan cried. "His name is Diego Santiago."

"Good," Daniel said. "Now what is your little organization's next move?"

"You expect me to know?" Juan asked, finally gaining strength to look back up at Daniel. "I'm just muscle. They don't tell us shit."

"Damn," Daniel said. He bit his lip and looked away.

Rachel spoke up. "I know why he's so confident,"

"Just figured it out, did you? You're a little slow."

Rachel got up beside Juan and reached into his jean's pocket. She pulled out his phone. "This is his ace in the hole."

"A phone?" Daniel asked. "What about it?"

"This thing has a gps in it. They know where we are now." She moved back to the door leading outside as she spoke. "We were in such a rush to get out of there, we didn't empty his pockets. Deal with him quickly, Father, if you want my advice," she said before flinging the door open and sprinting toward the larger building, leaving the door open."

"I want you two to put him in that barrel and light it on fire." He pointed to a corner of the room containing an oil barrel sized drum. "Give him a proper burial of his people."

Juan's eyes went wide and stared at the drum as the two men went to follow the order. "Wait a minute! I'll tell you what you want. Just shoot me or something else. Not that!"

Daniel reached the door before stopping and looking

back, one foot out the door. "Live by the sword, die by the sword." He turned and left the three alone."

Warren undid Juan's right ankle lock and then passed the key to Chris to unlock the other. He wrapped his arms around Juan as Chris moved the drum over before removing the top.

"This is going to be gnarly," Chris said.

"I'll pay you both two hundred thousand dollars if you let me go," Juan said, his voice shaky. "Don't cook me, man."

"Orders are orders," Warren said. "Secure that barrel." He lifted Juan's lithe frame up and dunked him into the liquid inside while Chris held the container steady from Juan's frantic kicks. The fit was a tight one, taking a full minute to even fit him into it.

"No! God no!" Juan's panicked voice said. "Anything but this!" His arms were pinned down at his side in the narrow container. He struggled and groaned in the black liquid.

Chris held out an engraved metal lighter and flicked the wheel, producing a flame.

"I'll do it," Warren said amid incoherent screams. He grabbed the lighter and dropped it into the liquid.

The barrel roared to life as both men backed off immediately out of the room. Inhumane screams met their ears as they left the room. Smoke billowed out of the doorway as they both looked back at their handiwork.

Chris watched as Juan's flame covered body jerked around along with his howls of anguish. "I have to say, it's the first time I've done this." He spat on the ground and turned away. "I don't like it."

"Oh, the smell." Warren covered his nose and turned away while gagging, leading the duo away from the execution site. He recovered his composure and spoke again. "It's what they do to their enemies. It's also easier disposal."

"What a way to look on the bright side you have."

Inside the tech room...

"At least I got an hour of rest." Lee sat up in bed to see Rachel already at one of the computers he had on a desk. "What are you doing here? What time is it?"

"Good, you're awake." Rachel turned the chair around. "We have a situation."

"I'm hearing that phrase too often nowadays." Lee rubbed his eyes and got up. He walked over and took the phone that Rachel held out to him. "Who's is this?"

"Our newest prisoner's."

Lee took it over to one of the desks with tools and set to work. He disassembled the device under Rachel's watchful eye. "You know this still has its gps tracker in here, yes?"

"That is what I was worried about," Rachel said. "Alright then. I need you to rip any possible intel off that. I'm going to go prepare everyone for what could happen."

"What's that?" Lee watched as Rachel moved to the door leading into the hallway.

"I don't know. That's the scary part." Rachel left him alone with those words and made her way into the hallway. "God, I'm tired. I'll stop by Ben's room real quick and then get some sleep. He deserves to know what's happening." She saw her father walking toward her in the hallway after she turned a corner.

"What's the news?" Daniel asked, causing her to stop next to a nearby window.

She looked out into the forest as she spoke. "It still was trackable. I'm having Lee deactivate it and pull any relevant intel out of it. It's the best I could do. I'm sorry, Father. It was a rookie mistake. We were so focused on getting out with our newfound prize, we didn't take his phone."

"It was a mistake for sure," Daniel's voice was stern. "There's nothing that can be done about it now though. If they know where we are," his voice turned softer, more solemn, "there's only one thing to do. I'll call in everyone we have and get them over here. We're turning this place into a goddamned fortress. I don't think they'd attack tonight seeing as it's already almost three in the morning, but tomorrow it could happen anytime."

"I'll help get everyone armed tomorrow. We need plans for how many personnel we're going to have where."

"I'll take care of that part," Daniel said. "No offense, princess, but I'm far more experienced in this sort of thing."

"It's fine by me," Rachel said. "How many men and women do we have once we call them in?"

"By my count," Daniel said, "we have around two hundred men and women. "It should be enough to guard this place. This house is far enough out in the middle of nowhere that we shouldn't have to worry about cops. That's one less thing to worry about."

"I need to find a room without windows," Rachel said.

"Why, pray tell?"

"I don't want Roger anywhere near windows that could shatter if they attack."

"You need to put him in my saferoom before it starts."

"I can get La-"

"I said you for a reason," Daniel said. "The syndicate will need their second in command if anything happens to me. Think of it like if the President goes into a dangerous situation. You know how the vice-president and a bunch of the higher ups separate? It's like that."

"Won't they just think of me as a coward if I do that? I'd

much rather help direct troop movement and coordinate the defense. If they win and take this villa, we'd be trapped in there until starvation."

"True enough, but you're going in the safe room. It's in my work room. I'll brook no disagreement on this. Changing the subject, what do you think of Bristol? You were out there with him on that job. Does he live up to the hype?"

"He gets the job done, if that's what you're asking. I just personally find his personality grating. Why do you ask?"

"Do you think he could lead men in battle?"

"I have no clue honestly. He followed orders to a 't' in the only battle I saw him in. I'd guess yes if I had to," Rachel said, stepping forward and planting a hand on either side of the window. "Why do you ask?"

"I needed to know if I could trust him with a group if they attack. I think I can now after what you said. He'll have a squad of his own then in the attack. Be sure to get up early tomorrow. We're having a meeting tomorrow morning and briefing the personnel."

"I'll make it there," Rachel said, taking a step around her father. "I'm going to go get some rest."

"Good night," Daniel said from behind her.

"Good night, Dad," she said. She kept walking through the twisting opulent hallways until she finally reached Ben's door.

She saw Elizabeth exiting his room with a wipe of her mouth and a visible swallow. She saw Rachel approach and gave her a fake smile. "You don't have to worry, sweetheart. He'll be asleep soon. Believe that."

Rachel glared at her aunt. "Then get to sleep already. Tomorrow will be busy. Believe that."

"Don't be jealous, sweetheart." She walked off, laughing to herself. "I'm leaving already."

Rachel watched her aunt leave with a sour look on her face before entering the room herself. She saw Ben getting under the cover in nothing but a pair of boxers. "Did you just have some fun with Auntie?" she asked in a sickeningly sweet voice. She pulled out a small device and ran it over the room as she spoke. "I already know the answer."

"It wasn't my idea," Ben said. "It just kind of happened. I swear."

"I told you not to piss her off." Rachel waved the sensor over the bed, exposing her belly for Ben to see. "If you'd declined her, it'd have done just that. I don't like that it happened though. She didn't do anything too bad, did she?" She put the device away.

"She didn't go all the way, no." Ben blushed. "More like third base."

"I figured as much. She's recently given birth after all." Rachel sat down on Ben's bed and sat next to Ben. "Our time is approaching." She reached out and played with his hair with a smile. "I was on a job earlier you know."

"How did that go?"

"We killed the target and got an unexpected prisoner who is giving us intel. There's only one problem."

Ben tilted his head. "I don't follow. That all sounds great."

"We forgot to remove his phone. Namely me," her voice grew soft. "I forgot to have the guys get rid of it. I was too damned focused on the getaway. I saw lights coming on and got us out of there just as people were coming out to see what the noise was. We're working under the assumption that we'll be attacked here soon."

Ben got to a sitting position with a groan. "I'm able to fight, don't worry."

"No." Rachel leaned forward and delivered a peck on his lips. "For you, I have something very important."

"Anything," Ben said.

Rachel kissed him again. "Do you want to be together with me? Yes or no? Don't think about Dad or any of that shit. Do you want to be with me as a couple?"

"Yes."

She guided his head to her lap and caressed his cheeks. Her voice was low, sultry, almost hypnotizing. "There's only one way that can happen. What is about to happen tomorrow doesn't need to merely be a setback. It can also be an opportunity for the both of us. Tomorrow I want you to go to my father's room when I tell you, armed. He'll more than likely order you to help him if the assault's started."

"I think I see where this is going. Are you asking me to do the same thing as Ms. Morris? Are you..." his voice fell to a mere whisper. "Are you asking me to kill the boss? Your father, that is."

Rachel stopped her motions and stared off into the distance. "Wait, what? She asked you to do this too? God damn. I suppose Dad not getting her kid out and the demeaning manual labor was the final straw."

"In her words," Ben said, "I want you to kill him." He looked up into Rachel's eyes. "She claimed she'd take over since she was his sister."

"The hell she will," Rachel said. "Davis, yourself, and most of the rank and file would recognize me as the successor. She's not even initiated." She stopped moving her hands and merely cupped his face in her hands. "You know, dating the boss would have a great many benefits."

"I'll tell you the same thing I told her."

"That you'd do it? You actually told her that?"

Ben's face reddened. "What was I to do? Tell her no? She'd have claimed I had the conspiracy if she's the type of woman I take her to be."

Rachel paused and eventually nodded. "Yeah, I could see that. She'd take you down for her own plot. She's done it before. She is despicable. At least with me," her voice turned sensual as she leaned in close to his ear, "you'd know I'd take responsibility for my own actions." She sat back up, her voice cheery. "There is also the other reason you'd say yes. You know Dad will kill you for being involved with me. Never you mind the whole relationship thing you're pretending to have with his sister. Let her imagine you're doing it for her." She gently got him up to a sitting position. "What do you say? I need to hear it."

"Yes, I'll do it for us," Ben said. "I'd like to see where this goes. Besides, the strong motivation is I don't want to die."

"Good." Rachel got off the bed. "Lay down then. You need your rest. When the time is right, do what I say. Have your phone charged, on you, and always turned on."

"I understand. I'll be ready." He looked over at the holstered pistol laying on the nightstand. "Make it look like an accident?"

"If it's during the siege, just have it be a bullet. Preferably make it quick. He's a bastard, but he's still my dad."

Ben got under the covers and closed his eyes. "As you order, so shall it be done."

Rachel bent down and gave him a long good-night kiss. "Sleep well..."

17

"**G**ood morning, beautiful," Chris said to Elizabeth as he entered the kitchen.

"Who are you supposed to be, talking to me like that?" Elizabeth looked up from her cleaning duty. She held a cloth in her right hand and a bottle of cleaning solution in her left. "You have balls talking to me like that."

"What is it with women recently saying something like that whenever I try?" he asked. "All I'm doing is delivering a compliment."

"Well," Elizabeth got back to scrubbing the tiled floor clean. "Forgive me if I'm not in the mood as I break my back to keep this place clean." Her voice got softer, but Chris could still make out what she said. "I can't believe he's got me doing this demeaning shit job."

"Who? The boss? Aren't you his sister or something?" Chris scratched the back of his head, admiring the view of Elizabeth's backside as she was on all fours.

"You put that together all by yourself, big guy?" Elizabeth sat back on her knees and wiped her brow with the back of her arm and a loud exhale. "What gave you that clue? The rumor mill spreading about how the former leader of the Morris family is reduced to this bullshit? Or maybe it was my mugshot being on every major cable news station in this country? Stop me when I get it right. It's not like I have anything better to do than play the guessing game with some guy right now."

"I'm surprised the boss has you pulling cleaning duty. Didn't the news say you just had a kid?"

Elizabeth did nothing but level a silent glare his way.

"You look fantastic by the way. A lot of women put on weight afterward. Not you though."

Elizabeth followed his eyes down her body and looked back up at him. "Who are you, and how old are you, tough guy?"

"I am Christopher Bristol," he said. "I am forty-three years old, and it's been a long time since I've seen a woman in as good a shape as you. I don't say that lightly."

"You're a shameless flirt is what you are. Don't you have something better to do than flirt with women you find around the place? Isn't there a meeting for everybody soon?"

"I have time to kill beforehand. Now if I remember the hubbub about you, didn't you use to be the big boss woman?"

"In a different life, yes." Elizabeth got back to work, cleaning under the bar in the tough to reach spots. "That was a different time, with different people. Everything's different now."

"Some things stay the same." Chris got down and helped.

"What are you doing?"

"I'm not busy right now. I figured I'd make it easier on you is all." Chris flashed her a smile as he cleaned. "There's nothing wrong with talking while you work."

"You're an odd one, and not entirely wrong. It's infuriating."

"Where there are men and women, some things will never change. Like when a man recognizes a beautiful woman and wants to get to know her."

"Get to know her or her body?" Elizabeth asked. "Those are not always one and the same."

"You might be right. What an exploration that would be with you though," he said, turning to her with a wink. "Now," he said, scratching a white patch of his stubble over his chin, "don't get me wrong. I'm not a total walking stereotype of being horny."

"I'd never have guessed," Elizabeth said with a sarcastic edge.

"I like making women feel good is all."

Elizabeth stopped working and stared at him. "Seriously?"

"Oh, I didn't mean like that, Ms. Morris. Well, not entirely like that," Chris said. "Think about it. Do you remember the first time a boy flirted with you?"

Elizabeth got up from her knees and to her feet. "I remember bits and pieces of the experience, sure."

Chris hefted himself to his feet with a grunt. "Do you remember the warm feeling of happiness you got when he hit on you? Because I remember the first time a woman came on to me. It makes a person extraordinarily happy, even if we don't want to admit it to ourselves or others. I just like making people happy."

"I'm sure physical pleasure has nothing to do with your decision-making process," Elizabeth gave a cocky smile, "or the sensations they'll give you after you make them happy."

"I won't deny enjoying their appreciation," Chris said with a shrug. "What kind of healthy man wouldn't? You can't trust a man like that. They're dishonest if they say that."

"Uh huh." Elizabeth looked him up and down. "Come on then," she led him over to the coffee machine. Its pot was half full. She grabbed a cup from the nearby cabinet, filled it, and handed it to her newfound helper before fetching one for herself. "You remind me of someone."

"An old lover perhaps?"

"You are actually right for once." Elizabeth took a sip from the cup.

"Oh?"

"Yep. He was also a complete jackass that led me on and used me for my body. You'd like him. His name was Bruce. He was in the exact line of work as you, hit on me the same as you, and was a lifer to this lifestyle." She took another hard look at his rugged features and prominent scar running across his face. "Just like you."

"Did you love him?"

"For a time. Then something better came along, or at least what I thought was better. That bit me in the ass later."

Chris drank the whole cup in one go before placing the container into the nearby sink. "We're not all the same I bet you anything. Maybe you should put yourself out there again. Who knows? You could find happiness again. What have you got to lose?"

Elizabeth grabbed her cleaning supplies and went to leave the room. "Unless you want to join me in the bathroom, this conversation is coming to an end. Besides, don't you and everyone else have a meeting in an hour? It's already past six. It's almost light out. I happen to know for a fact you're going to need all the energy you can get for today. I'll tell you what - if you survive the day without giving up, maybe I'll give you a chance."

Chris watched her leave, his eyes wandering lower. "I'll hold you to that..."

An hour later at 7am...

Daniel stood above the large crowd of men and women below him on the grass. He placed his hands on the guard rail on his porch and spoke in a loud commanding tone. "Some of you may be wondering why I've called all of us here on this fine morning. As you all know, we are at war. Now I'm doing everything I can to end it, but we have reason to believe we are going to be attacked here soon. It is better for all of us if we work together and overcome this. If we were to stay spread apart, we'd all be in far more danger."

Daniel took a deep breath amid the assorted mutterings in the crowd. "Quiet! I'm not finished. In order to maximize our chances of everyone surviving, we have some work to do. We are going to transform this place into a veritable fortress with everyone's help. That way, no matter what these savages throw at us, we'll be able to withstand." He pointed to a man in the front row holding up his hand. "What is it?"

"We are talking about the Crag Cartel, yes?"

"Yes, sir," Daniel said. "Now, we are going to construct barricades of bags full of dirt around our defensible positions. I've already drawn up plans for each and every one of you in what jobs you're going to undertake today. Multiple groups will go out and buy the required supplies needed for this undertaking. Once they're back, those of you with trucks will go with groups to fill said bags and bring them back, while yet more build the actual defensive positions. While all this is going on, others will be securing this place. I want you to talk to Mr. Davis." He pointed toward Warren down on the grass. "You can also ask my daughter. They will tell you what you need to be doing. I remind you this is no time for slacking off. Our very lives depend on our hard work here. If we catch anyone slacking, the reprimand will be severe. Am I understood? I will not tolerate laziness."

"We understand, sir!" the choir of voices answered.

"Good. We think the attack will come after dark. There's no way they'll try an assault in broad daylight. It would be suicide. Regardless, to be safe do not leave the premises alone. Always go with protection. I don't care if you need to take a piss in the woods when you're filling bags with dirt - go with someone else. I don't want anyone dying due to stupid mistakes. We're better than that. Also, as a one time thing, while doing all this manual labor feel free to dress appropriately. Formal wear will only slow down our progress to being ready. Make sure you have them back on before tonight though. I do not want friendly fire claiming casualties because you couldn't tell friend from foe. Uniforms do just that."

He paced back and forth on the wooden patio as he continued. "At five o'clock tonight, I will come out and inspect the fortifications. At that time, everyone here is expected to go to the basement to get equipped. Then move to where you're assigned. If you follow the plan, we'll be fine. Every man and woman here will be expected to fight. We all knew the danger of the life we chose - now it's time to prove your mettle." He clapped loudly. "Now get to work. I have to go get us some reinforcements as insurance. Mr. Bristol, I want to see you in private, so don't head off too quickly."

The crowd formed two lines in front of Warren and Rachel respectively while Chris climbed the wooden stairs. "Yes, sir?"

"I'm giving you command of a group for the battle tonight. Are you comfortable with that?"

"It wouldn't be the first time I've had a command, boss. I can handle it. Who am I commanding exactly?"

"Pick a group. I don't care which. God knows we have enough manpower here today. Grab up to twenty people. You are going to be stationed out back."

"May I ask why the back?"

"If you were going to attack this place, would you come in the front? It's too obvious. I want competent defenses in the back. Davis vouched for your skill. You will prove it to me by keeping us intact if they sneak up on us. Is that understood?"

"Got it. Shall I undertake building the defenses on that side as well? I can help with that."

"Go for it. I want it fortified. You're going to be the ones there, so set it up how you see fit. Now that means no slacking or flirting with the personnel like you did my sister earlier this morning."

"Sir?"

"You think people didn't notice? You were in the kitchen, Bristol. It's a common room. I hear things. I'd rather you not get involved with her, but she's a big girl and can make her own decisions. Just know what you're getting into if you go after her. I will not tolerate someone toying with my sister's heart. Do you understand me, son?"

"Crystal clear, sir."

"Then get moving. We have a lot of work today." He turned away from Chris and saw his daughter and Warren directing the people one by one on their job today. The lines moved quickly with people jogging off toward their directed duty one by one. "I love a well-oiled machine..."

A few hours later...

A black jeep appeared on the dirt road approaching the villa. Numerous men and women stood behind the fences and fledgling fences being built, pointing their weapons at the vehicle.

"Hold your fire!" Daniel yelled, walking over. "Open the gate."

The guards did as instructed, and the jeep pulled inside before the gate was shut behind them. All the doors of the jeep opened as soon as it stopped. Oleg, Artyom, and five other men filed out of the vehicle and slammed their doors shut.

"What is all of this?" Oleg asked, motioning toward the men and women creating makeshift defenses.

"We're expecting company later. Whether it's tonight or tomorrow, it's always best to be prepared."

Oleg scratched his bald head. "This is more than just prepared, old buddy. Why did you call us here anyway? It looks like you're building an army outpost."

"Yes. Well that's because we heard some distressing news from our newest guest." He pointed toward the back of the property. "We had a cartel member chat with us earlier. He had some interesting news."

"Out with it already, Morris," Oleg said. "This place is making me nervous just standing here. Like bombs are going to start falling out of nowhere."

"Funny thing about that," Daniel said, a sheepish grin on his face.

"Here we go," Oleg said.

"We've received intel that we're being attacked tonight."

"That sucks. What's that got to do with us?" Oleg asked. "We're not involved in your day-to-day affairs."

"Yeah, so here's the thing. We were told from our late friend that as soon as they take us out, they're going after you all. They have your headquarter's location and everything. So, I figured we'd be better off crushing them here together. Then I have a plan to end this war inside of two days. We just need to hold here."

Oleg leaned back against the side of his jeep. "Son of a bitch. You're serious?"

"Does it look like I'm joking around?" Daniel asked. "Look, I'm not asking you and your men to be down in the trenches with us. Don't be mistaken. All I'm asking is for you all to be our ace in the hole. You would be ambushing them."

"How exactly would you even propose ambushing them? Shall we just go a few minutes up the road, turn off onto a dirt road, and wait for a signal? Just totally abandoning our plans for tonight and all?"

"I don't pretend to know your agenda. What I do know is you want this bullshit to be over. Once they're gone, we're free to do business with impunity. Now I haven't called on you all thus far in this war. All I'm asking is for help in one defense."

"Before you magically end this war with the cartel?" Oleg sneered. "You never did mention how you're going to do that. Explain that to me, and then I'll entertain this."

"We know where their shot callers are."

"In Mexico I'd assume. If not there, some other South American country. What?" Oleg asked. "Are you going to send a group to assassinate them on their own home turf? Tell me that's not your plan."

"Nothing quite so extraordinary. Think more intimidation. We've been systematically killing anybody who sends money back home to them."

"I think that's just going to keep them here to kill you honestly," Oleg said. He turned to Artyom. "What do you think?"

Artyom held his silence for a few moments before speaking up in a calm voice. "It could go either way. It depends on how dead set they are on having an operation here. If they're blowing a ton of money here, they could in fact pack up and leave for greener pastures. Or it could of course just piss them off. It's our best bet right now in my opinion, boss."

Oleg sighed. "Do you at least have a number to contact them? There's no way they're going to just quit without a push of some sort."

"We do. After we wipe them out, I was planning on taking pictures of all the bodies. I'd get my tech department to send them a picture of the carnage when I call them. I'm going to explain to them that it'd be in their best interests to move to another town. I've beaten a number of groups in my life, old friend. Trust me when I say this - the war will be over within a week."

"I'll trust your judgement on this. Fine, what would you have us do?"

"First, head inside and get some boxed lunches I had our cooks make for tonight. Your first guess wasn't that far off. Parking somewhere nearby off the road and hanging out would be the most advantageous. You'd be able to get here in a hurry and surprise the fuck out of them with a flanking maneuver. When we call for you, we'll tell you where they are and which way to approach. You may have to hike through a bit of woods, but we'd both rather you come up behind them and blow them away."

"It sounds simple enough," Artyom said. "It is tactically sound, boss. We have enough men to make a difference, assuming the enemy doesn't send more than a few hundred."

"I don't think they have more than a few hundred in this whole state," Daniel said. "You can also pick up some gas from the backyard just in case it gets cold, so you boys can keep the heater on in your cars tonight. We've stockpiled more than enough even for us."

"You're making it difficult to say no," Oleg said. "Fine. We'll help out, but this war better end."

"Feel free to help with the fortifications if you want. It'll help our success chances if you do," Daniel said. "We have cooks inside making a huge lunch you can also partake of if you help. That's assuming you boys like hearty stew."

"We are not strangers to hard work. Fine, we'll work hand in hand with the lot of you." Oleg extended a hand out toward Daniel who took it and shook with a firm hand-shake. He looked over toward the front door to see it open and Ben take a slow step outside while holding a large cooler. "Adams, get over here." He beckoned him over to the group.

"Yes, boss?" He asked, placing the cooler down and approaching them.

"Get these men settled in. They're going to aid us today. You can manage that even injured I assume? Then get back to keeping everyone hydrated."

"I'm feeling better, sir. It's not a problem."

"Good. I need to oversee the defense building. You take over from here."

"Yes, sir," Ben said. He watched Daniel walk off and give orders to the workers. He turned to their Russian allies. "Which job did you gentlemen want?"

"One moment," Oleg pulled out a cell phone and dialed a number. He raised it to his ear and spoke. "I need one hundred men to come to my location. Yes, I'm aware. Get them to the Morris estate, now. I know we're leaving some outposts with minimum personnel. Follow my orders, you ingrate! Yes, everybody bring their own vehicle or carpool. I don't give a fuck, just make it happen." He hung up and jammed the device back in his coat pocket. "Where do you want us?"

"They're working on the front and back yards. We need more people constructing walls on the sides of the place. How you split your group is up to you. You may be asked to help dig depending on how acquisition of the dirt is going. Be prepared for that."

"I think we can take it from here." Oleg looked at the rest of his men. "Let's go get this place ready then."

Ben picked up the cooler, circled around the house inspecting the progress, and handing out water bottles to a great many workers.

"Working hard?" Rachel asked him from the deck as he climbed back up the stairs.

"I'm just getting more water for everybody, boss. They're parched out there."

"Good, don't let me stop you. By the way, we've settled on your job when the attack happens. It should suit you, even if you are still injured. You'll be restocking ammunition for the men and women taking position from the windows. Remember that for tonight and save some energy. You'll be running a lot."

"I understand. I'll be ready.

Rachel smirked, watching Ben head inside and looked back at the manual labor happening under her direction. "I know you will..."

18

"Would you look at that?" Daniel overlooked the bags full of dirt built into walls. Each and every wall had multiple syndicate members behind it, a small box between them full of ammunition. A small wooden platform was built to the side with yet another makeshift wall atop of it for cover, made for shooting over the chain link fence, which had also been covered in barbed wire around the entire compound. "It's nigh impenetrable with the manpower we have."

Rachel spoke up, her voice quiet. "You know what they say about overconfidence, Dad?" Rachel asked at her father's side. "It's a slow and insidious killer. It's a damned sight better than it was, but let's not be arrogant. We still have to weather the storm, and we have no idea the firepower they may have."

"I am aware men and women will die," Daniel said, lowering his voice so only the two of them could hear. "They'll have explosives, no doubt. The fence will only act to slow them down. That's why we have dozens of men and women on each side with high ground to shoot them as they get near.

"Explosives will be the true test. No one in their right mind will try and charge the lines. Do we have a plan for that?"

"For dealing with explosives?" Daniel asked. "What the fuck kind of plan can you make for that beyond killing them before they deploy them? To get to use them without getting close they'd need a mortar or rpg. Otherwise, they'd have to be in the open and toss a grenade - which is exactly what we've set our defenses to stop." He looked back at the men and women behind the defenses. "This battle will decide the tide of the war, princess. If we hold here, we can go on the offensive and establish our dominance. They won't have a choice but to abandon their campaign if we kill enough up here. It won't be financially viable to stay up here."

"Going with the Japanese strategy on the islands in World War 2, huh?"

"They just didn't kill enough. They had the right idea in a war though. It's all about the execution of the plan."

"If there was ever a quote that would fit you, that'd be it, Dad."

"I'm just thorough, princess."

Rachel looked down at her shaking hand and grabbed it with the other, preventing it from shaking.

Daniel looked down and saw the offending hand. He placed a hand on his daughter's shoulder. "This is your first big battle, isn't it? Now don't worry. You're going to be up in my safe room. You know where it is, yes?"

"In your work room?"

"Correct. Do you remember the password to get in?"

"Of course."

"I've set up multiple monitors in there in case you want

to see what's going on. Do not come out of there until I give the say so. Do you understand me? I will not chance losing my only daughter on this. You keep yourself and Roger safe. That's your job."

Rachel took a deep breath, letting go of her hand to find it unmoving. "I'm not nervous."

"Of course not," Daniel smirked and looked back at his people's handiwork. "I was being silly is all." He spotted a group of four men patrolling around. "Hey, the lot of you. Yeah, you." He pointed at the group. "Stop lollygagging and fucking around. People's lives depend on you not joking around. Do you understand me?" he asked, his voice full of steel.

"Sorry, sir," the leader of the group said.

"You had best take this seriously. If you're caught slacking again, you don't want to know what's going to happen. Keep your eyes peeled and your heads on a swivel. I didn't assign four groups of patrol for shits and giggles. Now get to work, you bums."

"Lee and I came up with an early warning plan I think you might be interested in."

"Does it involve him working his computer magic?"

"It kind of does," Rachel said. "It even has a failsafe, but that's not nearly as reliable."

"Out with it."

"They're going to be coming in vans or high-capacity vehicles, right? Well, the plan is, if they're idiots and carry phones we'd be able to see a large volume of cell signals hurdling along the only road leading here."

"Mm," Daniel grunted. "What if they're smart?"

"Then we'd still see the car's computer system. It's less precise, considering it could be anyone driving on the road, but it's an early warning system nonetheless. The only way it wouldn't work is if they walk here or take bicycles. I told him to alert you if he sees anything. You do have your phone on you?"

"I always have it on me."

"He has it setup to send a text to everyone if he sees anything, so everyone will be ready."

Daniel spat down to the grass below them from the front porch. "Have him try to watch not just the road. For all we know they'll hike through the forest to get the jump on us. They're not stupid."

"He's only one man, Dad. He can't watch everywhere, and I'll be in the safe room. If I was with him, I could watch the woods while he watches the road."

"Then get up there and do so. When one of you sees something, you head to the safe room with Roger. You should have enough time before the shit starts."

"Roger that." Rachel turned around and walked to the nearby front door.

Daniel stared out into the now darkening woods around him. "I can feel it. It's happening tonight..."

Out back of the house a little later...

Chris ejected the magazine from the automatic rifle in his grip, inspected it, and reinserted it with a click. "Make sure your weapons are ready, boys. It's getting dark. You don't want to be caught with your pants down." He knelt behind the wall closest to the house, still on the grass.

"Sir, how bad do you think this is going to be?" a young man to his side asked.

"Don't think about that. What you need to be thinking about is doing your job. Focus on killing the people trying to kill you. Keep your damned head down when not shooting, and you're doing all that can be expected."

"That bad, huh?" another man asked from behind a wall not too far away.

"Probably," Chris said.

"Don't be a baby," one black woman in his squad said from down on the grass embankments. "We're trained for this. God knows we get paid enough. The boss knows what he's doing. This is better than getting picked off one by one."

"Listen to the pretty lady," Chris said, smiling toward her. "She's got a good head on her shoulders. What was your name again?"

"It was Jackie, sir."

"Are you familiar with the term, 'The calm before the storm'?"

"Yes, sir."

"That's where we are." He stood up, his voice raised loud enough to be heard by everyone in the backyard. "This will be a bloody battle, no doubt. We are the front line. We will hold, or a great many more men and women will die. Do you hear me? We will not falter! Not under our watch. We have brave men and women watching our flank, and by God, we will do the same for them. We are one unit, and we are unstoppable if we each do our jobs."

A raucous round of cheers followed his little speech.

He raised a hand, quieting the crowd. "Make no mistake, this will be hellish. That is what life is though when you think about it." He looked around at the confused look on their faces. "Without challenges, we would never grow and become better people. Try and use this to your advantage. I guarantee if you survive this, you'll better manage your stress in battle. You never eliminate it, but you push through it. That is true bravery. The fool who lives without fear is not brave - he is stupid. Do you understand me? Take it from a guy who's been in multiple gun fights, you can make it through this if you remain disciplined."

Another wave of incoherent voices answered him. A rumble in his pocket interrupted his impromptu speech. He raised one hand, quieting them again, and then fished the device out of his pocket. He looked at the message with a face of grim determination. He looked up as the others' phones blew up too. "It's starting soon. Remember to keep those at your side alive, and they will do the same for you..."

19

Chris overlooked the back yard as an unsteady silence filled the balmy night air. He stayed low behind cover on the elevated deck. "I don't like this," he said to himself. He peeked around the corner of the bullet shield. The brightly lit up backyard contrasted sharply with the tree line cloaked in darkness. He squinted, trying to will himself to see through the limited light. "Jackie?"

"Yes, sir?"

"Take one of your grenades and chuck it into that tree line.

Jackie didn't verbally respond but did take out one of the explosive devices from her waistline. She armed it by pulling out the pin and threw it over the modified fence and into the tree line.

A thunderous boom exploded in the night, the limited light from the lights outside illuminated enough to see a number of trees falling. A mist of dust came out from the murky treeline.

"Are they here?" a panicked male voice asked from behind him. "Was that them?"

"Negative!" Jackie yelled back.

"I'm not so sure about that," Chris said. He braced his weapon atop the makeshift cover and angled the business end toward the tree line. "Make ready!" His voice was commanding and unwavering.

"For what, sir?" Jackie asked. "There's nobody out there."

Silence took dominion in the night air. Everyone had their weapons at the ready, scanning the dark unknown.

Another deafening explosion made everyone jump. Nothing had changed so far as Chris saw, but the sound came from his left along with a choir of screams erupting into the night air.

"Watch the fence!" A male voice came from the same direction.

Chris felt the earth shake. His abdomen hurt as an ear piercing boom flooded his senses. The fence he had just been staring at was shrouded in smoke and dirt. "Open fire in short bursts. It's more accurate!" he said, squeezing the trigger in short bursts.

The dirt cleared to reveal three bodies dressed in dark clothes laying on the grass beyond a pierced fence. The structure remained whole but the explosion took out a solid few feet. What first only looked like a few moving figures in the shadows quickly multiplied as more bodies poured out of the woodwork.

Incoherent screams accentuated the barrage of gun shots being fired from behind them. Some were commands, others wails of pain and suffering, all intermixing into a perfect battlefield melody. "Keep your god damned heads down." Chris ducked down behind cover and yanked out the magazine before reinserting another from the pouch at his side, then pulled the slide back. He got to his knees and perched his weapon atop the cover, firing more rounds downrange.

Men charged at the estate into their fields of view, firing their weapons all the while. The lion's share of them fell, some continued crawling, leaving a blood red stain on the grass in their wake.

The men and women under his command continued flinging lead toward their targets. He surveyed the situation as he fired, his eyes darting from one target to the next. "Jackie, watch the right side! We have a few hostiles trying to catch us by surprise."

Jackie fell down behind cover and readjusted her position. She fired to the right as more bodies fell outside the fence.

The man to his right fell back with a thud against the sliding glass door. Blood spattered as he rolled down the now marred and chipped glass. "Shit," Chris cursed to himself. He kicked the dead body away before getting to his stomach. He left his rifle behind cover but pulled out his pistol before taking a deep breath. "This is crazy even for my dumbass." He rolled out of cover and immediately unloaded into the waves of assailants before rolling back behind cover after exhausting his pistol. He reloaded and got back to a knee stuffing the sidearm away before picking up the rifle.

Another in the yard fell, this time slumping forward against the cover.

Chris stole the ammunition from the dead man next to him and got back to work. He watched one of the syndicate's men near the fence on his side throw a grenade toward the tree line.

This time the explosion elicited a horrified scream from Jackie as body parts rained down around the syndicate forces.

"Steady!" Chris said. "Do that again!"

Another of the young men near the fence tossed a grenade past a few brave cartel soldiers and into their previous cover.

Another explosion and yet more body parts were airborne. Most of the trees that were hiding their attackers had been knocked down now, leaving the outside of the compound more open.

Another of his men caught a bullet on the field below, immediately going limp before the exiting bullet had even left his head.

"Hold, we have the numbers to hold fast!" Chris continued his onslaught against their attackers. Amidst the cacophony of gunfire, the sound of an engine met his ears.

"Someone get that damned truck!" a voice said from behind him.

"Everyone get down!" The engine sound was quickly moving to his right. He gripped one of his own grenades, pulled the pin, and tossed it toward where the sound was soon to be from his own calculations. Success! Right before the colossal explosion a truck ran over the tiny device.

Following the explosion a tire rushed above his head, past his battlement, and into the woods on the opposite side. The main frame of the truck tumbled out of control past the fence, eventually rolling over several Cartel members before coming to a stop. A young man was trapped under the hunk of now useless metal. He clawed at the weight pushing down on his body before a stray bullet pierced his skull, mercifully ending his life.

The earth shook below them. More yells followed by the one phrase no one wanted to hear that night. "Take them down! They're getting too close."

"Fucking shit," Chris cussed to himself. "Jackie, take command here. I need to fix this shit. I can't let them flank us."

"Yes, sir." She yelled at nearby men to snap out of it.

Chris took a deep breath and waited until he saw most of their attackers dead in his field of view before taking off into a sprint around the corner of the brick mansion and dove behind the nearest L shaped man-made cover spot they had created earlier in the day.

He found a dead man already laying beside him and got up. He peeked around the side and laid down as much fire as his fully automatic rifle could muster toward the large group of young men charging at them. He could hear bullets rush by his head with a dull woosh near his ears before pulling his head back. "This is way more than a couple hundred, boss. Try a fucking thousand to be more precise." He took his remaining grenade and tossed it without looking behind him. His efforts were rewarded with nothing but the death of his enemies and the raining of body parts better left to the imagination.

"Use your explosives for God's sake, you morons. It's what we gave them to you for!" He spotted two men huddling behind their cover, not even attempting to fire. "Shoot, God dammit!" They did not follow his orders, instead still crying and trying to sink into the ground. "Get in the damned house, you cowards. It's right there." He pointed toward the door, a good dozen feet away from their position.

The men needed no further coaxing. They got up from their position and made a mad dash for the door, or what was left of it.

While they did so, Chris got up and fired. The sounds of

bodies to his side indicated the young men had died. While they did so however, he had a clear shot at their murderers. He eradicated them from this plane of existence before taking cover again and reloading. "I found a use for you boys yet," he laughed to himself. He saw Lauren atop the nearby patio. "Are you good here now, ma'am?"

"As can be," Lauren said.

Without needing instruction, he dashed back to his original position. "Hey, old buddy." He kicked the body leaning against the punctured, nearly shattered glass door. "Bad day?" He fired a few blind shots around the cover as more cries into the night echoed all around him. "Yeah, me too."

"We're holding, sir!" Jackie's voice made it to his ears.

"So I see."

At the same time inside of the house...

Ben placed four fully loaded magazines near the table by the window. The man beside the opening was firing out into the blood-soaked battlefield. His weapon clicked, and he got out of the line of fire. He grabbed one of the magazines and reloaded. "You saved my ass, man."

Ben didn't respond verbally, choosing instead to dash out of the door into the hallway. The nonstop cracks of gunshots accentuated his running toward his next destination. He ducked into another doorway.

"It's about time you got here." A woman holstered her pistol, grabbing the magazines out of his hand and picking up the rifle leaning against the wall beside the window before reloading it. "I've been out for ages."

"I'm going as fast as I can, ma'am. Speaking of which, I need to keep the rounds going." He left the room in a hurry. Once he was out of the room, he tried to catch his breath.

"This never ends." He checked the contents of his pouch to only find a solitary ammunition magazine left in it. "Fuck. Time to resupply.

He took off into a sprint and descended the nearby stairs as fast as he could. He kept low to the ground as he moved, eventually entering the room Daniel dubbed the armory. He loaded as many resupplies of ammo as he could in the pouch before beginning another go around.

He dropped another bundle in the nearby room before his phone rumbled in his pocket. He took it out as he ran. Once he'd delivered that bundle, he looked down at the message. "Go to his room, now." He continued up his usual route and dashed up the stairs. He tossed magazines into various doors as they passed with a quick apology. Once he'd reached the familiar double doors his pouch was again empty. He patted the back of his belt line, ensuring his side arm was still there before pulling it out.

He swung open the door to find a pistol leveled his way along with a sigh and a shake of the head from Daniel. "What the hell are you doing here? Oh, it doesn't matter. Come over here." Daniel pointed at the small monitor on his desk. "Do you see that?" He pointed at the scene of carnage unfolding outside. "I need you to go and resupply the north side of the manor. The ammo guy on that side bit the big one." Daniel looked up at Ben. "Do you think you can manage that?"

Ben nodded, not saying a word.

"Good. Get going then, and keep your damned head down. We can't afford to lose any more couriers. Get one of the lazy bastards downstairs to replace him while you're there. Use my name if you must." Daniel returned his gaze to the monitors

"I'm on it, boss," Ben said, his voice calm. He stepped

back five or six feet. His right hand raised, aiming the weapon squarely at Daniel's head. Without hesitation he fired.

Daniel's body fell back into the swiveling chair, a newly minted hole in the side of his head.

Ben put the murder weapon away before dashing out of the room as quickly as he could. He'd turned a corner when he saw another man running toward him.

"What was that noise?"

"I don't know," Ben said, gesturing toward the pouch hanging at his side. "Out of the way. I need to get more ammo to pass out." Ben pushed past him and sprinted toward the direction of the armory on the first floor...

In Daniel's room just after...

The paneled wall slid to the side along with the almost imperceptible whir of a motor. A door appeared from behind. A beep came before the door opened to reveal Rachel. She looked back at the playpen in the corner of the room. "Mama put your bottle in there with you, sweetie. You'll be fine. Mommy will be right back." She closed the door again and pushed in a sequence of keys on the keypad to the side of the doorway. She took a step back as the wall shifted back into position, obscuring the door once again. She saw the recent corpse of her father slumped in the chair.

"Good shot," she mumbled to herself. She pushed the chair away. The sound of glass cracking underneath them from the shards of the once pristine glass windows behind the desk was the only noise aside from the constant unre-lenting sound of gunfire, screams, and the occasional explosion. She bent over and pulled the laptop on the desk closer to her. She clicked, changing the camera to another angle, and then to the next. "They're leaving?" She couldn't hide an involuntary smile. "They're retreating." She took use of the app her Father was using and sent another message. "Backyard, move toward the front side once you've cleaned up." She hit enter before changing the recipient list and changing it to all syndicate members. "The enemy is retreating," she typed. "Stay safe, do not be heroes. Allow them to disengage, but defend yourselves if necessary." She hit enter and got back around the desk and kneeled behind it.

The gunfire that she had once swore would never leave her head suddenly became sparse. More tortured wails could be made out over the sound of unrelenting death that had previously been raining down all around them. "Now for the hardest part of this whole scheme." Rachel looked over at the dead body of her father.

Before she even had a chance to think of much else, she found tears escaping her eyes. Her throat seized up and a wheezing yelp left her. She forced herself to her feet and threw open the door. She closed it behind her. She found a group of two young men awaiting her on the other side. Not even allowing them to speak, she did so first. "My father is in that room. Once we're sure the enemy's gone, I am taking over duties."

"Ma'am?"

"He caught a bullet, you fucking simpleton," Rage filled her voice as tears trickled down her face. "I am in charge of this syndicate now. Do you have a fucking problem with that?"

"No, ma'am," the young man said, looking away.

"Good. Clean up the body for now," Rachel said. "Once

the rest of the cartel retreats, we'll clean up the rest of the dead. Since you two boys are free, then you can start on that after moving my father's body. Gather the cartel bodies and go create a mass grave in the woods behind the place. Dig a big hole, cover it in gas, and do a mass cremation. I want the syndicates' graves far away from the cartels. Is that understood?"

"We just came here to..." The same young man's voice stopped, seeing the look on his new boss's face.

"To what, pray tell?" Rachel asked, planting her hands on her hips. "To tell the old man the enemy's retreating?"

"It was what Mr. Davis said to do."

"Fine. You have your new job. Now hop to it and recruit as many to your cause. I want this settled before anyone beds down. If you see Mr. Adams, send him to my room at once. Him, Mr. Davis, and Elizabeth Morris. Make it happen." Without further words, she pushed past the two men and made her way downstairs. She saw Lauren dragging an injured man in through the nearest back door.

Rachel called out. "I'm glad to see you made it through alright." She looked down at the injured men lining the room. "I'm sad to say too many died at the hands of my father's plans. Go and get Roger. He's in my father's safe room. You know how to enter it, yes?"

"Of course. Your father taught me how to open it just in case."

"I need to go and let everyone know the dire news." Rachel stepped outside to see the lion's share of men and women. She raised her arms and raised her voice. "You have done a good job tonight. I only wish my father could be here to share this victory with us."

Warren pushed his way through the crowd of men and

women gathering near the wooden porch below. "What does that mean?"

Elizabeth stepped out the door behind Rachel. "Yes, dear niece. What does that mean exactly?"

Her voice lost any shakiness and escalated into a yell. "I am now leader of this syndicate!" She took a deep breath and lowered her voice to a sterner, calmer tone. "My father died during the battle. I came out of the safe room to see him slumped in his chair. From the angle, as best as I could tell, a bullet came through one of the nearby windows and clipped him in the head. He went down directing his men like a true leader."

"Son of a bitch," Warren said.

"Now, we need to focus on moving forward, and I know exactly how we're going to do that."

"It better be good, sweetheart," Elizabeth said, leaning against the damaged guardrail.

"Quiet," Rachel said in a lower voice. "Now, I am going to do what my father never could." She paused a few moments. "I'm going to barter a peace."

"Do you actually think you know the type better than him or even I?" Elizabeth asked.

"I think I am a far better negotiator than my father. Now be quiet."

"You couldn't be much worse to be fair," Elizabeth said.

"I want to see you two." She pointed to Elizabeth and then to Warren. "Inside, now. As for the rest of you, you're on cleanup detail. We can't leave our brothers and sisters laying out to rot. I want a decent burial for each and every one of ours. As for the cartel, dig a mass grave and burn them. They deserve nothing better. Nobody beds down until the bodies are taken care of. I will not have the rest of us die to some disease from dead bodies. Is that understood?"

"Yes, ma'am," the crowd of syndicate members bellowed in unison.

Rachel turned and stepped back into the house. She waited until both Elizabeth and Warren were behind her. "Come on then. We need privacy for this." She looked over at Lauren. "Have you seen Adams recently?"

"Last I saw him, he was frantically running around handing out ammo. He's probably around here somewhere," Lauren said.

Rachel led the trio up the stairs back to the scene of her father's death. She stopped halfway into the room and walked over to the side of the room with the safe room. She reached up to the bookshelf and picked up a knickknack.

"That is a lot of blood," Warren looked over at the window and down at the stain on the carpet. "Yeah, it was definitely a gunshot. Judging by the glass on the ground, you're right."

"Of course I'm right," Rachel said placing the decorative bookend back on the shelf. "That's not why I brought you two in here. We need to make sure this transition of power goes smoothly. Aunt..."

"Yeah?" Elizabeth asked.

"I can't have you second guessing me in public in front of the men like that. I know you and Dad had a beef about your duties. I waive you of the cleaning duty."

"That's a good start."

"Warren, I have your support. Yes?"

"You're the daughter of the man, so yes. I know you can handle this shit. I'll follow you the same as your father."

Rachel moved to behind the desk. "Good. Now I need a second in command. No offense, Davis, but I need you as my head of security, so no promotion for now."

"Who are you picking?" Elizabeth asked. "Your new boy toy - Adams, was it?"

"No," Rachel said. "He will be my personal bodyguard. If anything, my father's death has taught me the value of one. You, Auntie, will fill that role."

"Me?" Elizabeth asked. "I'm not even in the syndicate."

"You ran the Morris family. You'll do fine. I know for a fact you've killed and can keep secrets. I just need you to back me up and advise me as you see fit. Dad promised you we'd get your kid back. Assuming I can get this peace deal, I'll do the same."

The meeting was interrupted when Ben entered the room. "I'm sorry I'm late." Ben closed the door behind him and stepped forward toward Elizabeth and Warren.

"As I was saying," Rachel continued, unabated. "Meet my new bodyguard from now on. Mr. Adams, you are alright with this, yes?"

"Of course, boss," Ben bowed. "I'll do everything in my power to keep you from harm."

Warren raised a hand before he spoke up. "With all due respect, boss, how are you planning on making peace with those people? They're not exactly civilized."

"Civilized?" Rachel asked. "Maybe not. Are they good at making money though? My answer to that is yes. If they decide to keep this war going, we will break out the big guns."

"Meaning?" Elizabeth asked, tilting her head.

"We go after their bank accounts. Every organized crime organization has money. Most of them want to use that money for something legitimate afterward. At some point in the line, there's a real account involved. We have a dedicated tech specialist. They would guess that already since Dad's family always had one. It came out in the court case, remember?"

"Of course I remember," Elizabeth covered her face with a hand. "That damned digital evidence kept me up for countless sleepless nights in the pen."

"Therefore, it wouldn't be a hard sell to convince them that we can go after their digital livelihood. Guns, bullets, and manpower is their strong point. Dad went about it all wrong. We need to be smarter."

"That might work," Warren said. "They got what they wanted - your father's death."

"They save face," Elizabeth said. "After proving their point, they don't want to keep the heat rising. It's smart."

"Davis, send Lee in here. I have a job for him. Now go," she pointed behind him at the door.

"Right away, Boss." He nodded and turned to leave the room.

Once the three were left, Rachel cleared her throat. "As for the last term of our arrangement..." Rachel moved around the table. She angled Ben to look at Elizabeth and flashed an impish smile, wrapping her arm around his side. "You keep your hands off what's mine, and we'll get along great, Auntie. Is that understood?"

Elizabeth looked down at the arm cradling Ben and up to Rachel's eyes. "I get it. It was fun though. Right, stud?"

"None of that either."

"You need to lighten up, dearest niece. This job will give you a heart attack if you let it. Take it from me." She took a few steps back, approaching the door. "If you get my Bernard back, we're good. For now, you focus on sweet talking our soon to be friendly acquaintances." She took her leave and left Rachel and Ben alone.

"Was that really necessary?" Ben asked.

"I'll not have her harassing you. I thought you'd be thankful."

"I am. I just hope she's not a petty person is all," Ben said, looking over at the recently shut door. "I've only heard stories about her. Not many of them were flattering."

"She's a piece of work." Rachel placed her hands on either side of Ben's face and gently redirected his attention back to her. Her voice fell to a whisper. "You did great today. Dad was planning on killing you. You know that."

"I had my suspicions."

"He was not blind. He knew we were still seeing each other. It's why it had to be done when it was. It was the perfect cover." She pulled him in for a kiss. Her voice was breathy. "Best of all, it looked like a natural gunshot wound." She gestured toward the shattered glass on the floor and carpet. Her voice went back to its usual tone and volume. "You will always be at my side, Mr. Bodyguard. Is that understood?"

"Always?"

"I meant what I said." She accentuated her statement by slapping his behind. "Now follow me. That is an order." She grabbed his hand and led him toward the door. "If anyone asks, we're doing research on the cartel leadership."

"What about Lee?"

As if on cue, Lee opened the door.

Rachel let loose Ben's hand and glared at her tech specialist.

"Yes, Ms. Morris?" Lee asked, barely getting inside the door before Rachel pushed him further out into the hall.

"Come with me, the both of you." She walked down the hallway, occasionally the crunching of glass underfoot from the nearby windows and occasional faint chatter from outside made it to their ears. She stopped in front of a particularly wide window on the second floor. "Do you see that outside, Lee?"

Lee looked down on the site of dozens of men and women moving bodies in assorted pickup trucks. "Yes?"

"We will not have this happen again. You are key in this. I need you to find me a bank account linked with the cartel."

"Oh, is that all?" Lee asked, sarcasm apparent in his voice. "Shall I send you to the castle in a pumpkin too?"

"What about cryptocurrency? Lots of these outfits south of the border sell drugs on the darknet. The crypto chain can be traced, yes?"

"Yes," Lee looked ahead blankly. "It certainly can. Come to think of it, that guy Bert was buying some crypto last month. I could trace where that went and get that address."

Ben spoke up from the middle of the group. "Does that help though? They'd have their wallet locked down and encrypted."

"That is true, but we don't need to drain the money ourselves." A devious grin appeared on Rachel's features. "Do it, Lee. This will be the bargaining chip we need to broker a peace deal. Mark my words."

"I'm on it right away, boss. The sooner this shit is behind us and we can just earn, I'll be happy," Lee said.

"Then don't let us stop you. Get a move on," she shouted toward Lee as he jogged off. "The sooner you get it done, the sooner you get an assistant. Remember that."

"He seemed excited," Ben said. "He must really want someone to boss around."

"Now before we were so rudely interrupted..." She grabbed his hand and dragged him in the direction of her room. "Lauren's got Roger all taken care of. We deserve a rest after all this crap."

Ben allowed himself to be dragged around a corner. "God knows I could use one after today," he said.

"I need one before I enter the virtual lion's pit of those negotiations. I expect you to help me relax, Mr. Adams. Then maybe once things calm down, maybe even invite little old me over for a dinner with your parents. They were so sweet." She led them to a now familiar hallway. She quickened their pace toward her door and threw it open, pulling him inside. She slammed the door shut behind him.

She pressed a hand on the door beside his head, effectively pinning him to the door. "Tell me how it went down." She lowered her arm, tugging at his coat. She led him over to the bed and sat down.

Ben sat beside her and looked at the floor. "He damn near shot me when I entered the room. He told me to get over there. I waited until he looked at his monitor, then aimed..." He made a gun shape with his right hand before firing. "It was over just like that. I immediately left and continued my ammo runs."

"You must be exhausted," Rachel said. "I can still see bruises from your accident." She helped him out of his formal coat and threw the garment on her floor before doing the same for herself.

"The pain is manageable. It's not that bad," Ben said, taking off his shoes. "I did run into a guy after the whole thing went down. I was well out of the room by this point. He asked me if I heard a gunshot from the boss's room."

Rachel threw her shoes under her bed. "There is no damned way a guy could differentiate one gunshot from the hundreds going out.

"I dismissed him, showed my empty pouch, and pushed past him."

"That was the perfect play." Rachel leaned her head onto

his neck and scooted closer. "Everything's gone to plan. I'd rather we'd not been attacked, but we work with what we get."

"I heard one of the girls who was tending to the wounded say the body count for us was close to forty tonight.

"What about the enemy?" Rachel asked, angling her head to look up at Ben. "It looked like over a hundred."

"She was more concerned with keeping us alive. I don't have that number. Sorry. Regardless, their permanent resting place will be in the forest behind us. We're seeing to that. The rank and file will be drained for days. We'll need to schedule some rest time soon, or they'll be running ragged."

"Exhaustion will be the least of their worries. Besides, leave that to me." She grabbed him by the shoulders and pushed him onto his back. She crawled over top of him and stared down into his eyes. "I need comfort. You will give it to me. It's your first job as bodyguard. Hop to it." She lowered herself on top of him and laid her head on his chest.

He wrapped one arm around her, resting it on her back while the other found it's way to the back of her head and patted. He could feel a wetness seeping into his shirt and squeezed harder.

A high pitched, muffled noise escaped his chest as it escalated in volume.

Ben moved the hand from her head to wrap around her back, totally enveloping her in a hug. They remained like this for untold minutes - one comforting, the other being soothed. Eventually the crying stopped, being replaced by silence.

Ben looked down at his boss as soft snores replaced the muffled wailing. He relaxed his neck onto the pillows and looked up at the ceiling. "It's over and done." His voice was barely audible to even himself. He rubbed her back, "Maybe one day I'll forgive myself. He was going to kill me though. That's self-defense."

Rachel wiggled in his embrace.

His voice turned soothing. "Shh, relax. I've got you."

His boss stopped fussing.

"Sorry, boss…"

20

"I can't believe they have us doing this shit," Chris hopped out of the truck and down to the grass below. He looked up at the moon above him and then at the group of men and women around him.

"Stop whining, you big baby," Jackie said. "We can't have bodies all around the place."

"At least we could be digging graves for our own men." Chris reached into the back seat and grabbed shovel after shovel, tossing them to various people. "We get stuck burying the same bastards that tried to kill us not even an hour ago. It just pisses me off is all." He handed out the last digging implement and grabbed the one he'd set aside for himself. "We're going to be digging all night." He pointed toward a relatively small clearing nearby off the dirt trail. There's as good a place as any. It's big enough to dump that many bodies."

He and the five helpers all started digging.

Chris looked over at Jackie. "At least there's some eye candy with this work anyway."

"You are a hopeless flirt. Did anyone ever tell you that?"

Jackie brushed a strand of hair behind her ear and kept digging. "Does that approach ever work? It's so old fashioned."

"Old fashioned?" Chris hefted a load full of dirt over his shoulder, the grey patches in his beard barely visible in the dim light. "What other way is there? You express interest and see if they reciprocate. It seems like common sense to me."

"It's like I'm talking to my dad," Jackie said.

"Do I look that old?"

"My dad's in his forties. How old are you again?"

Chris didn't immediately answer.

"I didn't hear an answer."

The dirt behind him was growing larger all the while. "I'm in my forties."

"I knew it. You need to be more subtle for some women. The only kind of girls you'll get like that are the ones with low self-esteem." Jackie looked over her shoulder at another truck arriving with yet more people filing out. Its truck bed was filled to the brim with dead bodies, the same as theirs. The smell of death, fetid decay, and human waste was overpowering.

"Are you supposed to be a dating guru, Miss Jackie?"

"It's Jackie Thomas."

"It's a beautiful name." Chris flashed her a daring smile.

"You need to learn time and place. It's far less effective when we're both digging ditches."

Chris saw their reinforcements finally get equipped and join in on the work. He moved closer to Jackie amidst the rapidly growing mass of manpower. "I don't know if you noticed, Ms. Thomas, but life can be quite short in this line of work. Living in the moment is paramount if you ask me."

"That is a fair point. Maybe I'm just old fashioned."

"I like an old-fashioned girl."

"I'd be careful if I were you," Jackie said. "A little birdie told me you were seen flirting with the now number two of the organization. Do you think she'd want you flirting with others after her? The stories say she's quite vicious."

"I find that sexy," Chris said. "There's nothing better than a woman who knows what she wants and gets it."

"You really are hopeless. She's a man eater."

"You're cute when you're jealous."

Another truck pulled up. With this one the back compartment was loaded to the brim with dead bodies too. Warren exited and slammed the door shut. "How much longer until the hole's ready?"

Chris looked over his shoulder. "We just started, Mr. Davis. We're making good progress, but with this many people..." Chris looked up at the stars for a moment. "I'd guess an hour or two and we'll be ready."

"Then let's not waste time." Warren grabbed a nearby shovel laying in the grass and got to work alongside everyone else. "There will be another truck getting up here momentarily. We'll have them buried before sunrise if I have anything to say about it."

"What about our own dead, sir?" Jackie asked, still working.

"They're at another site getting a proper burial, one to a hole. We take care of our own. Mr. Bristol, I heard you led with heroism tonight."

"I just did what experience taught me to do - to try and keep as many of my men and women alive as I could."

"Bullshit," Jackie said with a laugh. "You saved another group's ass when it was going to shit, and then came back to do the same for us again. It was quite the spectacle, sir. I'm sorry you missed it."

"Spectacle she says." Chris shook his head as he jammed the shovel head into the soil below. "My bravery was done out of desperation. I couldn't let us get flanked through no fault of our own. Besides, I heard more than my fair share of bullets whizzing by my ear. I honestly thought I was going to die. Just like in every other damned firefight I've ever been in."

"It never goes away," Warren said.

"Aren't you two just bastions of joy. We won. Shouldn't we be happier?" Jackie asked.

"I am optimistic the new boss will end the war," Warren said. "I don't think I can ever be happy when I'm digging a mass grave though, Miss Thomas."

"Well shit," Jackie said. "When you put it that way..." She trailed off.

The group of manpower dug for the next half an hour in relative silence, finishing ahead of schedule.

"Now comes the fun part," Warren said. "Thomas, get in that truck. Chris, you are with me. We're getting in the back."

"I don't want to get in there with all the dead bodies." His complaint died on his lips as Warren shot him a pointed glare. "Fine, I get it." He climbed into the bed of the truck.

Warren grabbed hold of the sides and looked through the open window as Jackie climbed into the driver's seat. "Now back us up until I say stop. Go very slow."

"I understand, sir."

Chris braced himself, trying not to touch the numerous dead bodies underneath him. He grabbed hold of what he could to steady himself as the truck started backing up toward the large hole they'd just dug.

"Slow," Warren said. "Go slow."

The truck approached the soon to be grave.

"Stop now," Warren said.

The truck stopped its backing up just shy of the hole.

"Good job." Warren stood up as Jackie put it in park and engaged the parking brake. "Let's get this shit going smooth. Bristol and I will knock the bodies down. The rest of you move them as they fall. We don't want them all stacked below us. It'll be slower now but quicker later. Does everybody understand?"

The crowd of men and women below them made it clear they understood verbally.

Without warning, Chris kicked a dead body into the hole. "Move that shit over there," he pointed toward the other end of the mass grave.

The group eventually settled into a routine of dropping a body down, two people below would move it over to another spot before another would fall. A half an hour later the back of the truck was empty. Chris and Warren hopped over the side of the truck and back down to earth. "Ms. Thomas, move this truck out of the way. You," Warren pointed toward another young man. "You get that truck," He pointed toward the other truck that showed up while they worked, it's back full of dead bodies like the first. "You bring that one over here where this one is."

"Yes, sir," the young man said, making a run toward the vehicle.

Warren watched the manpower follow his orders. This time he stayed outside and directed traffic from the grass. He guided the new truck to where the old one sat and halted it. "You're good there."

The truck stopped its reverse movement and came to a halt. He directed two new people to get up and dump the bodies out as he oversaw the process. The process was repeated two more times with the third and fourth trucks.

Once all the bodies were spread out relatively evenly across the whole grave the group looked out over their work.

"Good God, how many are in there do you think?" Jackie asked.

"Did anybody count?" Chris asked. "Because I didn't."

They had to double stack the bodies to make them fit, but the hole was sufficiently deep that it didn't really matter.

"Now before we fill this shit in, we have one more thing on the agenda. For those with a weak stomach, you have leave to take off. You're not going to want to stick around. Those with a strong stomach, feel free to stay. You'd better come back if you leave to help fill in the hole. Bristol, help me get the gas tanks out and douse the bodies."

"Right away," Chris followed Warren over to the truck he came in on.

Warren opened the back seat and handed two red gas canisters over to Chris before getting two more for himself. He slammed the door shut and walked over to the hole. He saw most of the manpower scrambling to leave back to the villa. "I don't blame them. They've put in a whole night's work and more." Warren yawned, his hands still full.

"Why are we burning them boss? With all due respect, if we're burying them six feet under, isn't that redundant?" Jackie asked.

"Possibly, but we're in the business of being overly cautious. Burning the bodies destroys any evidence that could be found if they're ever dug up."

"That makes sense." She watched the men circle around the hole in opposite directions, splashing gasoline on the dead carcasses below all the while. "Do you both believe this war will really end soon?"

"I'm not sure," Chris said.

"I'm one hundred percent sure," Warren said, tossing

away one gas canister and using the other. "The boss has a foolproof plan."

"Do you think she has the balls to make it happen though?" Chris asked. "It takes a special kind of person to stand up to an organized crime cartel and make demands. She strikes me as strong and all, but nothing like her father."

"Watch your fucking mouth," Warren pointed to Chris with his now free hand before continuing. "I've seen her work. I've seen what she can do. They cut her finger off, and she never even let them know it hurt. That's the kind of boss she is. Do not underestimate her, Bristol. Her fighting skills are not to be underestimated either. I saw her kill a traitor with her own hands using a knife after he pinned her down. You do not want to mess with her."

"Have you told her about your crush yet?" Chris asked, a grin plastered on his face until he looked over at the angry look on Warren's face. "Sorry, I'm just the new guy. I'll take your word on it."

"You're damned right you will. Don't let me catch you disrespecting the boss again. We need to band together during a transition of power, not undermine and make jokes."

Chris chucked the second gasoline container to the side. "My side's done."

"As is mine," Warren tossed his aside as well. "Everybody take a few steps back and cover your noses. This will be bad." He reached into his back pocket and took out a box of matches. He took one out and struck it against the side of the box, igniting the small stick. He tossed the match into the pile of bodies.

A few moments later the fire spread across the hole, engulfing body after body into the hellish blaze. Within a minute the entire hole was covered in fire with smoke rising into the night sky.

The three remaining members all covered their noses and mouths.

"Oh God almighty," Jackie said.

"I'll never get used to that stench," Chris said. "I thought burning bodies from bombings were bad, but this takes the cake."

"I'm going to signal those guys to get back here," Warren used one hand to dig out his phone and start texting. "We're not going to fill all this shit in by ourselves by morning. By the time they get here the burning will be nearly done."

"Really?" Jackie asked. "I'd have thought it'd be a while."

"I don't want them falling asleep. They'll be fine with their windows up if they have a weak stomach. This will be done before morning. I don't care if they're grumpy. We're all making sacrifices right now. This is hopefully a one and done kind of thing."

"If you're right, Mr. Davis, it will be." Chris gazed into the burning flames dancing atop the dead bodies. He did not avert his gaze as he spoke. "Let us pray you are right..."

21

"Report," Rachel said, staring across the desk at Lee, Warren, Elizabeth, and Chris. Ben stood at her chair's side, his hands behind his back. He held a stoic expression.

Lee took a step forward. "I found a cryptocurrency address they've used for drug deals in the past. Once I caught wind of that, I did some more investigative work and found where they got their startup capital."

"Explain."

"To get started on a lot of these darknet sites, you need to verify yourself with a small fee of cryptocurrency to prove you're serious. It turns out, they used one of their member's bank account to buy a little bit and didn't mix it properly. Meaning, they didn't cover their tracks. With this revelation I found some very interesting info." He laid down the manila envelope on her desk. "I'm sure you can leverage what's in there to our advantage, Ms. Morris."

Rachel flipped open the envelope and started reading. "Good job, Mr. Lee. Mr. Davis, you're up next. Report," she said still looking down at the new intel.

"The dead bodies of the cartel are disposed of in a mass grave deep into the forest behind this mansion. We burned them and then filled the hole in over top of them. As far as our casualties, they received a proper burial at a separate location. What shall we do with the defenses we constructed?"

"Nothing right now. If I do my job right, then we can demolish them. Not a moment before. Am I clear?"

"Crystal clear, ma'am."

"Aunt Elizabeth, do you have any advice for my upcoming negotiations?" Rachel looked up at Elizabeth.

"You're asking for my advice?"

"You are the one who has the most experience here running a syndicate. I thought you may have wisdom when it comes to negotiating. Am I wrong?"

Elizabeth shifted her weight. "If it was me, I'd portray strength. If they sense weakness, they'll pounce on it. I'd leverage that financial information you have there and make it be known it's in their best interest to end this war. If you call and beg for peace, it'll only elongate this war. If you threaten their pocketbook, they'll want it to end as badly as you do. Does that make sense?"

"I agree with Ms. Morris," Warren said.

"We're in agreement then," Rachel said. "I see you found a phone number here," she placed her prosthetic finger on the series of numbers. She looked up at Lee. "Who's is this? It doesn't say here."

"The guy who bought the crypto for the initial investment had that number on his phone. It was the only number. My bet is it's for a supervisor to let them know the business is up and running. I'd use that if you want to reach the shot callers," Lee said.

"It could just be his favorite fast food place," Chris said, snickering.

Rachel leveled a glare in his direction, shutting him up before looking back at Lee. "You couldn't run a check on this?"

"I did, and if you look below it," Lee pointed at the paper. "I traced it back to a rich neighborhood in Mexico. Which is what led me to believe it was a shot caller's place. It's the best we're getting, ma'am. I was up all night getting that intel and validating it."

"Go and get some much deserved sleep then. You've done well, Lee. You're dismissed." She flashed a momentary smile at him.

Lee thanked her and exited the room in a hurry.

"Now for the fun part." Rachel picked up the landline her father had been using just the previous night. She took a deep breath before immediately dialing the numbers on the page in front of her.

A gruff male voice answered in Spanish.

"Put your boss on the line, now," Rachel said. "Spare me the ignorant act and save us both the time. I know you're affiliated with the Crag cartel."

"Who the hell do you think you are?" the voice answered in nigh perfect English, obviously tinted in a Spanish accent.

"I am the boss of the syndicate you are at war with. Connect me with your boss now. I have important news he will want to hear. You wouldn't want to be the one responsible for him remaining in the dark, would you?"

"One minute," the voice said before the line went quiet.

A new voice belonging to a seemingly older gentleman picked up. "Is this the syndicate leader?"

"The new one, yes."

"Have you called to surrender?"

"Not quite. See, this can go one of two ways." Rachel tapped her finger on the paper below. "One, we keep this nonsensical war going and we eviscerate each other until we're both poor and possibly in prison. The other is we work this out like adults and make some money."

"What about the third option?" the suave older male voice asked. "The one where we obliterate your so-called syndicate and take over your city."

"You could try that," Rachel said. "I wouldn't, considering what we have on you; but it's certainly an option."

"What does that mean?" the voice asked, obviously annoyed.

"It means, señor Jefe, that I know where your money comes in. I know where it goes. I know who's running your little darkweb operations. I know who goes to pick up the money. I know, because of recent political shifts, that the US special forces are now allowed to operate in your fucking country. I can only imagine what they could do if this intel anonymously found itself in their hands. Do you understand me? Or no habla ingles?"

"You fucking cunt," the voice on the other end growled.

"Look, you all proved your point to your rank and file. Your little blood feud with my father is over. You won - he's dead. You get to go back to business as usual and claim a win. We both get to stop burying our dead. So? What do you say? You want this shit to continue? Or do we both want to be adults and do business while staying out of each other's way?"

"You don't have any of what you claim. Do you think I was born yesterday, little girl? Who's to say that old fool's dead anyhow?"

"You're calling me a liar now?" Rachel laughed loud

enough to be heard. "Let me see here. I'll make sure Manuel down in Celaya down there knows he's going to have a very loud visit from some soldiers soon. I'm sure your lieutenant Pedro will be disappointed that his crypto investment will lead to some prison time. I'm also sure your home in Acapulco will be destroyed by some very loud flashbangs soon. I can rattle off the specific addresses if you still think I'm lying." Her voice turned sugary sweet. "Do we have an understanding, Jefe?"

Very loud Spanish could be heard over the line. Rachel could have sworn she could make out some of the words, namely the few Spanish curse words she'd learned in high school. The ranting and raving went on for quite some time before the line went quiet. A calmer voice was heard conversing in their native tongue before he spoke English again. "I have your word he's dead then?"

"I saw his body myself," Rachel said. "You all achieved your promise. You took him out. Tell your men that if you must. Now you all can continue your drug game in Toledo. I don't give a flying fuck about that business. All I ask is you stop selling guns. We'd even give you a discount as a show of good faith if you needed such supplies."

"You have a deal. Now if you'll excuse me, I have some plans I need to rewrite and manpower to reassign."

"Just remember what I said. No guns, stay out of our way, don't go after us, and we'll all make money. I bid you good day." She hung up the phone and looked at the eager faces looking at her.

"The war's over. See how hard that was? Why didn't Dad ever do that?"

"Good work, kid," Elizabeth smirked.

"Fantastic job, boss," Warren said pumping his fist in the air.

"Which reminds me," Rachel said, pointing at Warren. "I need you to put together a team of sorts. Pick your best and brightest."

"I definitely know I want this guy," Warren jabbed a thumb in Chris's direction.

"I have a suggestion, sir," Chris spoke up. "There's a woman under my command that proved herself last night. She goes by the name of Jackie. I think you should consider her. She can handle herself. I can attest to that."

"Do you know that from personal experience?" Elizabeth asked.

"Oh, don't be jealous. It wasn't that kind of fun experience," Chris said.

"I'll check her out today. How many people are to be on this team?"

Rachel closed the intel file on the desk and pushed it away from her, leaning back in her chair. "Large enough that you can perform bigger jobs. At least three, preferably four or five. I leave that to you."

"I have a few ideas."

"You are all dismissed. Make sure business goes back to normal. We have another scheduled buy this week. I'll set up getting another property to build the guns. It'll take a few months, but for the time being, we can do it here."

"It's risky doing it all here," Elizabeth said. "One cop follows a member here, and we're made."

"Do you have a better idea? Our warehouse is gone. The police know of its location. Thankfully father didn't have anything incriminating there, but the location is dead."

"Anything but here would be better. Hell, buy a random house and it'd be better."

"I'll take that under advisement," Rachel said. "Moving forward, we need to get back to a normal routine. I've already set up our next shipment. Let's put all this foolish-ness behind us and get back to making money again. You are all dismissed."

Once everyone left, Ben looked down to his side at Rachel. "It's kind of hard to believe it's over just like that from one phone call."

"It's surreal, isn't it?" Rachel asked. She leaned back in the chair causing it to squeak as it reclined back under her lithe frame. "It's amazing what a simple conversation can accomplish when both sides don't resort to force to impose their will. Father was too old school for this new era. To get ahead now leaders must be tech savvy, quick witted, and vicious. I aim to do precisely that and keep us out of the fire."

"My mother and father always did say everything happened for a reason."

"Do you still believe that?" She looked up at him.

"I have to, or I'd go insane. As far as I'm concerned, this was all destined to happen."

"It's always been my opinion that it's foolish to ponder such cosmic ideas," Rachel said. "It never leads anywhere substantial. It's better to focus on the here and now. You'd do well to remember that."

"Yes, boss," Ben said.

22

"M s. Thomas, was it?" Warren asked as he and Chris sat down across from her in the living room.

"Yes sir, Mr. Davis?" Jackie asked.

Warren motioned over to Chris. "I've heard from Mr. Bristol here that you're a woman who can get things done. Let's call this an interview for simplicity's sake."

"Fire away, Mr. Davis."

"That's what I want to hear." Warren cleared his throat. "First off, let's ask the obvious question. Would you be interested in joining a team I'm putting together. Your pay would be higher than right now, but the jobs would be more demanding. Keep in mind, this group would be sophisticated, meaning we'd have tech support and overwatch."

"You're damned right I'd be interested, sir."

"Good," Warren said. "Next, I understand this could be a private thing, but I have to ask potential recruits to my team. Why did you join this syndicate? The only reason I ask is I like to know the people under my command."

"Money was the main motivator, sir. I grew up poor in what most would call a ghetto. I watched people get evicted from their homes, take out loans from loan sharks, and get their legs broken if they couldn't pay. I'm an only child, and my mom's the only one I've got left. She's gone senile at her age, so I pay for her bills."

"I see," Warren said, giving her a once over. "Mr. Bristol recommended you, but I would still have to take you to a shooting range and see for myself. We're constructing a makeshift one behind the house as we speak. Would you be willing to prove yourself, so to speak?"

"Name the time and place. I'll be there," Jackie said, her voice brimming with confidence.

"That's what I like to hear," Warren said. "I'll tell you what, when they get it set up I'll give you a ring. Until then, keep working hard," he said as he stood up. "If you'll excuse me, I have more work to tend to."

Jackie and Chris watched as Warren walked off and exited the room.

Chris looked over at her with a shit eating grin. "That's not too bad for a new guy, huh? I've only just joined, and I already got you a promotion."

"You got me an interview. I don't have the job yet," Jackie said. "But thank you nonetheless."

"I know I portray a certain look, but I didn't recommend you just because you're pretty. You really did impress me last night. You took command while I had to go fix the west side's mess. You held the men and women together while their leader was temporarily absent, even though you were no doubt worried yourself. That takes a certain intangible that not many have in the heat of battle."

"I was just doing what I had to. If they'd panicked we'd have buckled, and all of us would have died."

"That's probably true," Chris said. "It doesn't change

what I said though. I see great potential in you. I hope to live long enough to see it come to fruition."

"I'd be careful then," Jackie said while looking over at Elizabeth across the room watching television. "If you get involved with her, you might not live as long as you want to."

"You're just paranoid. What could have possibly happened to her last boyfriend?"

She made sure her voice was low enough so that only the two of them could hear. She looked around, making sure no one was eavesdropping. "Rumor has it she was responsible for her last boyfriend of sorts. I hear his name was Axel. Posthumously she blamed him when she was the one who gave the order. She's only concerned with what's best for her. I'd watch yourself if you still decide to go for it."

"I hear you. She's also not a woman you can say no to though."

Jackie reached into her coat pocket and pulled out some chap stick before applying it to her lips. "Also true. Just watch out."

"If you're jealous, I don't have to get with her you know." Chris leaned toward her only for her to push him back with a laugh.

"In your dreams, old man."

"You already got a target, huh? I knew it. All the pretty ones usually do."

"That is for me to know, and you to not find out."

"I'll find out one day - mark my words."

"You will try..."

Later that night...

"How has he been?" Rachel asked while picking up

Roger from Lauren. "I'm sorry about the extra time, but it's been busy the past few days."

"That's an understatement," Lauren said. She moved toward Rachel's bed and sat down. "Everything went okay from the looks of it. When's your father's funeral?"

"Tomorrow," Rachel said. She rocked Roger in her arms as he fussed. "I have him in the basement surrounded in ice now. I'd rather he not smell to the high heavens for our little ceremony." She took a deep breath and steadied herself. Her voice came out weaker than before. "I can't believe it's real to be honest. Dad's gone." She sat down beside Lauren. "I knew intellectually it'd happen when I told Ben what I did. It feels surreal."

"How exactly did you convince him anyway?" Lauren asked. "Ben doesn't strike me as the kind of guy to do that."

"I told him Dad was planning on killing him. That he was convinced he was ravaging his daughter."

"I can see why he did it now. I didn't know your dad hated him so much."

"He didn't," Rachel said. She grabbed a nearby green dinosaur toy on the bed and handed it to Roger. "I made that part up. Dad was annoyed, sure. He wasn't that mad. The timing worked perfectly as it happened. He had just got his ass tore up by Dad about seeing me."

"I bet you're glad you picked him now and not Davis, huh? I guess you were right on that detail. I would have sworn you'd have had a better chance with him. Not to mention he's hot."

"God, are we reliving our high school gossip sessions?" Rachel couldn't help but laugh. "I picked Ben because I know his type."

"Don't tell me this is about that Uncle figure of yours," Lauren said. "I was hoping it was just a rumor."

"A little bit, but that's not the whole story." Rachel got up and put Roger down into the playpen. She moved over to the now open window. She gazed out at the night sky as she spoke. "If you're going to conspire to what we did, you need to be sure your accomplices are trustworthy."

"You trust Adams more than Davis?" Lauren asked. "I'm not sure I agree with that. Davis is a lifer. Adams is yet to be proven."

"What easier type of man is there to control than the trusting underling? All he needed to hear were the words out of my mouth before he agreed. He's timid but not stupid. He knew the threat of Father killing him was quite possible," Rachel said. "He was just defending himself. He never wants this to come out. Davis would have seen it for what it was - a power play motivated by revenge. Ben's kind, caring, and considerate. I just wouldn't go to him for advice for strategy outside of a fire fight. Do you get my meaning?"

"That is cold and calculating, boss." Lauren stared at her boss. "I didn't know you had that in you."

"You haven't seen anything yet."

"Answer me one thing about your choice."

"Shoot," Rachel said.

"How is Ben handling all this? You are his girlfriend now, yes? I imagine he feels guilty about all this. He has to with his personality."

"He seems to be doing fine from what I can tell."

"You're going to want to keep an eye on him. That whole kind, caring type you like so much generally has issues with murder. I'd watch him if I were you."

"He's my bodyguard. I don't need him to do much besides keeping us alive. He's got a sweet gig now. I'll have more than enough time to talk this out. Any other concerns about my personal love life, Ms. Nosy?"

"I was just worried. He's the only other link in our little plan. I do not like taking chances. You knew that when you brought me in."

"You need to focus on the future. We'll recover from this and make more money than you ever thought possible. I have some ideas for our expansion soon."

"Tell me more..."

23

"Is there any other business we should attend to this morning?" Rachel asked the small group in her office. "I'll call Oleg and set up another sale after this."

"I have one," Elizabeth stepped forward. "When are we going to get my Bernard back exactly? You said you would, but I want to know when."

"Not anytime soon," Rachel said. "Have you listened to the news? Everyone and their mother is searching for you across the country. They're going to be watching that kid. Our best bet is taking him back once he's placed in a foster home. It's a simple breaking and entering then."

"That's not good enough," Elizabeth said.

Warren and Chris both looked at her with open eyes before looking toward Rachel.

Rachel frowned. "Are you really complaining right now?"

"For that matter even if you do get him back, where the hell would we even stay? Just get a few men to build me a place on the property. I don't need much."

"That's not happening right now," Rachel said. "We have

other priorities. You know, like getting our enterprise back off the ground after this war your brother got us into. Now you are dismissed. I have to get ready for my father's funeral, and I suspect you all do too. We only have a few minutes before it starts."

"Wait a minute, this isn't over," Elizabeth pointed at Rachel. Her voice grew louder as Warren left the room behind her and closed the door.

"You need to understand your situation, Auntie." Rachel's voice was cold and firm. "You are public enemy number one. I got you out personally. Have enough decorum to not complain to me that your golden cage isn't nice enough. Frankly I have other things to worry about."

"You little bitch," Elizabeth said. She grit her teeth.

"Know your good fortune when you have it. If it wasn't for me, you'd still be cleaning floors and toilets. Is there anything else, or must I mother you too?"

Elizabeth stomped out of the room, fuming inside her own head. *That little tart*, she thought. *You enjoy that power while you can. It'll be mine soon enough if my own plans come to fruition.*

A devious grin appeared on her face as she approached her personal room. She walked over to the dresser, already filled with assorted clothes. She picked up an especially formal dress and held it up to her chest, admiring her figure in the nearby mirror. She thought to herself as she undressed and put the new one on. *I still have the looks, I still have the reputation, and I damned sure still have the tactical IQ to beat your disrespectful ass. It's all about how you treat people, and you're going through your power trip phase. That's my advantage.*

She reached down beneath her bed and retrieved a pair of black heels. She put them on and left the room. Her inner monologue continued as she passed Ben and Rachel further down the hallway. *All I need is a good man to help me. Luckily, I have two good candidates.* She walked out the back door to see Warren standing near a closed casket. A nearby tripod was lined with wreathes of flowers surrounding a giant portrait of Daniel from his younger years alongside Roger and Elizabeth.

Her eyes settled on Warren. *He's an option. I know he can get shit done. He's savvy, and he's selfish enough to agree. My other option is more of a wildcard though.*

Her eyes wandered a few rows back and spotted Chris sitting beside Jackie. He turned around and waved to her with a wide smile. *The man portrays himself as a sexist oaf, but there's something far deeper to him. I can tell. He's quickly gaining a reputation. Now which one would fit my needs better?*

She interrupted her inner monologue and walked over toward Chris. "Why don't you join me up front?"

"Yes, ma'am." Chris got up and escorted her to the front row of chairs among the damaged earth below them. She took her seat two deep in the row and watched as Chris sat beside her.

"I'm sorry about your brother, Ms. Morris," Chris said. "I've only served in this group for a short time, but he struck me as a good leader."

"At times he was," Elizabeth said. "He tended to let power go to his head though. He was a tactical genius in a gun fight, the likes of which you or I could only dream of. He only had one person that could rival him there, and he's long dead." She didn't notice when a tear escaped and trailed down her pale face.

Chris followed the tear and his gaze darted back to her eyes. He didn't want to interrupt her, so he stayed quiet.

She wiped the tear away. "Anyway, I will say my brother

was a man of his people. He knew how to treat those under him, most of the time."

"I wish I could have known him longer."

The conversation was cut short as Rachel and Ben stepped out of the house. They walked over toward the casket. She rested a hand on the closed lid. She stood there for a full minute as the rest of the crowd quieted down behind her.

While this was going on, Ben leaned over and whispered in Warren's ear something Elizabeth couldn't make out.

Warren nodded and moved to take a seat in the front row near her while Ben took his place up front near Rachel.

Rachel finally turned around and spoke in a loud voice. "We all know why we're here," she said. "The war is over now. My father led us into this fight, but we finished it in his honor. I will not stand up here and lie. I cannot tell you people won't die in the future. This business is dirty and ugly, but it is what we do. We do our best to be professionals and keep it pleasant. I will endeavor to do just that."

Elizabeth zoned out as Rachel continued on in her speech. *She's a smooth talker. I need to make note of that. She could inspire loyalty, which means I need to account for that in my plans. I'll just have to be Miss Congeniality. She'll be short with people from time to time, and I'll take advantage.*

She looked over at Warren and then the other way toward Chris. *Which one of you will best suit me? Which one of you is capable? I'll keep the Morris bloodline pure. My baby Bernard is the true heir, not that Roger kid. I owe it to him and me.* The crowd around her clapped as Rachel finished her little speech. Elizabeth clapped along with them. *My work here is only beginning...*

THANK YOU FOR READING!

The adventures of Rachel, Ben, and the syndicate will continue in book seven. If you'd like to help support this work, please consider leaving an honest review or rating on Amazon. Have a great day!

ABOUT THE AUTHOR

Alex J Fischer has been writing for close to a decade and has won five National Novel Writing Month challenges in a row.

Alex grew up in a small town in Ohio and still resides there. Hobbies include writing, video games, and watching crime shows.

ALSO BY ALEX J FISCHER